Bitcoin and the Ritual of Kyudo Archery

Bitcoin and the Ritual of Kyudo Archery

a novel

Beau de Rubempré

Anton Gunzburg LLC

Copyright © 2021 Anton Gunzburg LLC

The characters and events portrayed in this book are fictitious. Any similarity to real persons, living or dead, is coincidental and not intended by the author.

No part of this book may be reproduced, or stored in a retrieval system, or transmitted in any form or by any means, electronic, mechanical, photocopying, recording, or otherwise, without express written permission of the publisher.

ISBN: 9798570257009

Imprint: Independently published
by Anton Gunzburg LLC

Cover design by: Art Painter
Printed in the United States of America

to Maurizio Mambrin and Alessandro Chiolerio

> We can literally store our money in whatever way we want ... The most interesting of all the alternatives is the place where humans have been storing most of our information for the past 100,000 years: in our brains.
> – Vitalik Buterin, "Brain Wallets: The What and the How"

Bitcoin and the Ritual of Kyudo Archery

PROLOGUE

What age was he? Seven. Eight. It wasn't long since they had moved to Skokie near Chicago. He liked Skokie because they often got kosher sausage at a Polish take-out place, so Dad didn't complain like he always complained with Mom that she couldn't cook a decent kosher meal. No, she was not one of them. How long did they live there? Two years. Three. Dad hated the American celebration of Halloween, the Day of the Dead. He said it was kind of insane. "Death is not a game," he yelled, "not to mention that Skokie is a Jewish community, or is it not?" Which didn't help him understand Dad's view of it. He wasn't allowed to wear a Halloween costume like his friends. He liked the Darth Vader costume they sold at Target. Above all he liked that just by wearing a costume you could become someone else. He wasn't allowed to do Treat-or-Trick in the neighborhood either. Dad would turn off all the lights in the house, so, when children came knocking at the door that evening, they would pretend nobody was at home. The first time they did it, he had a hard time grasping why he couldn't be out there with his new friends, and at each wave of children knocking on the door, Mom told him, "Now we must talk softly, Anton, very softly." He did his best to whisper, if he found something to say, but mostly he wished he could just weep on his own. Next year, when Mom and Dad were shutting the windows closed and turning off the lights, the idea came to him of a new game. When he thinks back to that day, he's unrecognizable to himself: a full tiny vessel overflowing with love and good intentions, that's what he was. They would have fun too, he declared, they would play dead! Mom joined in eagerly, so, at each new wave of children at the door, he lay down on the floor, holding his breath with his eyes closed, till he heard the steps of the children walk away. Then he could breathe again. From behind his closed eyes, he took for granted that Mom and Dad played according to the rules of the new game. Mom, Varvara: *I bet you played dead for real, like I did. Lying on the couch, mouth and eyes sealed, totally silent, free for a brief moment from Dad's vexation. Were you thinking of Granddad, the Hater of the Jews?*

There was no third Halloween for them in Skokie. Next year they moved again. By then things had turned totally nasty.

Bitcoin and the Ritual of Kyudo Archery

BRAIN WALLET # 1

If my Michelin street map reminds you of a color-coded war plan, you aren't too off of the mark. For sure, it has little to do with the quadrant of distances and directions that lead a regular Parisian to his destination. But is there really still someone who consults a Michelin map to move around the city? How many people there can possibly be who know how to read a street map? Me, I'll use the iPhone's GPS to find my way around Paris, once I'll be there. Soon.

The way I adjusted my Michelin street map was certainly not meant to help me figure directions out. Directions to *where*, as I had no plan of ever be going to Paris at the time?

Once the idea got into my head (Daniel put it there) that the Paris street map would be my declaration of war on the hackers who keep a lookout for my bitcoin treasure, I brushed its grid off and gave in to *improvisation*.

Improvisation is not even the right word. I shuffle a certain street, a certain square, a certain crossroads, I do the trick of the sharper with a deck of marked cards, shuffle and reshuffle, till I funnel those hackers into a maze of dead ends. And me, I travel meanwhile the invisible straight road that leads… No, it's neither to the Eiffel Tower nor to the Champs-Elysées. It leads to a precise coordinate in crypto space, the spot where I go dig whenever I need to get a few bitcoins out of my treasure. Or add some new ones to it. The millimetric location of my cache is hidden in plain sight on the Michelin map, such that nobody but me will ever find out.

It may sound like magic but it's just math: improvisation degree-zero. Without my secret compass, any direction is as good as the next, and none leads to the right place. It's like I wrote the location of my cache on a pinhead and hid the pin in a haystack as large as a supernova. All that the hackers get out of my map is innumerable paths to the treasure, each with probability zero.

The day I decided I'll leave Palo Alto and move to France, Paris was but that street map to me. I had never even dreamt I'd visit the French Capital one day.

There it is, my Michelin map, the same whose picture I taped to the cover of the black Moleskine notebook I'm writing on. It hangs from the wall of my study in Palo Alto, facing my desk and me sitting at it. Why don't you grab the Moleskine and take a look at it? Don't be shy. See how the map is pierced by a load of colored flag pushpins (blue red orange purple) and crisscrossed by three long colored ribbons (black red green)? How long ago did I stick it to the large cork panel that supports it, you wonder? Six years. Make it seven.

In a few months I'll see the real Paris with my own eyes.

Sophie Renault Hosnani, place de l'Alma, corner rue Jean-Goujon, Paris, France.

I'll stay at Sophie's place the day I get to France. My Mac, my bows and arrows travel with me. The black Moleskine too. Demoiselle Dambreuil has been notified. The Paris map requires special care. I consulted a specialist in transport of artworks: the cork panel must be packed in a custom-made box that will travel on its own. Just in case, I took several close-up pictures of the map with my iPhone.

It would be so much easier to explain all of this with an algorithm.

Bitcoin and the Ritual of Kyudo Archery

You must've figured out by now that what we've been talking about all along is a Treasure Map.

Remember Captain Hook? *You go by the Mermaid Lagoon, cross the Cannibal Cove*, and then... And then Captain Hook is stuck because he doesn't know how to decrypt the rest of the treasure map. And he doesn't know it for the simple reason that the secret code was never written down, it's buried in someone's memory. The map will keep hiding its secret under his nose till the day Captain Hook will squeeze the secret out of this someone. Nothing new under the sun, in sum (if Daniel's fate is any evidence): you don't break the code, you break the man.

Memo for later: *Captain Hook wasn't the least of my English instructors, teaching his lessons, long ago, from the screen of our first American TV set. That flat classroom full of marvelous colors... As my father complained in Russian to my Mom Varvara of the incomprehensible talk they spoke to him in the streets downtown Chicago, where he went job hunting, I tried my hand at calling him "Dad," like a regular American kid would, but he didn't seem to hear me.*

I don't remember too well the day I set up the map in front of my desk and if I bought it online or in a bookstore. The reason why I did it was clear from the start, though: it'd be my solution (Daniel's, to give credit where it's due) to bitcoin's main shortcoming.

It's hard to believe it for newbies to bitcoin, but all there stands between your bitcoin cache and the next hacker is an *Open Sesame* of sorts, your secret passphrase: not just two words as in the case of Ali Baba and the forty thieves, but twelve. You must hide those twelve words from the hackers' prying eyes like your life depended on it. If you don't want to end up like the forty thieves, that is. It sounds easy but it's far from it. Listen.

Some guys break their twelve words into distinct groups, copy each group on a file card, and then rent safe deposit boxes from different banks and in different locations, to hide one card per box. Some guys do the same but use metal plates instead of cardboard, to preempt damage from natural or nuclear disaster. When in need of their passphrase, they get ahold of their safes by showing an ID card to the bank employee. Some guys store the *Open Sesame* in a specially designated offline computer, virgin of any interaction with humans or other machines, and when in need, they unlock it with a secret password. Still some other guys, who trust machines blindly, adopt a tiny gadget called hardware wallet and designed to remember the *Open Sesame* in their stead, which leaves the owner in a state of blissed ignorance and is unlocked with a secret PIN number.

All these solutions are based on a chain of regressions from secret to previous secret, granted your ID card or PIN number, as terminal items in the chain of regressions, are, believe me, easy-to-crack secrets. And one breaking point is enough to compromise the security of your whole treasure.

My way out of that forced pathway – from secret to previous secret to the breaking point of no-secret-at-all – is the street map of Paris on the wall in front of me. My *Open Sesame* is there on the map, buried in that certain combination of square, crossroads, and bridge. But the ultimate source of everything, the matrix of the code, starts in here: *knock, knock*. I got it into my own head.

Bitcoin and the Ritual of Kyudo Archery

I borrowed the method of the street map from Daniel after adjusting it to my own mental scale. Daniel claimed he had the memory of Pico della Mirandola, a fellow who could remember just about everything, forwards and backwards. And Daniel could too, till the day he couldn't anymore, and they started calling him Jesus. Daniel would recall the words of his passphrase with the help of the street map of Dublin, his hometown. His ribbons and flag pushpins traced the meanderings through the city of a character from a novel by his favorite Irish writer.

I thought I was the only person who knew of Daniel's secret method, but someone else must have been in on it, or I wouldn't be writing on this black Moleskine. He's gone, he's turned into Jesus, rambling Jesus, and all I'm left here in Palo Alto is you, the confidant privy to my secret mission in Paris.

Your lips are sealed. You don't even exist.

CHAPTER ONE

It drizzles. The porter at the Charles de Gaulle airport pushes his cart to the taxi stand before casting Anton a puzzled glance. Anton doesn't get a word of the porter's French but the obstacle they just bumped into is obvious. The wooden box with his bows inside is too bulky to fit into any cab. Anton gestures to the porter to set his box and his two backpacks by the door of the Restaurant Avion Bleu. He pays the porter and then touches Sophie's contact on the iPhone.

"Monsieur Anton?" It's the voice of demoiselle Dambreuil. "Madame is sleeping."

"Good morning, demoiselle." He explains the situation.

"Where are you right now, monsieur?" she replies, and then she tells him not to move from there. He sits down on the wooden box and Dambreuil calls him back shortly later. "Please, be patient." Bashir is rushing to his rescue. "Madame will be happy to know you are here!" she adds with a quiver of trepidation in her voice.

He has been waiting for about half an hour, sitting on his box, when a waiter steps out of the restaurant and asks him if he wants to order something. He is not exactly hungry, but the Apple watch tells him it's 7:12 AM of February 5, 2019. They negotiate in sign language, the waiter retreats with a prolonged nod, walking backwards, and five minutes later Anton has a tray in front of him holding a cappuccino and two fragrant croissants.

The moment he is done with breakfast, he hears a din all around, raises his eyes, and there he is, Bashir, his profile in the side window of a rental van, double parking by the taxi stand.

Bitcoin and the Ritual of Kyudo Archery

Bashir runs toward him trading abuse with the taxi drivers. His spirited handshake tells Anton that all past grudge between them was buried by time and distance. How did Bashir find it in himself to forgive those long hours he had to spend on the sidewalk of Cowper Street, waiting for Anton and Sophie to return from the beach?

They lift and carry his luggage to the van in a hurry.

The drive to Paris doesn't impress Anton all that much at first. In a while, though, the sun pierces the clouds, houses and cars grow denser, and Bashir announces, "Boulevard Diderot! ... Pont d'Austerlitz!" Anton lowers the window and a springy breeze brushes the leaden scent of the Seine against his nostrils. He throws a deferential glance at the opaque water slowly flowing from under the bridge.

Bashir drives with preternatural calm, steering the wheel with one hand. "Jardin des Plantes! ... Pont de la Concorde!" The van's radio plays an old Radiohead hit. Anton whistles along. Bashir casts him a glance and, when the refrain starts and Anton sees Bashir's lips pucker like he's going to kiss the air, he humors him: *But...* they sing in unison. Bashir even slows down the van to enjoy their duo: ... *I'm a creep, I'm a weirdo. What the hell am I doing here? I don't belong here.* Some of the cars that pass them by have their windows lowered. Those Parisians must be thinking that the Arab and the Slav aboard the rental van got it badly wrong if they took that song for a migrant's lament. *I wish I was special, you're so fucking special...*

"Pont de l'Alma! Rue Jean-Goujon!" They go through a gate, down an underground garage ramp, and park between a powder-blue convertible and a black SUV. Demoiselle Dambreuil is there waiting for them, blonder, thinner, and more shriveled than Anton remembers her. They have known each other, he muses, for longer than ten years.

He helps Bashir pull his box out of the van and then follows him out of the garage, holding his side of it. Dambreuil holds a door open on a sight that leaves Anton speechless: in front of him is a state-of-the-art kyudojo, a virtual duplicate of Daniel's kyudojo in Palo Alto. Same shooting platform on one side, same target resting on a bank of sand on the other. The only missing components are the glass windows through which daylight came into Daniel's pavilion, replaced by neon lights.

"This is the kyudojo," Dambreuil tells him with a proud swipe of the hand, pronouncing *kyudojò*.

He and Bashir put the box down on the shooting platform, and Bashir volunteers to pry the box open.

Anton looks around himself and notices an incongruity: there is a table on this side of the shooting platform and on it there is a half-empty whisky bottle. Stunned, he takes a second look: there is a glass too, with a dark dry crust on the bottom, and an ashtray full of cigarette butts.

He can't hide his irritation. "Who left this stuff in the kyudojo?" he tells Dambreuil.

"*Moi, j'sais pas, monsieur...* I don't know, I wouldn't know..."

He asks Bashir to help him move table, bottle, glass, and ashtray to the garage.

He walks to the van to get his backpacks. Back in the kyudojo, he asks Bashir to place his bows side by side with Sophie's on the bow rack. Dambreuil walks him into an elevator that climbs to the apartment on the third floor. While she shows it to him, room after room after room, Dambreuil tells him that the first-floor apartment, with a garden on place de l'Alma, is Sophie's, the three smaller apartments on the second floor are assigned to herself, Bashir, and Sophie's cook – *the spy*, she calls him – and this third-floor apartment will be Anton's during his stay in Paris.

His apartment is more than twice the size of the one he just moved out of in Palo Alto. He takes a giant curved monitor on the desk in the study as evidential proof that this must've been Nessim's apartment when he still lived with Sophie. The Eiffel Tower's bulk looms through the windows. Still wet with raindrops, the funereal black of its iron framework sparkles under the sunrays.

Anton puts down his backpacks on the floor of the living room. In a backpack there are cables, machines, and his black notebook, in the other a kyudojo uniform, an extra pair of black jeans, some t-shirts, a black hoodie, and a heavy sweater.

"Monsieur travels with no luggage?" Dambreuil asks.

He doesn't get her question at first, and after she asks again, he points a finger at his backpacks. His gesture leaves her puzzled, but only a minute because she is soon pulling a yellow-tape measure out of her pocket and then takes his measurements (waist, chest, shoulders, arms, and legs), jotting them down in green ink on a small green notebook. Nobody ever took his measurements this way. She'll take care of it, she says, without explaining what she's talking about or why she's shaking her head as she says so.

If this were a black-and-white movie, now would be the time for demoiselle to discreetly withdraw and let Anton rest awhile. But her hesitancy is palpable.

"Demoiselle..." he whispers with a note of encouragement in his voice, and she opens up at once, as though the throbbing heart in her chest couldn't hold back anymore.

"*Bon*, monsieur must help me. Monsieur is the only person who can help. Every day the TEXOR engineers call me asking for the algorithmics, they say they can't accomplish anything without the algorithmics. And I've run out of excuses!"

Algorithmics... "And what do they want these algorithms for?" he says.

"*Moi, j'sais pas...* I don't know!" A bitter, gap-toothed smile on her lips. "I have no idea."

"And, who do they want these algorithms from?" As he asks this question, the half-empty whisky bottle in the kyudojo pops into his head together with the obvious answer.

"*Mais, mais, j'sais pas...* but from madame Sophie! It's madame in sum who... it's she who writes the algorithmics, isn't she?"

It's been several months, he is being told now, since madame Sophie did any solid work, took something at heart, or even lived an ordinary life. Listless, lethargic, ill tempered... Dambreuil widens her eyes in a strange, vamp-like way as she explains that things have taken a bad turn after monsieur Nessim, on a business trip to Yemen, picked *une fille fertile* to bring back with him to Paris.

"*Une fille fertile?*" Anton tries unsuccessfully to mimic the sound of Dambreuil's French, but gets his explication from her anyway:

"Back from Yemen, monsieur Nessim showed up with *une fille fertile* in tow, a fertile girl."

Bitcoin and the Ritual of Kyudo Archery

Fille fertile… The expression sounds offensive, yet the lecherous way Dambreuil widens her eyes when she says it is too funny. Why funny, though? Anton feels his responses are out of sorts owing to the jetlag. But her alarmed tone of voice seeps through eventually, when he recalls that whisky bottle and the incrusted glass in the kyudojo.

I'll see what I can do, he tells her, shrugging his shoulders. Dambreuil insists: at this point, everything depends on monsieur Anton, nobody else can save the situation. He couldn't imagine the happiness of madame when he emailed that he would soon visit from Palo Alto. She was her old self for a whole week. She had painters come in and redecorate this apartment, and furnished it from scratch.

Anton's jet lag must be taking a heavy toll: he hasn't paid any attention yet to the primary colors of the walls – Daniel's colors: red, blue, and yellow – crossed diagonally by the morning sunrays, and the minimalist, cloister-like furniture.

It's almost two PM when they hear a beep from Dambreuil's iPhone. He peeks into the screen and see that it's a WhatsApp – he had been warned that WhatsApp is a must-have in Europe.

Madame woke up and is asking to see monsieur Anton, Dambreuil announces, her gap-toothed smile joyfully wide. They take the elevator to the ground floor and Dambreuil steers him to the kitchen, where they find a large tray holding a stack of tramezzino sandwiches, a bowl of fruit salad, a thermos bottle full of coffee, cups and saucers, spoons and teaspoons. After putting the tray unceremoniously in his hands, she shepherds him through a couple of rooms, followed by a long hallway leading, he presumes, to Sophie. At the end of the hallway, she opens a door and steps aside, giving him a knowing look.

The bedroom is in semidarkness. He makes out a broad bedframe with the mattress lying sideways on the floor, covered with a mess of bedsheets. He makes out a small table displaying a sealed whisky bottle. He pushes the bottle aside and puts down the tray. Just in time: popped out of nowhere, Elvis, Sophie's three-legged hound dog, jumps on him waving his tail. A merry heap of black muscles.

"Anton?" Sophie's voice reaches him through some soft music.

"Here I am."

Sophie walks barefoot out of the bathroom, wrapped in a white bathrobe, her hair disheveled. Anton doesn't get the hug he was expecting. An uncertain smile on her lips, she goes sit on the mattress on the floor and pats it on her side. Elvis is faster than Anton and curls up there. Anton moves the tray at her feet, near an ashtray filled with butts, and sits on the mattress by her other side. Sophie's downcast eyes avoid his gaze. She lights up an unfiltered cigarette – the blue packet reads *Gauloise* – and its acrid smoke makes him cough.

"Did you eat?" she asks.

"Yes."

"Are you hungry?"

"Yes."

He can study her up close since she avoids returning his gaze. Her hair is longer. Her cheeks are fuller, so much so that they drown her dimples even when she drags on her cigarette. She blows smoke out of her contracted nostrils, peevishly, as though she was trying to put out a forest fire. The dim light makes her look younger; the miracle repeats itself and he is ready to swear that this new version of Sophie is prettier than before. She's a whiter shade of pale for sure than her palest days in California, though, and her eyes have lost the intentness he was used to.

She makes a move as if to offer him her cigarette for a puff, but pulls her hand back right away with a shrug. He wishes she looked into his eyes.

The throaty R's of a French singer dances through the cloud of smoke floating around them.

"Brel," she whispers in answer to the question he hasn't asked. "Jacques Brel," she whispers again, withdrawn, her eyes frowning and staring into space. "Rickety kisses and small-time eternities."

He pours himself a cup of coffee, then he changes his mind and starts with some fruit salad instead. He serves himself a portion into a fruit cup and it's delicious, so he goes ahead and eats the rest of it straight from the bowl using a serving spoon. This gets a laugh out of her.

She stretches out her arm to take hold of his untouched cup of coffee. As she does it, one of her shoulders slips out of the white bathrobe – white on white – but she makes no effort to cover her breast nor does she try to stop his hand when he takes the cigarette from her fingers and puts it out in the ashtray while he pushes Elvis off the mattress.

BRAIN WALLET # 2

Memorize your *Open Sesame*, get it into your head… I won't pretend I can't hear the professional hackers complain. There are machines for that sort of task, machines that enjoy the advantage of absolute memory over humans. A well-trained machine can even recall a memory it never had. Of all people, those hackers complain, it's one of us, Anton Gunzburg, who pretends he doesn't know about it.

I raise no objections, machines have the advantage of absolute memory. But that's precisely why I don't trust them with my *Open Sesame*. Machines always remember those twelve words, even when I want them to just forget and shut up. Whisper your *Open Sesame* to your machine, and you turn it (the machine) into a honeypot of seizable wealth. It's not for nothing that those same hackers train so hard at breaking into it.

When the chips are down, only human memory is hackerproof. Mind you, this holds true only as long as no one knows that your magic words are coded within your own skull. Otherwise, some evil hacker, a black hat, a Captain Hook of sorts, will find a key to get inside your skull too. They don't break the map, they break the man. Or at least they give it a try: Jesus knows a thing or two about it. Strike that: Jesus *would* know a thing or two about some stranger forcing his way into his skull, if only he had a shred of a memory of the day it happened.

His brain too was, earlier and longer than mine, the matrix of the code. Not anymore: Jesus was still Daniel then.

Bitcoin and the Ritual of Kyudo Archery

What happened to Jesus, I take it as a lesson. A cautionary lesson I try not to muse too often about because when I do, I become a stranger to myself. And then I can't write on this Moleskine anymore. I can't code anymore. I can't eat, walk, sleep. I can't shoot my bow anymore either. All I can still do is feel my heartbeat: *lub-dub, lub-dub, lub-dub.* It reminds me, that dumb heartbeat, that there is a piece of me in there that's not been totally crushed yet, not even by what happened to Jesus. Not even after a good chunk of it was crushed by Sophie's betrayal.

This is where the cautionary part of the lesson kicks in.

If you are accustomed to seeing Jesus sitting on his usual bench downtown Palo Alto, where he spends, delirious, most of his days, you'll find it hard to believe that this big and tall homeless guy has ever been a brilliant software engineer of Silicon Valley. Just like you'll find it hard to believe he isn't fifty yet, when he looks at least ten years older. Technically speaking, he is not homeless, but almost everybody in town thinks he is.

Aside from his alleged resurrection, a local legend, Jesus owes his nickname to his long, hanging-down hair and thick blond beard: greasy and disheveled, they give him the air of a scruffy hermit. The hair on the back of his head hides the entry hole of the nail that's still stuck inside his skull.

Jesus is beginning to lose it. He is not one of those lost souls who inject in the street or anything of the sort, but his looks and outfit get worse by the day. Not long ago, it gave me a heartache to see his pants slide down to his ankles while he was getting up from his bench. That's Daniel, I told myself, the friend who taught me that one must always act and think with *the calm elegance of flowing water.*

Beau de Rubempré

How much wasted talent on that bench! And the frustration I feel every time I cross paths with him and powerless remorse overthrows me.

I've spent endless hours sitting on that bench near Jesus, listening at first, and later recording on my iPhone those rambling, never-ending monologues of his. It's evident that he doesn't recognize in me his devoted friend and disciple Anton. To the contrary, he doesn't even seem aware that someone is sitting by his side.

He goes on and on with his monologue like he is all alone, or maybe face to face with his words' secret addressee, his assailant maybe. I transcribe as I can from my iPhone: *Nuk. Brékek. kékek, kékek, kékek. Kóax, kóax, kóax. Ualu, ualu, ualu.*

At times he utters words that seem to convey some dark secret meaning. I transcribe again: *Infernal machinery, serial number, bully's acre, dig care a dig, killy kill killy, a toll, a toll.*

It was this sort of statements that made me decide it was time for me to join Sophie in Paris.

Once in a while, Jesus leaves his bench and wanders up and down University Avenue, or stops by Starbucks or Café Venetia for a cup of coffee, which he pays for with his American Express Platinum card, or pushes his way a few blocks further south to buy his lunch at Whole Foods – which he pays for with the same prestigious credit card. Some nights, he sleeps in a homeless shelter, some others, wrapped in cardboard on the sidewalk by the door to the J. P. Morgan's offices. Infrequently, he shows up at his downtown luxury apartment, where he reacts with the stubbornness of a wild animal if one of the caregivers, who take turns waiting for him there, tries to be of service to him. His older sister has become his guardian since the aggression. She settles his bills with American Express and all other expenses.

It's unlikely yet not impossible that Jesus is still one of the wealthiest men in Silicon Valley. I have no way of finding out if his attacker yanked the passphrase of his bitcoin portfolio out of him. As I said, he remembered the secret passphrase with the help of the street map of Dublin, his hometown.

His full name is Daniel Dunne, purebred Irish, and he holds two PhD degrees, in computer science and in theology. The day we first met at Café Venetia, I didn't think of myself as a college dropout yet, but in time I've become one. Nobody called him Jesus then: a Nordic-looking guy, tall and well shaven, his head crowned with a sizable, almost caricatured pompadour. Daniel was the first person I became acquainted with in Palo Alto. No sooner did he sit down at my table on the boardwalk, that first time, while I was succumbing to an overcaffeinated panic attack, than instinct told him we two shared the same passion for pure machine code: those laborious concatenations of hexadecimal instructions that speak the language of metal and silicone, without need for the clumsy intermediation of Python or not even of modular codes like C++. Afterwards, we took a walk on University Avenue under the cobalt-blue sky I wasn't accustomed to yet. That was the first time I heard him use the Japanese term *suki,* which he used to define the vulnerability of the coder who focuses excessively on a section of the program at the expense of other sections: the juncture, he explained, where high labor intensity undercuts itself.

As we were taking leave of each other, Daniel asked, "Do you trust me?"

I nodded.

"And you are right. Yet, it's me who knows you are right to trust me," he said in a disconsolate tone. "How could you possibly know?"

I couldn't find an answer to that.

"Think of it," he said as we shook hands. "Trust… I think of it all the time these days. We waste so much of it and it's in such scarce supply."

It was a nice springtime day. Downtown Palo Alto was flooded with sunlight under that cobalt-blue sky. I was whistling on my way to my place when, on the spur of the moment, I walked into the barbershop of the Cardinal Hotel. I kept whistling under my breath as I waited for my turn, looking at myself in the mirror. I could get rid of that reddish stubble and also of those curls that reminded me of a rabbi. When it's my turn, it turns out that the old barber, a Cuban refugee, detected the trace of Russian accent that still plagues my English. He refuses to shave my stubble and slaughters my hairdo on purpose. As soon as I walk out of his barbershop, I'm back to my whistling: to hell with communists and anti-communists.

BRAIN WALLET # 3

All my life since I can remember, people have been asking me where I am from. They still do. A girl in Pittsburgh told me it's an aggressive question and I should answer, "I'm from here." I tried it a few times, but it doesn't work all that good with me. *Here.* Here, where? Is Palo Alto still here or already there with respect to … Chicago? … Skokie? … Petersburg? I'm more at ease when I say, "I come from Russia." That's the truth, and besides, that's what they expect me to say from the way I speak. It's not really a malicious question, I don't think. Things turn a bit fuzzy when they ask, "What city?"

The last time I saw my father was on a winter day in the lobby of the Drake Hotel in Chicago, where he bummed a hundred bucks off me. No sooner did I hand him five twenty-dollars bills than he called a waiter and ordered himself a fifteen-dollar drink. At that moment, I wondered, not for the first time, if I'm truly his son.

As though he had been having the same thought, he said in Russian, "You are the son of a fallen wall. The day they tore down the Berlin Wall, I was passing through Moscow bound for home in Leningrad. Varvara lived in Moscow, a student in accounting." He downed a mouthful from his glass and concluded, "We were all in the streets of Moscow that night, a festive mob, everybody wasted."

Then he closed in on himself, staring at the bottom of the glass he was busy emptying fast.

It didn't add up. If they had conceived me on that night of November 1989, I'd be almost one year younger. With a sort of bleak smugness, like it was my turn to tear down the remains of that wall in Berlin, I ordered him another fifteen-dollar drink.

It loosened his tongue a bit.

"The next morning, I woke up on the couch in some strangers' apartment with my arms around Varvara. She burst into tears saying she couldn't go back home. She had lost her mother as a child. Her father loved her insanely. He would kill her the moment he learned she spent the night with a Jew like me. I asked, 'Are you sure you spent the night with me?' and she cried even harder. I suggested we should elope to Berlin. We rushed to central station, but once there we realized all they had torn down was a wall in Berlin. You still needed papers to cross the border, and neither of us had them. So, we boarded the next train to Leningrad, bent on covering her tracks. We left Moscow bound for Leningrad and got to Petersburg instead, because in my absence they had changed the name of my hometown."

He'd done it again! Enough with his incongruous dates! I ventured one of those arithmetic objections which, since the days I was a child prodigy, were sure to tick him off. "I was born at least ten months before the fall of the Berlin wall, Dad. In Leningrad, maybe?" I had spoken in English. I never learned to hold a conversation in Russian.

He gave me a calm bovine stare but no answer. "Varvara never recovered from our flight from Moscow," he said out of turn. "She never, never, never got back in touch with her father."

"My grandfather…?"

"The Jew Hater… He died of heartbreak."

"And Mom?" I ventured the taboo question, counting on the effect of that second drink.

"Mom… What are you asking about Mom?"

"What did she die of since she died that I was so little?"

"You can't find a black cat in a dark room, if the cat is not there, Son. This is something Varvara could never grasp," he declared in a tone that invited no argument. Then he tilted his head back, downed the rest of his drink, and was ready to leave. I followed him out of the hotel's lobby.

When we parted ways, I looked at him for a long time as he wandered along the edge of the beach of Lake Michigan. Between his path and the leaden waters of the lake there rose huge blocks of ice, iceberg-like. He had become a faraway dot when I got to thinking that the direction he was walking didn't lead anywhere. Now I knew even less than I did before, as to the way I came to be born, or why.

For a moment I deluded myself, that winter day at the Drake Hotel, that a fist of dollars would buy me the truth.

Would he be astounded by my move to Paris? Impressed?

That I've been living here in Palo Alto for the last ten years, he learned a couple years back from a tweet of mine.

CHAPTER TWO

Anton opens his eyes in the middle of a dream: a hailstorm rages on the Eiffel Tower. Sophie's eyes are gazing into his as in the old days. Their heads rest on the same pillow. He hears the soft voice of that French singer, Brel. The song is the same he was singing before Anton fell asleep.

"You haven't changed at all," Sophie says with her usual smile and her usual tone of voice. "And me, do you find me changed?"

"No… Except your hair."

She is going to reply something when he hears the hailstorm's noise again.

"Is it a storm?" he asks.

"A storm? Why on earth there should be a storm?"

"I hear hailstones."

"No, it's the Dimwits who throw gravel against my window shutters to wake me," she answers with a curt shrug, and her mood dampens again.

He takes a shower in Sophie's bathroom. He puts on yesterday's clothes and finds the bedroom's French window wide open on the garden. Behind the garden's fence, a breeze shakes the branches of a few big trees, and above their crowns peeps out the semicircle of the roofs looking out over place de l'Alma. Sophie is lying on a beach chair, a glass in her hand. Two other beach chairs are taken by the couple, he surmises, she just called the Dimwits. They too hold a glass in their hands. Several empty glasses are scattered pell-mell on the gravel at the foot of their beach chairs. How long did they wait here in Sophie's garden, throwing gravel at her window? A couple of patio heaters warm up the air around the party.

Nobody gets up when he appears in the garden, except Elvis who runs to lick his hands. Sophie makes introductions omitting to mention his name. His presence must've been announced while he was under the shower.

"Michel and Ursula."

Michel and Ursula. The Dimwits.

A burly Japanese man pops out of the shadow holding a cocktail shaker and improvises a weird tarantella – *shake shake shake* – with an inscrutable expression on his face. Anton is still standing. While the Japanese man pours the pink contents of the shaker into four fresh glasses, Sophie utters, "Masao." Her voice is addressed to no one in particular; at first Anton thinks she's mewing like a cat, then he realizes he just met the third member of the personnel, the cook Masao.

What did Dambreuil mean by *the spy*?

Masao nods at him with the same inscrutable expression on his face. Anton helps him pick up the empty glasses scattered on the gravel under the beach chairs, even if he knows he is breaking some rule of etiquette. Masao disappears holding a tray loaded with empty glasses.

The patio heaters are too hot. Anton pulls his chair on the grass by the hedge next to the fence. It's too late when he realizes that this position cuts him off the threesome party, whose chairs are facing the building. From where he sits, if he looks straight in front, he can see the car traffic in the square through the tree trunks. He sniffs the pink liquid in his glass and then puts the glass down on the grass without tasting it. Elvis approaches and sniffs it too: it seems they are of the same opinion. He must make an effort not to be totally absorbed by the sight of the traffic on the square.

Michel and Ursula. First impression: they are younger than they try to look. Twenty-one, twenty-two at most, which makes them not quite ten years his juniors. He is blond, she is brunette, but the hair of both is dyed, so who knows? Michel's dark jacket has a very thin lapel, he wears an equally thin tie on a white shirt, his hair seems to have been sculpted around his skull, and his cheeks are pink with makeup. On his lap sits an old-fashioned Compaq PC with the lid down. Ursula wears a pink polka-dot dress cinched at the waist, the skirt so wide that it hides most of her chair. Her black hair is piled up in a conical shape, beehive-like, her lips are coral pink, and her eyes are lengthened at the sides by two dark commas of mascara. It looks as though they were runaways from the Fifties – or Sixties? He's handsome, in his own way. She's not.

"Ursula… May I have your opinion?" Anton hears Michel speak to Ursula but meaning to be heard by the rest of the party. He speaks English. "Do you think we are still having fun in Paris?"

The jingle of ice cubes from his glass tells Anton he is downing a mouthful.

"No," Ursula answers. "We are not having fun anymore in Paris, not at all."

"Then I have no regrets," Michel says. "I was right to go do my studies in Oxford."

"You are a thousand times right," she says, with a suction-like noise that makes Anton turn his head. While speaking, she keeps sucking on her drink with a straw. "That's why I went do my studies in Geneva."

Bitcoin and the Ritual of Kyudo Archery

"In Paris, you know," Michel says, still addressing Ursula, "I feel I am a ghost."

With another jingle of ice cubes, he raises both arms and gives a long howl.

Anton has no idea what they are talking about. But he feels suddenly propelled onto an alternative reality where he himself is the ghost. He has a hunch that he arrived much too early on the scene of Sophie's new life in Paris. Or maybe he hasn't arrived at all yet. Is this someone else's life, perhaps that of some character from a Belmondo's novel?

As this conversation goes on, Sophie stares into the bottom of her glass, sniffs it, sips from it, stares into it again: she pretends she isn't aware that Anton is looking at her.

Bashir comes out of the same shadow into which Masao has vanished a bit ago, to report that Sophie's SUV is parked in front of the entrance to the building.

Sophie snaps out of her musing and speaks to her two neighbors: "No, tonight we go out on foot for once!"

Anton is not 100% sure he is invited to join the party, but is cheered up by Bashir's voice, singing under his breath as he passes him by: *I'm a creep, I'm a weirdo...*

"Pont de l'Alma," Michel says as they cross the Seine, walking arm in arm with Anton. Anton is tempted to ask him why he is in Paris in February, and not in Oxford *doing his studies*, but he keeps it to himself: a few ill-intentioned words mean always more than you say. He lets him do the talking. Michel wears a green wool herringbone coat over his jacket.

"Place de l'École Militaire," Michel says while they circumnavigate that square. He points a finger at a Music School on the left. "I am a musicologist," he explains.

"Are you enrolled here?" Anton ventures asking, most of all because he hasn't heard the sound of his own voice for too long. Maybe here in France, American words don't mean more than they say.

"If they want me at Oxford, they take me on my own terms."

Negative test: Michel felt his hostility. And besides, are they truly in Paris? As far as Anton is concerned, he could be in any European city in the company of three perfect strangers.

He put on his sweater before going out, but it's not too cold at this late hour. The night traffic gets thinner and thinner. The streetlights flash their lights – red green red green – for nothing and nobody, just them.

Sophie and Ursula walk arm in arm too. Sophie wears a wide fur coat and holds Elvis by a short thick leather leash with her right hand. Ursula wears a green wool coat that traces the outline of her polka-dot dress.

"Boulevard des Invalides... boulevard de Montparnasse..."

Sophie lets go of Ursula's arm and walks toward Anton with a pleased smile on her lips. She unbuttons her fur coat and enwraps him in it with a hug. He can feel the heat of her body and doesn't mind her cheeks swollen by alcohol and her candy-smelling breath. Elvis' one front paw rests on his lower back. It occurs to him that Sophie was waiting for this moment, and this walk was taken in his honor. But why? He hugs her back, his arms under the silk lining of her fur coat.

She speaks into his ear: "This green store is the Tschann Bookstore."

Bitcoin and the Ritual of Kyudo Archery

They break the embrace to look at a couple of darkish windows, chock-full of books. Is the idea that this is where he can buy his Belmondo novels?

Her right arm is around his waist. "See those windows above the bookstore? Your idol lives there."

"My idol…?"

"*Mais oui*, Belmondo!"

Anton raises his eyes and in one of the windows on the second floor sees a white-haired man who is looking down at then. He looks really tall.

"You are lucky," Sophie says with a strange music in her voice that reminds him of something. "There he is."

Anton checks his watch. It's almost three AM. He raises his eyes again and Patrick Belmondo is still there, looking down. Anton raises his index finger above the eyebrow. Belmondo returns the military salute.

Paris! Now at last – yes! – the network of streets and squares they just walked through adjusts as if by magic to a section of Anton's Michelin street map – the flag-dotted map that right now is flying on a cargo plane toward him. He feels as though he reached his destination for good. He is in the city of his new life with Sophie, and starts breathing a bit easier.

Paris.

Their two faces are very close to each other. He turns Sophie's, holding her chin with two fingers, till their eyes meet. The contraction in her nostrils slackens and the light in her eyes angles for her Palo Alto shine, intently, bit by bit, like a wreckage emerging intact to a lake's surface.

Anton forgot for a long moment the presence of Michel and Ursula. He hears Ursula whisper, "The writer at the window is fit for a straitjacket." He discerns her words, they are spoken in the language he speaks, but they don't mean a thing. Not a thing. He pictures himself lodging into his Paris street map the flag pushpin destined to commemorate the night of his homecoming to this city. He wheels around, lays his left hand, still beneath Sophie's fur coat, on her shoulder, and raises her left hand with his right one. The idea is to dance her smoothly toward the corner of the building –he saw Fred Astaire do that sort of move countless times at the Stanford movie theater – but his feet get entangled with Elvis' legs. He is afraid of stepping on his paws.

Sophie takes things in her hands, pushes her pubic bone against his, and steers the three of them in sync toward his chosen destination.

At the corner he memorizes the coordinates of the next flag on his Michelin map: "boulevard de Montparnasse" on this side, "rue de Chevreuse" on the other.

Bitcoin and the Ritual of Kyudo Archery

BRAIN WALLET # 4

At the time of my move to Palo Alto – ten, eleven years ago, give or take – there was no rambling Jesus yet, sitting all day long on that bench in University Avenue in front of the J. P. Morgan's offices. Everybody still called him his real name: Daniel.

Next is my first meeting with Daniel, in the Spring of 2008. *I cut and paste (literally, with tape and scissors) a page from my journal.*

I'm sitting at a table of Café Venetia on the sidewalk of University Avenue. I've just been hired at Google. I won't start my new job for another week. Yesterday I rented an apartment in downtown Palo Alto, close to Café Venetia. My hands are shaking, all of a sudden. I moved out of my room on the Pittsburgh campus without letting my resident assistant know. I dropped four computer science classes without notifying the instructtor. I forgot to pack half of my belongings. It's at least a year that girls give me stomach cramps. And it occurs to me, who knows why, that at my age, eighteen, my parents were still considered minors in Petersburg. I type on the keyboard of my Dell PC at a panicky pace, the acid of too many espressos in my throat. Before leaving Pittsburgh, I could have asked for a partial refund of my college fees. I could have taken a one-year leave from college. I could have given a call to the girl I got drunk with that last weekend. Of all possible plots, it's the most arbitrary one that unfolds. Not even this new job at Google makes sense: better and older students had applied from Pittsburgh, and Google picked me instead.

A hand brushes against my fingers, like it's trying to slow me down. I jump in my chair as I pull back my right arm. Then I look up and meet the gaze of two pale blue eyes.

The stranger, his head crowned with an old-fashioned pompadour that reminds me of a yellow cockscomb, whispers with a smile, "You think of the code you are writing as a finish line, but it's just a reflection of yourself." Then he adds in a good-natured tone, shaking his head and pointing a finger at my Dell, "On the other hand, with that type of machine…"

A little later, Daniel is telling me that in every ritual the form of the tool is crucial to the result. Apparently, he puts coding on a par with religious rituals. Steve Jobs, he adds, has brought formal balance to the world of computational science, shucking off its inherent aggressiveness – and giving the lie, on top of it, to those who claim Jobs is a bully. For the same reason, Daniel worships Enzo Ferrari, an automotive innovator from Italy, passed away long ago.

A few weeks later, he gives me my first Mac.

Bitcoin and the Ritual of Kyudo Archery

BRAIN WALLET # 5

That I'm using, as my treasure map, the Michelin street map of the city I'll soon be moving to, is a mere coincidence. The day I bought that map of Paris, I had just finished reading *Deeper than Forgetfulness*, a novel by Patrick Belmondo that is set there. The protagonists are three twenty-year olds: Jean, Jacqueline, and Van Bever. My move to France was not even in the cards yet.

You want to know how my treasure map works?

Take, on the map, the tiny wedge in the Latin Quarter, south of the Seine, whose corners are marked with three orange flag pushpins. The pushpins are linked to one another by a red ribbon that traces the sides of the wedge. On each of the three orange flags, I've written an address in black ink: rue de la Tournelle, rue des Bernardins, rue Dante.

The rest is in my head.

The hotel where Jacqueline and Van Bever share a room is on rue de la Tournelle.

The hotel where Jean takes a room shortly after making the acquaintance of Jacqueline and Van Bever, is on rue des Bernardins, not far from rue de la Tournelle.

The café where Jacqueline and Van Bever meet at dawn, on the nights after he tries his luck in some out-of-town casino, is on rue Dante.

On boulevard Haussmann, further north than the red wedge, there is another orange flag linked to the flag on rue Dante by the same red ribbon. Pierre Cartaud holds a dental office there, on the Right Bank: 160 boulevard Haussmann. Jacqueline sells herself to him in his office on the days when

Beau de Rubempré

Van Bever comes back empty-handed from the casinos. Pierre is fifteen years their senior.

In Belmondo's novel, Jean steals a briefcase from Pierre's office, supposedly full of cash, at Jacqueline's behest. Jean and Jacqueline plan to go hide in some Mediterranean sea town. Unbeknownst to Jean, she has designs on an American man who lives in Majorca. They run away to London, instead, when it turns out that the stolen briefcase holds just a slim sheaf of banknotes. Jean writes a letter to Pierre promising to return the money.

In Paris, Jacqueline was Van Bever's girlfriend. In London, she's Jean's.

I based on that wedge south of the Seine the first proof of concept I executed on the Michelin street map. All it takes is, you append a short string of words to a place on the map. I understand that a certain Hugh of St. Victor, back in the Middle Ages, used a diagram of Noah's ark to the same purpose.

My *Open Sesame* includes twelve words. Here we go.

When I look at the orange flag pinned on rue de la Tournelle, I think automatically of the first three of my twelve words: *long hair whisper*. Well, it can't possibly be as simple as that, I hear you say. Indeed, it's not. This is how I see it. I look at the orange flag pinned on rue de la Tournelle, and a gate opens in my mental picture of the streets of Paris from the map. I walk through that gate and I see Jacqueline, my idea of her on rue de la Tournelle, where she lives: her long hair down to her waist, her lungs going into a coughing fit at each cigarette she smokes, her gravelly whisper luring Jean into petty crime. That's how I piece together the first three words of my passphrase: *long hair whisper.*

Bitcoin and the Ritual of Kyudo Archery

The same way I revisit the café of rue Dante to picture Van Bever starving for coffee and croissants at dawn after a night spent playing number 5 on every available roulette with his martingale method, and I piece together: *number method dawn coffee*.

Next comes the hotel on rue des Bernardins where I picture Jean's ill-humor when Jacqueline is absent, the heavy doses of ether he takes in bed with her when Van Bever is out gambling, and I piece together: *humor heavy dose absent*.

So, I string together the resulting eleven words, and then (a trick of the trade, sorry) I pick once again the third word, *whisper*, as the twelfth in my twelve-word list. That's my *Open Sesame*.

Here we aren't in the fairy-tale land of Ali Baba, the forty thieves, magic caves and magic spells. We are in the real world of cryptographers and secret passphrases. I warned you: it sounds like magic, it reads like magic, it works like magic, but it's just mathematics, plus a pinch of theory of chance. The one thing that doesn't change with respect to fairy-tale land is that there is a sealed crypt – Крипта, *Kripta*, in the tongue spoken by my mother – which you want to make unbreachable.

Now for the home stretch. My twelve-word list reads: *long hair whisper number method dawn coffee humor heavy dose absent whisper*. I add a pinch of salt to it (trick of the trade number 2), and type the salted version into an apparatus in my Mac that generates this string of characters:

xprv9z4GrGcomPtKSyk36rcGFfiWFEcnR1nxYBt2iby7DP6tvB8o Vpei17fe5bF6ivvh9vdhUkYjiu8arV17e4XaQpP4uKwFpnxnHWW G4H1kwkm

This string, called hash, is the secret key to my treasure. The hash travels up and down the blockchain till it opens – literally, one by one – all the virtual vaults which I hold my bitcoins in: mini crypts inside the Mother *Kripta*.

Not for nothing that hash is called *secret key*: whoever knows it, can open those mini crypts and claim ownership of all my bitcoins. When in need, I revisit, guided by the orange flags, my mental picture of Paris' streets, walk through those same gates, meet again with Jean, Jacqueline, and Van Bever, recall one by one the words of my passphrase, use them to generate the secret key, and finally use the secret key to get ahold of my bitcoin crypts. And then I forget it all again, till next time.

Some hackers would have it that my bitcoin secret key is tantamount to several crypto-identities: one for each stash of bitcoins I hold in one of those crypts. Everybody can see the contents of those crypts, because each one of them figures in this or that block of the blockchain, yet nobody, unless I choose otherwise, knows that it's me who holds the key. My own anonymity entitles me to as many crypto-identities as there are crypts in my account, multiple ID's of sorts. I don one of my many crypto capes and become someone else.

Mind you, the long hash I transcribed above is a mere proof of concept, it doesn't open the crypt to any real treasure. No bitcoins in there, last time I checked.

I'm twenty-nine years old and never forget a thing. Not a thing. These mnemonic exercises won't let me down for many decades. Turning the map of a strange city into an archive of secret codes is hardly a new solution, if that Hugh of St. Victor was already doing something like that back in the Middle Ages.

Bitcoin and the Ritual of Kyudo Archery

I'm refraining from defining it one of the best solutions in the crypto space – even if I think it is – because sooner or later you meet the hacker who is better and faster than you. And I don't need to tell you if you're in the hacking business, you'll be hacked to pieces sooner, rather than later, if you can't resist boasting of your bouts of ingenuity.

What happened to Jesus, I take it as a lesson. I must have already said that.

BRAIN WALLET # 6

Fate or chance brought me, one morning a couple years ago, to the scene of the crime. It's me who found Daniel in a pool of blood on the floor of his Palo Alto apartment – with a nail stuck in his skull, as I later found out. Several months later, Daniel walked out of the Stanford hospital like he was risen from the grave, a half-witted idiot inexplicably steady on his feet. I don't know who, at the time, gave him that nickname, Jesus. Jesus, the homeless guy you always find sitting on the bench facing the J. P. Morgan offices in University Avenue. Beforehand, everybody in the crypto space knew him as Daniel Dunne.

Based on the most elusive of clues (a nail stuck in his brain to this day, a stolen Mac, and, maybe, the theft of some hundreds of thousands of bitcoin), I must guess the plot that leads to the crime.

Guess doesn't even seem like the right word here. I must tell myself, backwards, a story all of which I know is the end.

You need an oracle of the sort used by cryptographers – a machine, in sum – to guess a certainty out of an uncertainty. But how do I turn myself into a machine, and of all possible plots leading to Daniel's fate, pick the right one? And even assuming I could turn myself into a machine at will, and reach absolute certainty as to the fate suffered by Daniel, would I really want it? What does a machine know of love? Of loss?

Since the moment I discovered Daniel's lifeless body on the floor of his Palo Alto apartment, my heart's been gnawed by such a pain that what happened to him is totally incomprehensible to me. As a child prodigy, the left side of my brain never needed much training; to this day, it serves me like a well-tuned machine. My brain's opposite side is linked to the heart, though, and that part must've been left half-empty, back at home in Chicago.

Does this make sense to you?

That lifeless body, that pool of blood, that nail stuck in Daniel's brain, that inconceivable, new-found idiocy of his: it's all like a tall, blood-red stony wall splitting the lengths of my heart in two. *Lub-dub, lub-dub, lub-dub.* That wall blinds me to the evidence. It keeps me from crossing to the dark side, where hides the face of a stranger peddling horror. Whenever I'm visited by the sight of Daniel's lifeless body, which happens in a totally randomized way when I least expect it, I can't write on this Moleskine any longer because my fountainpen feels like it's filled with blood, and I can't eat my meal any longer because my plate feels like it's filled with raw flesh. And I can't shoot my bow either, because it's Jesus who's the target.

Guess is positively not the right word for this stage of my mission. The plot I'm seeking to reveal lives in the private memory of the stranger who assaulted Daniel, and is forever inaccessible to me. There may be thousand alternative ways of retelling that plot, all leading to the same last page, the same unhappy ending. Guessing the best string of words to tell it is not even the point. The point, my mission, is to climb above and beyond that blood-red wall till my heart sinks knee-deep into the scene of the aggression against Daniel. I must live through the aggression with the right side of my brain, with my whole heart – face to face with the face of the stranger. Words won't matter any longer then.

I know no right name for this endeavor.

Beau de Rubempré

Find me, if you can, the word that will thrust my heart into the blind randomness of a necessary crime. *Necessary*: that which we can't undo? That'll be the word I'm looking for. A word with zero entropy.

First I lost Sophie, then I lost Daniel. I'm not left with one good enough reason to keep living in Palo Alto. Except the compilation of this Moleskine, the exculpatory evidence I'm entrusting to you, whatever comes next. Whoever you are.

Memo for later: *Sophie jumped up abruptly to her feet, picked up her bow and arrows, and left the pavilion without a word, the wind gust that blew through the door threw me off-balance. I had to support my weight with the left arm not to fall sideways.*

Bitcoin and the Ritual of Kyudo Archery

CHAPTER THREE

Anton wakes up around two PM in Sophie's bed. While they were out on their walk, someone lifted up the mattress from the floor and put it back up on the bed-frame. Sophie is still asleep. Followed by Elvis, he walks out of the room on tiptoe, puts on his same old clothes, and they both get into the elevator to his apartment upstairs.

There is an email from Nessim in his iPhone: "Welcome to the city of lights." Anton must feel free to use Nessim's Bentley in the garage, it says. "It's a good thing I forgot to get rid of it, you can have it now, *mon ami*!"

So, the powder-blue convertible down in the garage is a Bentley. Nessim's.

Anton's primary target, coming forward of his own will?

Anton and Nessim have met several times when Sophie's husband was, in a fiscal sort of way, a California resident. Nessim can't have totally missed Anton's affair with his wife at the time, but here he is, making the best of the situation: the day Anton moves in with Sophie, he puts his expensive car at his disposal. *Nessim knows everything… Nessim collects information with the automatism of a robot.*

Lesson learned at Google: the most star-crossed hacker is the one who is unaware of being hacked by his own target.

Of all local terms of endearment, *mon ami* is among the few within reach of Anton's inexistent French. Is Anton acting paranoid when he wonders how could Nessim know that?

There is a professional espresso machine in the kitchen. *Modnyye veshchi*, fancy stuff.

Beau de Rubempré

Anton takes a shower, gets himself a pair of briefs from the backpack on the floor of the living room, puts on his kyudo outfit, and gets into the elevator to the basement floor. Elvis seems determined not to lose sight of him.

As he faces the bow rack, he muses over the prospect of solitary archery: it's the first time ever he practices all by myself. Think of it: it's the first time he handles a bow since the aggression against Daniel. All this time in Palo Alto, Daniel's sister's generous offer of the kyudojo went unheeded. Just the thought of setting foot in there – Anton's coming-of-age gymnasium, sort of – terrified him.

But this new kyudojo is a different story.

He picks Daniel's favorite bow, a lacquered shigeto-yumi wound with patterned strips of dark wood, and strings it.

Elvis curls up in a corner of the shooting platform.

He hits several good shots. After each shot, the vibration of the bowstring makes a sustained sound that brings him back to the days when Daniel used this bow to practice with him and Sophie. He doesn't need more than half an hour, most of it spent kneeling in the kiza posture, to restore his center of gravity.

He can even afford to get rid of his paranoia. No, Nessim doesn't even care if Anton's French measures up to his terms of endearment. French is lingua franca in Nessim's world. And no, the Bentley is not a Trojan horse.

He and Elvis make an inspection of the garage. The Bentley is a recent model. The top is down and the key is in the cubbyhole under the handbrake. He leans against the door to check if it has push ignition. Under his hands, the smooth car body gives the impression of touching powder-blue porcelain.

Bitcoin and the Ritual of Kyudo Archery

The moment they reach the third floor again, he is WhatsApped by Dambreuil. She noticed he is up already. Monsieur has instructions for her? Presumably madame will sleep for several more hours.

No, Monsieur has no instructions for her.

Thanks to Nessim's offer of the Bentley, he can make a first exploratory tour of the city. He and Elvis go back down to the garage and he messes about the Bentley's GPS as he consults *Google Earth* on the iPhone. He needs to search his memory before remembering that quai de Passy, which runs by the Seine, is called avenue du president Kennedy now. Avenue de Versailles runs by the Seine too, but a chain of tall buildings shields it from the bank of the river. To reach porte d'Auteuil on boulevard Murat from there, he'll need to take boulevard Exelmans first. A smile comes to his lips when he remembers this is the first Parisian itinerary he learned by heart on the Michelin street map, without ever setting foot in the city.

Boulogne-Billancourt's townhall is not too far from porte d'Auteuil.

Every time he thinks back to Belmondo's *Deeper than Forgetfulness*, it strikes him that there are people who don't have to think twice when in need of a birth certificate. In 1979, passing through Paris, Jean, the novel's protagonist, walks to Boulogne-Billancourt, near the Bois de Boulogne, to get his birth certificate from townhall. Then, the certificate in his pocket, he walks back to his hotel on avenue de New York. All of this is documented on Anton's Michelin street map with orange flag-pushpins. As he walks, Jean mulls over the signature on the original document: the name of the father who, when he was a boy, arranged for the two of them to meet in restaurants of train stations, as though those transitory spots made it easier for him to get rid of his teenage son.

Jean goes through porte d'Auteil and walks in the direction of porte de la Muette. Before getting there, he rests on a bench, and sees Jacqueline get out of a parked car. He follows her till she walks into an apartment building. He had lost sight of Jacqueline since the summer of 1964, when they took refuge in London. In the British capital city, he had found his vocation as a writer. She kept trading her body against favors from older men. Her hair is shorter now.

That evening Jean goes back to where he saw Jacqueline. There is a hubbub of activity by the entrance to the building, small groups of people seem to walk in, one after the next, to go into a party. Jean decides to crash the party. The host is called Darius. Jacqueline shows up shortly later: still beautiful, elegantly dressed, her shoulders naked, escorted by her American husband and some friends. Jacqueline now calls herself Thèrése. When she smokes, she doesn't go anymore into her old coughing fits, and her voice is not so deep now. Jacqueline pretends she doesn't recognize Jean, but at the moment of taking leave of the party, with a pretext she joins him out of the building and volunteers to give him a ride to his hotel. While she drives her car down boulevard Suchet, bound for porte Maillot, Jean tells himself that's not the right direction to his hotel.

A few minutes later, Jacqueline's intentions become as clear to Jean as they remain obscure to the reader who is unacquainted with the city plan – as Anton was when he read the novel. Who would've known that their car was running alongside the length of Bois de Boulogne? Who would've known that a simple left turn stood between the car's two passengers and a quiet shadowy corner? Anton was reading and misreading at once… Nowadays, forty years later, the Bois de Boulogne won't be anymore – Anton's guess – the free lawless zone of yore. But on this August night of 1979, shadow and darkness surround soon the two lovers.

Anton climbs the ramp out of the garage without trying to find out how to lower the Bentley's top. Elvis is on the passenger's seat. He couldn't find any rag in the garage to cover the passenger's seat. The sun is not warm yet, but driving with the top down won't be a problem if he keeps his speed down. The sunlight shines like a sheet of glare on the surface of the Seine while he drives along its bank on avenue du president Kennedy, leaving the Eiffel Tower behind. He covers some distance on avenue de Versailles, then on boulevard Exelmans. A road sign on boulevard Murat reminds him that as he walks away from townhall in Boulogne-Billancourt with the birth certificate in his pocket, Jean finds himself in the vicinities of a racetrack. Porte d'Auteuil, boulevard Suchet. They orbit several times the rings of three adjoining roundabouts still under construction in the square of porte Maillot, before turning into the same street that in 1979 led Jean and Jacqueline-Thérèse to the shadows of the Bois de Boulogne.

He stops on the side of the road to taste his success, taken aback by the weird emotion he is feeling for being in the place where Jean held Jacqueline in his arms for one last time.

Then he follows the instructions from the GPS, ten minutes later he is circumnavigating the Arch of Triumph, and in a few more minutes he is parking the Bentley in the underground garage near Sophie's black SUV.

Bitcoin and the Ritual of Kyudo Archery

CHAPTER FOUR

Michel and Ursula's beach chairs face the French window of Sophie's bedroom. Michel's Compaq is on his lap, the lid wide open this time. Anton and Elvis enter the garden from the vestibule, coming from behind, so he can take a peek at the screen of the Compaq before Michel is aware of their presence. When Anton is by his side, Michel lowers the Compaq's lid with ostentatious speed, sort of theatrical, giving him a defiant smile. His smile adds the missing tassel to Anton's mosaic of evidence. Michel's screen showed the typical patterns of a keylogger, an application tasked with recording the finger movements on the keyboard of the hacker's victim. Old Compaq PCs of that sort are a perfect shell when it comes to hiding within, behind the façade of obsolete technology, the artisanal machine of a professional hacker: giant hard drives, esoteric operating system, secret partitions conducive to plausible deniability, dead man's switches, etc. But it's above all the defiance of Michel's smile that's unmistakable: Anton is dealing with the sort of hacker who can't wait to show off his own skills and recklessness. So much for the musicologist!

Michel's delighted anger at being found out discharges in a gibe at Elvis: "The sight of that dog gives me a neckache!" he declares.

Judging from Elvis' spiny hackles, the dislike is mutual.

As he trades pleasantries with Ursula, Anton gathers one more tassel in support of his intuition: Ursula and Michel don't wear clothes but costumes – uniforms of sorts. Michel is an identical duplicate of the pretentious boy I met yesterday, down to the same freshly laundered white shirt, same cufflinks, same tie, same socks, same shiny leather shoes, same thin-lapelled dark jacket. Even his makeup duplicates to a T the paleness of the skin against the pink shade of the cheeks. Ursula seems to have staged with accuracy every detail in her appearance, down to her mannerisms: same pink polka-dot dress, same coral lipstick, same beehive hairdo, same dark commas of mascara lengthening her eyes, and as she talks to Anton, she keeps sucking on her drink with a straw, making the same suction-like noise that made Anton turn his head yesterday. It feels as though these two were constantly modeling for the same photo shoot. Or rehearsing the same play on an imaginary stage at Burning Man.

Anton doesn't even try to count the empty glasses scattered at the foot of their beach chairs. The patio heaters warm up the air above them.

He is a bit dispirited at the prospect of the tough work ahead of him tonight, to fix the possible damage made by Michel to Sophie's router, WiFi, and Mac. Add to it the burden of his jet lag, which makes him hover between sleep and wakefulness. Add to it the burden of this house's routine, where waking and sleeping hours have been all but upended. Sophie is still sleeping but it's past six PM! Before the Dimwits monopolize her attention, when she finally gets up, Anton must squeeze all her passwords out of her. How can she possibly be blind to the sort of people she hangs around with at home? Hasn't she learned yet that ordinary people don't treat cryptography like an impartial exercise in pure logics, the way she does?

Anton must see this through, and fast.

Bitcoin and the Ritual of Kyudo Archery

He takes comfort in the almost certainty that Michel belongs to the sort of black hats who are too vain to be truly lethal. After all, he shouldn't brace himself for too tough a job, tonight. Just tedious.

If he deluded himself that he'd come to Paris, live under the same roof with Nessim, slip a keylogger into his machine, and drag out of it the proofs of his crime, well, this prospect is screwed for the time being. If he fancied himself an American Sherlock Holmes of sorts, fast at work on his Map of the Crime, well, he just crossed path with a rival Sherlock Holmes – Parisian, this one.

Anton wishes he knew for sure at least that Michel was put on his path on purpose. Nessim's Trojan horse?

When he takes leave of Michel and Ursula, Sophie hasn't made an appearance yet. He goes up to his apartment followed by Elvis. He needs to collect his thoughts. He doesn't want to miss Sophie when she gets up: he is in a hurry to rid her digital systems of all potential malware, so he needs to tackle her before alcohol and the Dimwits take possession of her. He opens one of the windows that overlook place de l'Alma to check if it gives him a good view of the garden from here.

The patch of gravel under the beach chairs is directly beneath the windowsill. He can't help noticing that the lid of Michel's Compaq is opened again. Instinctively, he opens his mouth wide and is on the verge of calling Michel's name at the top of his lungs. Then tactical patience prevails over spite, and he holds his tongue: never waste your stock-in-trade over a stunt.

He kneels down in the kiza posture to rebalance his center of gravity. Dusk is setting in. Through the open window, he keeps his eyes fixed on the Eiffel Tower: behind its framework, a raggy cloud shines its glow-in-the-dark whiteness against the darkening blue sky. From time to time, he hears the crackle of the gravel that Michel and Ursula throw at the window shutters of Sophie's room.

He rushes back down to the garden as soon as he hears Sophie's voice speak.

Masao the cook is already starting his tarantella – *shake shake shake* – and it's with difficulty that Anton manages to take Sophie aside. Her expression tells him anyway that he shouldn't count on keeping her away from her first drink for too long. He cuts it short and just claims that her router and WiFi are badly compromised. He refrains from mentioning his suspicions of Michel. They reach her study and she scribbles on a sheet of paper, without a fuss, all the passwords he demands, her Mac's included. Then she shows him the room where she keeps the router and the wireless access point, together with the printers.

When they step back into the garden, Masao is waiting for them, holding two glasses filled with a greenish liquid. Anton notices with some relief that he gives Sophie the same inscrutable stare he gives him. He puts his glass down on the gravel and listens to the conversation standing up. The walk they took last night was an exception in his honor, but Sophie agrees with Ursula that tonight they'll have to go back to their usual joints.

"… and perhaps discover some new joints to celebrate our new mate," Ursula says, winking at Anton. The straw she holds between her lips gives her an inflection midway between sorrowful and seductive. She isn't pretty but there's shrewdness in the vamp she made herself into.

Anton seizes the moment and explains that tonight he must do urgent work for his mining plants in Iceland, so, sorry, can't join them. It's a stupid pretext, but he doubts Sophie is clear-minded enough to connect his urgent tasks with the compromised state of her systems.

"I want you to promise you'll join us tomorrow night, though," Ursula fights back. "Tomorrow is special, tomorrow it's Thursday…"

"Thursday!" Michel shouts out with a toasting gesture, and he starts singing a Brel song Anton has heard many times already, in bed with Sophie.

Bashir and Dambreuil pop out of the same shadow which Masao vanished into. Bashir reports that the SUV is parked in front of the entrance to the building. Right away, Sophie, Michel, and Ursula get ready to go out.

Anton, Elvis, and Dambreuil walk them to the doorsteps.

"What time are you planning to be back, madame?" Dambreuil asks while Sophie climbs onto the back seat of the car, where Michel and Ursula are already installed. Dambreuil's voice resonates with the feeble concern of a mother whose daughter's life is at risk.

"Very late, demoiselle. Don't stay up for me."

"Yes, yes, I'll be here waiting for madame."

From behind the car's side window, Sophie waves at Anton shyly, and the pretense of confidence behind her smile seems to be begging for mercy.

No sooner does the black SUV vanish on the bridge over the Seine than Dambreuil reproaches Anton for leaving Sophie alone with those two Characters. The Dimwits, she calls Characters.

He shrugs his shoulders. "Where do those Characters come out of, demoiselle?" he asks.

For a whole month after Nessim moved in with his Yemeni sex slave, Sophie didn't set foot out of the house. Then, one day, she went out for a walk by herself, and on her way back, she brought the Characters along. From that day onwards, white nights became a constant habit for madame. "But I had seen them hang out near here several times, those Characters," she adds, "whenever Bashir and I came back from some shopping. It's Bashir who noticed them first, it's his job, you know. Always there by our fence, waiting for Godot."

"Whom did you say they were waiting for?"

If it wasn't the obsequious Dambreuil Anton is talking with, he'd say she's just given him an impertinent stare.

"I meant to say, monsieur Anton, that it looked as though they were always waiting for someone who never showed up…"

"Unless they were waiting for madame," he ventures.

This time he gets an appreciative look. They get each other, don't they? She tells Anton once more that everything depends on him, nobody else can save the situation, etc. "You know, monsieur Anton, there are still those TEXOR engineers waiting for the algorithmics."

Bitcoin and the Ritual of Kyudo Archery

BRAIN WALLET # 7

It occurs to me that the word I'm seeking is *revenge*, maybe. A scary thought, when you think of it.

The secret key of my real bitcoin portfolio is buried within the lopsided triangle of red ribbon marked with four orange flags next to the Bois de Boulogne on my Michelin street map. In Belmondo's *Deeper than Forgetfulness*, that's where the action between Jean and Jacqueline-Thérèse switches to in 1979, when she drives him through porte Maillot (by the fourth orange flag) on their way to the secluded grounds in the woods.

In this case, regretfully, I can't list the eleven words that make up the *Open Sesame*, spread three by three by three by two on the four orange flags (the twelfth word is picked out of those eleven, like before). They are the real thing, not a proof of concept anymore. The mnemonic logic is the same anyway. It lives (or dies) with me.

The black and green ribbons on the map (plus the zig-zagging cobweb of black arrows just north of the Eiffel Tower) link one to another the colored flags that match the *Open Sesame* of my portfolios of three other cryptocurrencies: ethereum, ripple, and zcash. To this day I'm an avid reader of Belmondo: each one of those densely flagged areas circumscribes the Parisian adventures of the protagonists of one of his novels.

Today I started writing on this brand new black Moleskine notebook: six entries so far.

Daniel gave me a set of two red Moleskines for my nineteenth birthday, ten years ago, together with a Pelikan fountainpen like his own. I've bought many more such

Beau de Rubempré

Moleskines since, and have been writing on each of them with that same Pelikan.

"In Italy they have two rare identical reds: Ferrari red and Moleskine red," Daniel told me the day of my nineteenth birthday, pointing at a pile of red Moleskines on his desk. "I drive on Ferrari red and write on Moleskine red."

He was fond of his red Ferrari. Later that day he showed me how to change an ink cartridge: I had never held a fountainpen in my hand before then.

Daniel would often encourage me to write by hand, always keep a journal, and even compose my algorithms without the help of a keyboard – just like he did on his red Moleskines. I heeded his advice. Most of the Moleskine notebooks I bought since, and on which I mixed liberally algorithms and journal entries, were red too, a homage to the Ferrari cult he converted me to; but not this one I'm writing on today, which is the color of grief.

It's Daniel, by the way, who told me of that Hugh of St. Victor who used the diagram of Noah's ark as mnemonic supplement. To the same purpose, as I must have said before, Daniel used the street map of Dublin, the Irish city where he was born. I was supposed to be the only person in the know.

I picked the Paris map for myself because I can't decide once and for all in what city I was born. My father says Petersburg. All of my father's tall stories have a pinch of truth to them, never more than a pinch, though.

At Google I coded in C++ and Java, but mostly they used me as a hacker: *penetration tester* is what you write on the job contract.

Bitcoin and the Ritual of Kyudo Archery

One day at Café Venetia, a few weeks after our first meeting, Daniel stared at me with his pale-blue eyes and said, "Anton, your codes are imbued with Russian melancholy."

This remark went beyond the logic of suki. "You are kidding," I told him with a silent glance.

I'm not a talker if I can help it.

"I'm not kidding at all," he replied, reading my mind. "I could rewrite some blocks of your code in one line. You brood over things, chew on them over and over, first bask in your bout of ingenuity and then give it up. You are the Raskolnikov of coding."

He was right, as I realized quite a bit later on, when, as a coder, I managed to get rid of the temperamental ballast which I carried within myself since childhood. Before meeting Daniel, emotional insecurity dictated the pace of my coding. I say, it's not everyone who can decrypt traces of an individual temperament out of a code written in C++.

As a software engineer, the guidance I got from Daniel for the better part of a decade draws from the rituals of *kyudo* archery, which he initiated me to.

Here are the basics. The motion of the fingers on the Mac's keyboard must match the rhythm of your breathing, the coding mind must be emptied of intrusive thoughts, head neck and spine must be vertically aligned, chest and shoulders must relax effortlessly, and the body's center of gravity must gradually slide toward the lower abdomen. When you think your code is perfect, it's a sign you're being charmed by your own skills: a suki sort of pride is putting you at the hacker's whim. When your code feels lacking, it's a sign you are on the short path to success: humbleness shields you from the hacker.

Beau de Rubempré

Now you see why I don't and can't boast about the degree of passphrase obfuscation obtained by my Michelin map? The truth of humility is in the method.

Daniel had studied *kyudo* for an unspecified number of years in a *ryu* or archery school in Tokyo. And for the duration of his Japanese training, he had refrained from touching a keyboard with his fingers. But it was at that ryu, he used to say, that he made the leap into the ritual of coding. A ritual coder codes on Mac because the kyudo's first rule is harmony in form and gracefulness in motion.

I wasn't nineteen yet at the time we met, I had never heard talk of Raskolnikov before Daniel mentioned it to me (I read *Crime and Punishment*, eventually), I had never much cared about the proper alignment of hand, wrist, and arm in front of a keyboard. Daniel was about thirty-eight, an avid reader of that favorite Irish writer of his. It's by his example that I developed a passion for books. Suffice it to say that on my way to Palo Alto, I had stuffed two books in my backpack: *The Hobbit* and *The Lord of the Rings*. Daniel pushed me further, let's put it this way. I discovered Patrick Belmondo on my own, though, by mere chance at Kepler Bookstore in Menlo Park. Belmondo tells of youths who are more like me than that Russian freak, that *urod*, Raskolnikov.

When Daniel told me he was recovering from a stormy divorce, I had a hard time believing him. It seemed such an oddity, Daniel quarreling with anybody. He was the older brother I never had. Coming from anybody else, his tirades on ethical coding would've left me cold. Worse than that, I'd have shrugged them off, as I had done more than once on campus in Pittsburgh with equivalent advice. How many pints of

Bitcoin and the Ritual of Kyudo Archery

whisky did I down, that first year in Pittsburgh! And what bad stomach cramps did I get from the girls who drank with me! In Palo Alto, with Daniel, I found my center of gravity.

CHAPTER FIVE

There was a weird side to Anton's job at Google. As a penetration tester, you always face two alternatives. You may fight a dangerous hacker by straitjacketing him right away, or you may give him enough rope to hang himself. In the second case, what your superiors register is, first, the damage done by a brilliant hacker, and then, your super-brilliant and timely countermeasures. It's only if you take this second road that you become a local hero: your heroism is proportional to the leverage you give the adversary before striking him. If you take the first road and neutralize the hacker right away, no damage is done to the company, no big brass notices anything: all you gain is the unconditional respect of the adversary.

The whole thing boils down to a matter of professsional integrity. And salary raise.

The two things clashing with each other more often than not.

When Anton tests the vulnerabilities of the mining plants in Iceland, this either/or alternative doesn't hold: he is his own employer. Same tonight: neither his salary nor his reputation is at stake. All he cares is restoring what's compromised as fast as he can — assuming the Dimwits have been up to the job of breaking into Sophie's systems and Mac.

He starts with the router and the wireless access point. No trace of intrusion. He changes all passwords just the same and writes them down for Sophie. He purges the memory of the printers, which is loaded like an elephant's.

Now it's the turn of Sophie's Mac. He reaches her study followed by Elvis, sits at her desk, types her password, and then stops abruptly, his fingers poised mid-air above the keys, puzzled by his own qualm.

He is reminded of Daniel's main lesson: in front of any major obstacle, you must act and think with *the calm elegance of flowing water*. Here he is, having just made access to the Mac of the woman he loves. Free to roam as he pleases. Which leaves him dazed and confused.

He counts to three. One: *calm*. Two: *elegance*. Three: *flow*.

He conforms the pace of his fingers on the keyboard with the pace of his breathing, recalling Daniel's lessons. He aligns head neck and spine in a vertical line, and slides his body's center of gravity down toward the lower abdomen, slowly, till chest and shoulders feel totally relaxed. While he becomes one with the apathy of the machine facing him, he detects the presence of a commercial keylogger installed in the hard drive, a stupid malware you can buy on Amazon: easy to notice because it's heavy on the CPU. He kills it and changes the Mac's password.

Michel is harmless. He didn't even complete the installation of the malware, so all the information stolen from Sophie's Mac so far was encrypted when he got it. The compromised files from the hard drive date back to before Anton let Sophie know he was coming to Paris: so, the Dimwits are not tasked with getting in the way of the American Sherlock Holmes? Are they Nessim's agents? If the banker-monk resorts to such amateurs to spy on Sophie, what's his opinion of his wife's technological savvy? Or does he see her as especially vulnerable to eccentrics like the Dimwits? Or like Anton, the boy-in-black?.

Beau de Rubempré

Between three and four AM, he allows himself a long practice in the kyudojo. Before going back up to his apartment, he peeks into the garage, but of course there's no sign of the black SUV yet.

While the elevator climbs to the third floor, he pictures Dambreuil sitting by her second-floor window, her eyes on place de l'Alma, waiting for madame's return.

Where the hell is Elvis?

BRAIN WALLET # 8
I cut and paste a page from my journal. Here we are back in 2011.

I haven't read the Bible yet, but Daniel knows it inside out. Today at Café Venetia, we were talking of the Google job I'll soon quit – breaking, I'm afraid, the confidentiality rules I'm still bound to – when, without warning, Daniel started talking of the Bible.

Google uses me mostly as penetration tester – a white hat of sorts. I attack our networks the way black hats would, and if I'm lucky, I find the security vulnerability before they do, saving Google from serious damage.

There is a secrete side to my tasks at Google. I'm authorized, informally so to speak, to counterattack when possible, infecting the machines of my dark rivals with spying malware. That way, by infiltrating their machines and their private lives, I've grown acquainted with the huge tribe of international black hats. At security conferences, I can tell them apart from regular coders. Some of them, I have to admit, make my task easier, seemingly eager to betray their own dark skills: their PC's camera blinded with a piece of duct tape, their looks evocative of Burning Man veterans, their blue or green or pink hair dusted with desert sand. They are, how can I put it, theatrical. I take discreet picture of them with my iPhone and later on classify them in my private archive.

Black hats love to leave behind a signature of their passage. There is sort of an artistry to them. Indeed, the bravura of any coder, even the best intentioned of white hats, may be gauged by their ability to brand their programs with an unmistakable yet totally elusive mark. I learned in time that an obvious signature denotes a harmless black hat, one of those silly souls who deal in the most cryptic operating systems, but then end up downloading some compromised patches and washing their dirty laundry in public.

Last year I went to Burning Man with Daniel – he and his former wife used to go there every year – and there I saw several prominent fellows from my black-hat archive. Burning Man brings together tens of thousands of people at the end of summer in the middle of the Nevada desert, and its climax comes with the burning of a large wooden effigy of a man. The festival lasts one week, and leaves you with your lungs full of playa, the desert sand's dust, and also of the smoke from the many ritual fires that are ignited before the main ceremony. Daniel and I agreed that Burning Man is not the right place for the contemplative discipline we practice in our kyudojo, so I don't think we'll go back anymore. But it is by far the favorite getaway and the single place of highest concentration for the black hats' international tribe.

The idea is that the burning man, the sacrificial victim is a proxy for yourself and everybody else. He is the king of the festival as well. So, costume-wise, everybody does their best to get into the looks of a Desert King or a Desert Queen from Weirdom. The weirder the better.

I'm unfit for that sort of role play. I never wore a costume, not even at Halloween. Not that I wouldn't give it a try, once at least, to feel what it feels like to hide behind a regular costume (my secret crypto identities are a different matter altogether). When it comes to my regular outfit, I'm blacker than any black hat: black t-shirt, black jeans, black socks, black sneakers, and a black hoodie when it's cold, which in Palo Alto isn't often the case. Formal or informal or Burning-Man outfit, it's all one to me. No one taught me how to dress different at home.

So, not that I didn't stand out at Burning Man in my own way. But it was for the wrong reason.

Today I was telling Daniel that of all the black hats I recognized last year at Burning Man, those with the flashiest outfits were also those whose signatures I classify as the easiest to identify.

And of a sudden, he starts talking of the Bible.

You go to the desert to expiate the past and undergo the rite of passage of your emancipation from the Monarch, he said. The rite requires the destruction of the gold which you stole from the Monarch. Afterwards, you are born again, you leave the desert a new man. But the Monarch appears under a new guise as well and claims the return of his gold. Which leads you back to the desert, to expiate once more the past by destroying the gold you stole twice from the Monarch. The Monarch loves you too much to let you go, you are the favorite. In turn, you hate the Monarch too much to do without him, or without the gold you keep stealing from him and then destroy in the desert. Hence, the cycle of debt and expiation repeats itself, always the same and always new.

"In my opinion," he concluded, "those harmless black hats you talk about, the ones who leave obvious traces of their passage, long for the constant attention of the parents they rebelled against and ripped off. Their parents were the first incarnation of the Monarch they ever met. But the attention of those parents has run out. Hence, they try to replace it with the attention of the Federal Government, or if not the Government's, then the attention of the all-powerful private companies that allegedly spy on them. Parents, Government, Google, Apple, Facebook: God's proxies, all of them."

"And how do you explain the self-revealing signatures?" I asked him with my eyes.

"You won't ever grab the full attention of God or Google or the Federal Government unless you are caught red-handed. Those self-revealing signatures are a sign of vanity. What's the worst fate for a black hat?"

"I wouldn't know."

"The discovery that he isn't bothering anybody, what else?"

The constant attention of your parents… I'd like to get into those hackers' head to know what it feels like.

There are innumerable Bibles online, but I ordered my own printed copy on Amazon.

Besides being acquainted with my passion for Belmondo, now Amazon knows a bit more about my bookish interests.

It's not that, the data I care to protect.

BRAIN WALLET # 9

The Google offices where I worked were at the heart of that tiny urban agglomeration which Palo Alto still was a decade ago. My apartment was a few blocks to the west of Google, toward the Bay, and Café Venetia, where Daniel and I often met, was a few blocks to the east, in the direction of Stanford University.

I hadn't learned to drive yet. Here I could do without a car – even if it thrilled me no end to ride southbound on Daniel's red Ferrari toward Big Sur, mile after beachy mile under a cloudless sky while the sun wrestled the icy color of the ocean.

Daniel knew all sorts of anecdote about a Henry Miller who spent the rest of his life in Big Sur after making a splash in Paris as a writer.

I would walk out of my place in Palo Alto wearing the outfit of a sort of Japanese monk, my long *yumi* bow in the right hand and the *yazutsu* quiver holding two arrows over my left shoulder. The bow was unstrung, yet every time I crossed paths with the policemen at the corner of University Avenue, I expected they'd stop me to enquire about the weapon I carried. But it never happened. Our pavilion – I had taken to thinking of the pavilion as *ours*, that is, mine, Daniel's, and Sophie's, right after the first few archery lessons. Clearly, there were no other pupils, nor did Daniel plan to admit any more besides us two. The pavilion, I was saying, wasn't far from downtown. We called it *kyudojo* – a sort of industrial warehouse in the vicinity of Whole Foods and Palantir, totally empty except for a wooden platform slightly higher than the cement floor on one side, and a target resting on a compact bank of sand on the other.

At first, I wondered how could Daniel afford the lease on such first-rate real estate. Later on, I learned he wasn't paying any lease, he had acquired the pavilion, together with plenty of prime real estate in town, at the time when the dot-com bubble burst, around the year 2000.

As I got closer to the kyudojo, the bonfire of Sophie's hair came into view from the opposite direction. She was wearing my same outfit with minor differences, the most prominent being a small leather shield above her right breast. Sophie is seven years older than me and fifteen or so years younger than Daniel.

Kyudo archery training is based on emulation. When you have mastered the many technical elements of shooting the arrow, you must still learn an elementary yet most basic aspect of the ritual: patience. The patient wait of your turn to shoot as you kneel in the kiza posture. You learn to become one with your own breathing: your gaze is straight, your eyes resting in mild concentration on the back of the archer in front of you. That way, without staring too hard, without analyzing too deep, you *watch* her shots from close by. And learn from it.

Sophie was much more advanced than me, she'd been attending the kyudojo for a few years already. I think I learned almost as much from her example as from Daniel's instruction.

Sophie's *kai* shooting position: her collarbone orthogonal to the target, her bare feet glued to the wooden platform, her legs apart, the white skin of her naked left arm sprinkled with freckles, her arrow notched to the bowstring. The instant before shooting the arrow: her left arm stretched out and motionless, the curvature of her spine S-shaped – spellbinding to me. The instant after the shoot: her left arm stretched out, still motionless, while the bow in her hand turned slightly leftwards and the bowstring brushed against her elbow's inside. You could hear a violin-like sound, one single steady note in the air. As her bowstring's vibration died down, and I knew my turn to shoot had almost come, Sophie kept both arms stretched out in a straight line, an extension of her collarbone: the left hand holding the bow and pointed at the target, the right hand, gloved, pointed in the opposite direction. For a short interval, never short enough not to stir my senses, she was holding the whole universe in her arms.

Would I ever be part of that universe of hers? I wondered. Would her arms ever lure me that way?

BRAIN WALLET # 10
I cut and paste a page from my journal. Here we are back to the very first weeks of my friendship with Daniel.

The blind archer shoots the arrow at the target. Afterwards, the blind archer is given the option to consult two oracles to learn whether he hit the target or not. One of the oracles always tells the truth and the other one never does, and they are otherwise indistinguishable from each other. How can the archer know for sure if he hit the target?

Yesterday, Daniel asked me this riddle with an email. One of his pedagogical challenges...

I replied: "The blind archer queries both oracles, asking each one how would his colleague answer the question: 'Was the target hit?' Let's suppose the target was hit. The lying oracle would say that according to his colleague the target wasn't hit, while the truthful oracle would say that according to his colleague the target wasn't hit. In the opposite case, both oracles would declare that the target was hit. In any case, the blind archer knows that truth is always the opposite of the unanimous declarations of the two oracles."

Daniel wrote back to me: "Anton, you start from the unfounded premise that each oracle is privy to the norm of the other's behavior. Did my riddle mention that premise? Not at all. Suppose that the blind archer asks the lying oracle whether he is aware of the norm of his colleague's behavior. He will say he is not if he is, and will say he is if he is not. The truthful oracle does the opposite. The blind archer always gets a yes and a no in response to this question, and is therefore unable to distinguish the liar from the truth-teller. The flaw of your solution is in the premise, Anton. For all my riddle told you, it's equally likely that each oracle is and is not aware of the norm of the other's behavior. Either way, the blind archer is always taken for a ride. Just as in real life."

I replied that I learnt my solution in a class of algorithmic logics in Pittsburgh. He sent me a smiley, followed by the words, "Trust in logics makes you blinder than the blind archer. And we both know what's a blind archer worth on the battlefield."

Today, as we are standing at the counter of Café Venetia, Daniel unwrinkles a green one-dollar bill on the hard wood in front of me and points at the motto "In God We Trust." I had never paid it any attention. Does it mean "We trust God" or "We run up God's bill"? Then he pulls out some more green bills from his wallet to pay for our espressos. He calls my attention to how wrinkled and threadbare those bills are. It's the first time I see him pay cash.

"Our collective trust in these green scraps of paper beats your trust in logics," he says as he shakes his blond pompadour. "And to think that from each bill like these a bank squeezes out ten, a dozen more… That's what we get from trusting paper money!"

I give him a questioning stare.

"For each dollar bill a bank holds in its vaults, it can lend a tenfold, a twelvefold figure to its clients. Moreover, there are derivatives and synthetic securities that increase even further this mass of credit. It's like minting money faster than the US

Mint itself, and it's private citizens doing it, the owners of the banks. You and I can't, though…"

CHAPTER SIX

Anton isn't really sleeping. The jet lag lets him doze off at best. He conjectures on the whereabouts of his Michelin map: carefully crated, flying to France in the belly of a cargo plane, or still stowed in some warehouse at San Francisco International? He kept it before his eyes for how long? Five, six years, give or take. Street by street, neighborhood by neighborhood, he mapped the adventures of Belmondo's characters in Paris with flag pushpins, and that way, he memorized the *Open sesame* of his secret keys. Now he is stretched out on a bed a stone's throw from the Eiffel Tower, the real thing. The tip of the tower traces a black outline in one of the windows. This afternoon he retraced by car the itinerary that in 1979 brought Jean and Jacqueline back into each other's arms at the Bois de Boulogne. Guided by the Bentley's GPS, he had the impression of being smuggled into Belmondo's world without the least hiccup. He covered those distances with confidence, like Jean. Then came the obstacle of the three adjoining roundabouts under construction in the square of porte Maillot, each ring wedged into the next. The GPS went crazy, there was no way he could tear the Bentley away from those concentric orbits, and he felt the ground shift beneath the car's tires. A bit later, parked in the Bois de Boulogne, he was watching a few Parisians meandering among the trees, a babysitter pushing a stroller half-heartedly, a police car patrolling the wood at an idling speed. He wondered what they were waiting for, all of them. After the quickfire disorientation of his concentric orbits on the roundabouts, the whole scene looked as though it was staged in slow motion. Driving by his

Beau de Rubempré

Bentley, the policeman in the driver's seat looked at Anton: all he saw was a young man in a luxury car parked on the side of the road. It may have looked as though Anton was waiting for something, but he was waiting for nothing really, just passing the time like everybody else around him. Something inside him clicked, and he knew he had stepped for real into the urban fabric of Belmondo's world – he had been smuggled in for real, this time. In Palo Alto, he derived mathematical certainties from Jean's adventures, based on a smooth and fluid Michelin map, unchangeable like a GPS. Day in and day out, he fed himself with equally unchangeable certainties: the *Open Sesame* of his bitcoin portfolio buried in a papery version of the Bois de Boulogne, his archery at Daniel's kyudojo, his meditation in the kiza posture, his rites of food preparation and consumption, his hikes by the ocean or among the sequoias of Wunderlich Park with Sophie, his walks from home to the kyudojo and back. A linear existence, as logical as a silicon chip. Jean instead, here in Paris, had to cope with this urban fabric and its lethargies: the traffic within those three roundabouts linked to one another had entangled Anton within a devious timeline, thick like a bath of molasses.

Walking from townhall in Boulogne-Billancourt to porte de la Muette – it's the day in the summer 1979 that he'll meet Jacqueline again – Belmondo's character, Jean crosses mentally a whole stage of his youth, that of his relationship with his father. Only to emerge gradually onto the more recent stage of his unfinished relationship with Jacqueline. In the time it takes to cover this distance by step, Jean covers the longer distance between him and his own youth. But to cover it, he can't refer, as Anton's GPS does, to the fixed network of streets shown on a Michelin map. He covers it by plunging himself into the overlapping layers of past days that encase the walls, the squares, the intersections, the bridges on the river.

A plunge amidst a thousand setbacks: as visceral as the squeeze in the belly that keeps Anton from falling asleep.

How long it's been since he ate some decent food?

He must've dozed off. A bluish light is coming through the windows. Maybe he is hallucinating, but a blue patch of the Seine spreads in tiny waves across the ceiling. He sees floating in it the faces of the protagonists of his investigation: Daniel, Sophie, Nessim, Michel, Ursula, Dambreuil, Bashir, Masao-*the-spy*. And himself as well. They all cruise along the same streets walked by Belmondo's characters, wade across the same squares, the same bridges, the same neighborhoods, enmeshed in the same molasses. In the eyes of an extraterrestrial, would the incongruity between Paris's smooth city plan and their devious paths through it stand out at all? In an extraterrestrial cartography of the city, wouldn't their individual stories end up blending in with one another?

He becomes aware that Sophie stepped into his room only the moment she collapses on him. Her forehead slams against his chest, and she falls right away into a deep sleep, slightly wheezy. The smell from her skin pores tells him she's drunk.

Now he is totally awake.

He gets up, tries to yawn to no avail, tries to stretch out his arms and legs to no avail, then takes off Sophie's shoes and undresses her. Her body, face down on his bed, is yielding like a ragdoll's. He covers her up to her neck and pulls the curtains to keep the daylight out.

Beau de Rubempré

The fridge in the kitchen is chockfull of delicacies. Masao must've come around sometime last night.

As stealthy as a spy?

He starts eating, standing silently in front of the open door of the fridge: he recalls the hasty meal in his kitchen the day he fell in love with Sophie. He hears the swish of the elevator door and Elvis walks into the kitchen. Dambreuil must've sent him up to watch over Sophie. He never fully suspected, in Palo Alto, the extent of Dambreuil's devotion for Sophie: they have been together for about fifteen years.

He leads Elvis to the bedroom and Elvis jumps to curl up by Sophie. He comes back to the kitchen to end his meal. He is about to tidy up but then thinks better of it: the house staff would feel defrauded. He leaves the kitchen as is, goes back to his bedroom, and settles in an armchair to figure out his best course of action. Sophie's breathing is less wheezy, he finds its pace relaxing. In this half-light, her cheeks are full and smooth like a child's. He is not blind to the fact that her new features are side effects of the alcohol in her veins.

It's not that love makes you blind: it's that if you love a woman there must be a reason, and that reason keeps you from judging her.

He tells himself he must figure out his best course of action.

He steps into the walk-in closet, finds his jeans and t-shirts amidst a grid of empty shelves and dangling hangers, puts on the kyudo outfit, and goes down to the kyudojo. His second solo practice. He keeps at it for about an hour using Daniel's dark bow, till a growing sense of well-being gets a huge yawn out of him. And he stretches arms and legs with utter delight.

His third day in Paris.

Back upstairs, he WhatsApps Dambreuil: "Madame is sleeping in my room."

"I know, monsieur. I sent Elvis upstairs."

"I must run an errand in town."

"You need some help, monsieur?"

"No. It's that I hate to leave madame alone for too long."

"Elvis will suffice for another few hours. And I am here."

Down in the garage, he messes about the Bentley's GPS till he hacks out of it the list of its most frequent destinations. The first one is rue Blanche 21. Judging from *Google Maps*, in current traffic that location is less than half-an-hour drive from here. *Google Earth* shows an Indian restaurant with a red front, but when he navigates a bit forward, he makes out a golden plaque at number 21. He rotates the screen ninety degrees and reads, in black letters on a golden background:

HOSNANI HOLDING LTD
Dynamic Registry Solution (DRS) Limited

He goes upstairs to get his black hoodie and the minimal machinery he needs for a first inspection. Nothing but quiet in his bedroom. Elvis uncurls just a bit to wave his tail when he peeks inside.

He drives the Bentley to rue Blanche 21, a cute three-storey Liberty building with the security flaw – a virtue to hackers – of huge windows on the street, then he drives some more till he turns into a parking lot on rue d'Amsterdam, five minutes from place de Clichy. He parks the Bentley, walks to the taxi stand on place de Clichy, and asks the driver to bring him to rue Blanche 21. The cab driver sounds annoyed at his English, even if he understands perfectly well what Anton wants. The black hood Anton keeps down his eyes doesn't help either. But he needs the hood: without its cover, Nessim and his Stanford collaborators would identify him at first sight. When they reach destination, Anton asks the driver to park just after the area reserved for motorbikes. He was going to add that he is waiting for a friend when the driver's prolonged mumbling silences him. No need for explications, even if Anton doesn't get one word of the driver's French: they could've parked just before the motorbikes area, but all spots were taken there, and here, after the motorbikes area, no parking is allowed. Anton pulls some Euro bills out of his wallet and, for the first time since he is abroad, tests the power of this exotic currency. They back out a bit and park across several empty spots reserved for motorbikes. The driver turns off the engine and makes himself busy playing with his iPhone.

Anton brought with him the Dell PC, which is more versatile than the Mac with Kali Linux, and sticks a USB wireless card to its lid with a suction cup. He types in the ritual passwords and commands. All he wants for now is to get a first impression of his target.

He is bombarded right away by an embarrassment of riches – as was to be expected from this urban environment. The list of WiFi systems active in the area is overwhelming, but once he discards the obviously vulnerable ones as well as the ones with silly names, cozy badges of domesticity etc., he is left with a tolerably small range of alternatives. And out of this limited number, the Hosnani Holding's WiFi systems, however pseudonymously named, stands out by a long shot: signal strength...

Bitcoin and the Ritual of Kyudo Archery

A little probing to test penetrability is all he needs. A routine job, really.

There, done.

Judging from the pace of his thumbs on the iPhone, the cab driver is absorbed in a chat room. This leaves Anton the time to browse the local Airbnb site.

He is lucky. Two apartments are available in a few days in the building to his left, facing the Hosnani Holding LTD: rue Blanche 38, second and third floor. The one on the third floor is quite large with three windows on the street. It's not certain that a location close to the target will be necessary, but if there's one thing he learned at Google, it's not to scrimp on resources: attack on all fronts at once. He reserves the third-floor apartment, starting February 11. On Amazon, he buys a remote-programmable video camera with telephoto lens and tripod.

When the chips are down, social engineering isn't just the fastest approach to hacking, it's often the best, especially when the target exposes itself behind huge windows. You just grab all that the target leaves unshielded. Even pickpockets are social engineers in the world of hackers. He'll have to find out how Nessim relates to those windows, you never know.

He shuts the lid of the Dell, steps out of the cab and reaches the opposite sidewalk to take a look at the windows of the apartment he just reserved, then comes back aboard and asks the driver to bring him back to the Bentley. In that sort of old buildings, the glass of the windows may make the interiors either visible or invisible, depending on the time of day and whether the sky is overcast or not. With today's overcast sky, the windows are totally see-through. The best option is to wrap the spying devices behind the window in the folds of some thick curtain.

From place de Clichy, the Bentley's GPS launches him toward the Eiffel Tower, the magnetic pole of Belmondo's world, and the traffic is as smooth as on a country road.

He is home in twenty minutes.

CHAPTER SEVEN

In Anton's absence the walk-in closet has been transformed. A few fancy suits of a sort he wouldn't wear if his life depended on it hang from the cloth hangers, there are coats and jackets for all seasons, a pile of shirts, white and not, ties, sweaters, fancy men's underwear, even Italian leather shoes his size. Even a selection of bedsheet, pillow covers, and linens. It was to be expected: Dambreuil had a sartorial goal in mind when she jotted down Anton's measurements. Does she picture his better-looking self as a wannabe banker-monk?

Apologies, demoiselle, that I don't have Nessim's oval face, or those frosted-glass eyes either.

The pile of his black t-shirts is relegated to an out-of-the-way corner shelf. He slips out of the one he is wearing and puts on a fresh one.

He walks into his bedroom, welcomed by Elvis' restrained tail wagging. He adjusts his eyes to the semi-darkness. Sophie is sleeping in the same position he left her. Totally disheveled, she has the sulky face of a cherub. He relaxes listening to the regular pace of her breathing: that irascible cab driver stressed him out more than he realized. Elvis rests his snout on his one foreleg, looking like a statue in black onyx.

He stays like this for an hour or so, sitting in the armchair and watching over Sophie's sleep. He can't hear the least noise from the street. The strips of light creeping in by the sides of the curtains give a false impression of sunlight pouring in. He ends up dozing off, cradled by the sleep-inducing lull of this house, where they all kill time, it seems, in wait of a dawn that rises only at sunset.

Beau de Rubempré

He goes downstairs and leaves the house for a walk. He has his keys: no need to warn Dambreuil. Nothing happens in this house without her knowing of it anyway.

Place de l'Alma: the sidewalk cafés are empty because of the weather. He realizes with some dismay that he doesn't have the iPhone on him. He wanders around aimlessly, careful not to lose his bearings. He crosses paths with rare pedestrians. The wind that blows in his face shakes the tops of the trees on avenue Montaigne: it's lively and not too cold, seems to blow from the seaside.

He walks the length of the gardens of Champs-Elysées. At one point he finds himself in a crowded area where everybody hurries to some destination in a harassed way. Near place de la Concorde he is taken by surprise by a snowfall, but doesn't feel like seeking shelter. A few minutes later the sun peeps through the clouds, just in time to change a myriad of snowflakes into as many floating gems.

He is backtracking along avenue Montaigne and the same wind from earlier on blows in his face, and it feels again as though he was approaching the seaside, even if he is walking in the opposite direction than before. Some seagulls glide above his head. When he reaches place de l'Alma, the sky is a leaden grey and the snowfall starts again with a vengeance. He finds shelter behind the glass window of a restaurant called *Chez Francis*, sits at a table and orders an espresso. The waiter takes him for a tourist and tells him in a reproachful English that he should've waited to be assigned a table. This is a regular restaurant and he is supposed to order real food, not just a cup of coffee. While the waiter speaks, Anton feels his pockets for the wallet to no avail: forgotten with the iPhone. He gives up espresso and shelter, and runs back home zigzagging among heavy wet snowflakes.

In his kitchen he finds the same large tray he carried to Sophie's bedroom the other day. How long ago was it? Time has a playdough-like oddity in Sophie's house.

Sandwiches, fruit salad, hot coffee, dishware, silverware: he carries the whole shebang to his bedroom and then gives Sophie a tiny shake. She opens her eyes a slit, smiles, and whispers: "Siri, play some Jacques Brel." Brel's by now familiar voice starts singing the same familiar song, the one Michel sang last night as he pretended to toast some forthcoming special event. Due tonight, if Anton remembers correctly.

Music in his bedroom? It doesn't take Anton long to recover from the surprise: the music comes out of a pod on a shelf. How could he possibly have missed it? It's not really a problem that Siri is programmed to obey Sophie's voice in his bedroom. That's easy to fix. The real problem is that this sort of wireless home devices is a hacker's open invitation, and Sophie's house must be filled with them. More work to be done at the soonest. He regrets he didn't throw a wireless RF detector into one of his backpacks before leaving Palo Alto.

Sophie's body adheres docilely to his under the shower. He forces her to eat one tramezzino sandwich. He puts on his kyudojo outfit and then, down in her apartment, helps her put on hers. She isn't too stable on her legs and complains of a headache. In the kyudojo, it's right away evident to both of them that she must start archery from scratch. Since the moment Anton set foot into this kyudojo, that empty glass incrusted with dried-up whisky, now removed to the garage, foreboded evil to come.

Beau de Rubempré

He strings her favorite bow, puts it in her left hand, and then adjusts her feet, legs, arms, back, and neck into shooting position, her whole body as pliable and weak-willed as the ragdoll he arranged on his bed a while ago. The woman he is handling is a far cry from the chatty Sophie he used to know. They exchange a look, shy yet intense, and he feels a tiny wave of confidence when she whispers, "… not quite from scratch," as though she reads into his thoughts, the way Daniel used to do.

Daniel, we miss you.

Her first shoot is pitiful: one more reason to stick with the kyudojo's protocol to a T, and not skip the preliminaries as they just did.

They kneel down in the kiza posture, facing each other as prescribed by Daniel's rules. Anton gets up and shoots his two arrows in sequence. Two good shots. Now it's her turn. She misses both times. The sound of her bowstring is dull.

Back to the kiza posture. It's Anton's turn to shoot again: one, two good shots. When it's her turn, he stands behind her. He holds his right hand on her collarbone so he can press his thumb against the base of her neck, and push the palm of his left hand against her lower back. It feels odd, shaping her spine this way, like playdough: a wary giggle comes out of her throat.

Shot after shot, her bowstring starts giving a less tentative sound. But the flight of her arrows is tired, hardly parallel to the floor.

Once more.

And once more.

Bitcoin and the Ritual of Kyudo Archery

They take a break after her last shot is followed by a longish, familiar, violin-like note. The arrow barely hits the target, but it's something.

BRAIN WALLET # 11

Daniel had me and Sophie use bowstrings made from natural hemp.

After each practice, we made a circle in the middle of the open space between the target and the shooting platform, kneeling in the kiza posture again, and Daniel explained how our progress that day could be applied to coding on Mac – both bodily and mentally. Then he would move on to more general remarks. That summer of 2008, his remarks dealt without fail with *trust*, the same subject he had tackled with me on our first meeting.

"We are three adults," he said one day, "each of us holding a lethal weapon within a confined space, and none of us seems to worry for his or her own safety. I ask you, why?"

Sophie: "Because we come here to practice archery, not to kill one another. Because we like one another. Because," chuckling to herself, "if we shoot at one another, this kyudojo is *fucked*."

Sophie was the opposite of me in everything. It felt like in that closed enclave, fueled by my introversion, her fantasy acquired butterfly wings. I pondered Daniel's question (indeed, why did I trust him, or why did I trust this Sophie, whom I barely knew, beautiful as she was?) and then I ventured my guess with a mute glance at Daniel – I knew he would decipher my body and eye language, and wasn't bothered by my silence. Sophie *was* bothered by it, and even more by my silent dialogue with Daniel, and didn't try to hide it. In my early days at the kyudojo, she must have thought me a complete idiot. Was it for a sort of deliberate compensation that she shot out her flurry of inane answers to Daniel's question, that day?

"All in all, I think you are right, Sophie," Daniel said. "None of us wants to wreck the kyudojo. Each of us derives greater advantage from not shooting at the other two archers than from doing it."

I couldn't help raising a perplexed eyebrow.

"It's no laughing matter, Anton. We are debating the solution to an old dilemma. It's called *consensus*: is it possible to devise a network such that the maximum advantage for each node brings about the maximum advantage to the network itself?"

"I don't get it," I said. "Why is that an old dilemma?"

He replied: "It's the dilemma of trust versus incentive. Take the American democracy. A democracy is a network whose nodes are called voters. Some people think that in America the collusion of a majority of voters coerces the richer minority into actions and initiatives that maximize the welfare of the majority. Some people think the opposite is true, it's a collusion among the minority of voters that coerces the poorer majority into actions and initiatives that maximize the welfare of the rich minority. Now, think how much better it would be if each voter's best welfare brought about the best collective welfare, so that by promoting his own advantage, every voter maximized everybody else's advantage. In this scenario, the incentive to do your best would feed off your trust in every other voter's doing the same."

"Isn't there a basic difference, though?" Sophie objected. "Networks are machine-like, democracies are subject to mob mentality."

Beau de Rubempré

None of us three belonged to a poor minority, but something in her words told me that me and Sophie came from opposite family backgrounds.

"I'm really talking of a network like this kyudojo, made up of human beings, each one handling a lethal machine, however primitive," Daniel replied. "What bothers me is that our network is flimsy. In the absence of an objective incentive to preserve mutual safety, the three of us trust one another blindly."

Were me and Sophie competing for the favors of the Master?

If we were, then there was a side to our competition which came to my disadvantage. It was the subject of her doctoral dissertation which had brought Sophie to Daniel, seeking his advice. He had the reputation of an unapproachable recluse among local academics. Sophie wanted to study the formal connections between modern cryptography and traditional cryptology of Holy Script – there is a rabbinic tradition in this regard, she told me later on, but she wanted to focus on the Koran. Daniel was notorious at Stanford for having argued that theology is an inferior form of mathematics.

We never practiced for less than two hours at the Kyudojo. Daniel stayed there longer than me and Sophie. In those early days, I hadn't seen him shoot more than a dozen arrows. Maybe he didn't want to show off his skills with two apprentices. Or maybe neither of us was up to the ritual ceremony yet. Or maybe I wasn't.

Out in front of the pavilion, me and Sophie would always hang a few minutes before parting and walking in opposite directions. We had no plausible reasons to socialize with each other. As the kyudojo's new member, I slowed down her progress in archery and interfered with her evident adoration of Daniel. From the heights of her academic credentials (prep school at Wycombe Abbey in the UK, Bachelor's degree at Stanford, doctorate in progress), Sophie must have thought me a complete idiot, good only for coding on Mac. And she had already made herself amply clear as to her dislike for my inarticulacy. It felt like those few minutes we spent together by the door to the pavilion were our shared tribute to Daniel's reliance in the solidarity among the kyudojo's members.

Or maybe there was some other motive on her part which I didn't get.

As to me, I couldn't tire of watching her strangely beautiful face. Even faced with my staring silence, she would never shut up, and replied compulsively to all the questions I didn't ask. Her nose was Arabian, her red hair and freckled skin were pure Norman, from the north of France: she was the final result of a matrimonial contract, often renewed, between two dynasties which were geographically remote and opposed as to religious creed. She hinted at her study of the Koran, taking it for granted that I knew a little something of Islam. She told me of the reasons why she didn't veil her head, taking it for granted I had ever seen a veiled girl before.

I thought to myself that she was seven years older than me. Could she still be called a *girl*?

Once, she covered her lips and nose with an arm and asked, "Can you picture me going around with my face hidden behind a niqab, like this?"

For the life of me, I couldn't reply her question. For one thing, I had never even heard the word *niqab* before. But I was

Beau de Rubempré

noticing specks of gold shining in the gray of her eyes: detached like that from the rest of her face, her eyes bewitched me.

Bitcoin and the Ritual of Kyudo Archery

BRAIN WALLET # 12
I cut and paste a page from my journal.

I walk out of my place toward the kyudojo. This time, one of the policemen at the corner of University Avenue signals me to stop. He comes closer. He wants to take a look at my arrows.

I reach out above my shoulder to get him one, but he stops me with a smile. "I take care of it myself if you don't mind," he says as he takes an arrow out of my quiver. "Not that I don't trust you, mind you," he adds in a tone meant to suggest he hasn't the least reason to trust the eccentric monk facing him.

He must have Hispanic blood, judging from the shape of his eyes. He is a few years younger than Daniel. At the sight of the matte metal of the arrowhead, a look of wonder comes to his face. He nods to his two colleagues on the sidewalk: ""Hey, guys, this arrow is better than our tasers." The two policemen keep chatting with each other without paying him much attention.

He gives me another smile and says: "This arrow looks like it's made to break through a wall rather than just hit a target."

I try to say a few words. "The head of normal arrows is sharper, this bulky one is for practice."

"I wouldn't want to cross paths with this sort," he counters. He strokes the metal head with a finger, then, instead of slipping it back into my quiver, he puts it into my right hand. He adds, as I raise the arrow above my shoulder and toward the quiver, "I've been meaning to take a look at your arrows for a while. I'm glad I didn't do it earlier on."

"Why, Officer?" I feel I'm supposed to ask.

Beau de Rubempré

"Because earlier on I couldn't trust your intentions and so, I would have confiscated them. Your arrows can be considered improper weapons. Thinking of it, they are real weapons. But I've seen you walk by so often down this way carrying this lopsided bow, and I have no indication you'll commit acts of violence with it. As a risk, you are beneath threat level."

He doesn't miss the spark of interest that lights up in my eyes. "Call it professional habit, that's the way they train us: always and above all, cut down public risk." He makes a sweeping gesture with his open hand. "All these people walking the street or driving through are potential criminal. Who do you trust? You trust those that pose a tolerable risk to the public. The less I risk, the more I trust. Can you think of a better solution?"

I take my leave with a military salute, sort of, my index finger above the eyebrow.

One day long ago, my father tried to tell me what it feels like to grow up in a country where policemen are a nuisance. To me, growing up in a Jewish neighborhood near Chicago, where it was policemen who helped me cross the street on my way to school, it sounded like an upended fairytale, too many ogres and no good fairies. If the tongue I speak in isn't my mother's, it's because of the fairytale characters I watched on our TV screen: Captain Hook navigating his treasure map, Ali Baba decoding secret passwords, Aladdin mastering the genie of the lamp, Basil cracking the crime map, Scheherazade telling and retelling one thousand and one versions of her story. They were my best friends. No ogres. No evil policemen.

I wish I had explained to that friendly policeman why my yumi bow looks lopsided, but he didn't seem to care all that much. Easier to keep my mouth shut than explain the reason for these two uneven humps. Compared to ordinary bows, granted, yumi bows do look weird.

At the kyudojo, after practice, I can't resist telling Daniel and Sophie of my exchange with the policeman. I've never spoken at such length before Daniel, much less before Sophie. She listens intently, her frowning eyes glued to my lips. When I'm done talking, Daniel stares at me without a word. We stay like that, sort of frozen, for what seems like a long time, kneeling in the kiza posture, everybody silent, till I realize Daniel isn't really staring at me. It's been a while, rather, since his pale-blue eyes quit seeing me. As this goes on, Sophie shows a compliant attitude I didn't know her capable of: her eyes half closed, her glance slanted downwards, her chest still like she's breathing only with the lower part of her abdomen.

Suddenly, a brighter light shines in Daniel's eyes. He shakes his pompadour, once, twice, and makes the instinctive motion to stand up. Then he stops in his tracks like he has just come back to his senses. He addresses himself to me:

"When you wait for your turn to take on the shooting position, Anton, you are aligned in a chain of archers. You hold a bow and two arrows. Why is it that the archer before you knows you won't shoot him in the back? Or if you come first, why is it that you yourself don't fear being shot in the back by the archer behind you?"

He stops talking and I know he isn't expecting me to answer him, not in speech for sure. As I return his stare, I try to picture that chain of archers linked by an unprompted pact of mutual trust. Daniel looks at me for another while, decoding the animation in my eyes. Then he speaks again:

"Right, Anton, one can talk of mutual trust, spontaneous empathy, I won't deny it. Yet, the ritual in the kyudojo is not as subjective as that, it's a sort of machinery rather, a network of incentives. Why should Sophie trust you, a virtual stranger? Now I see the point of your story, though: risk and trust are inversely correlated in our network. Sophie trusts you the more, the less you entail a risk to her in the kyudojo. And you are minimized as a risk factor when your incentive to trust her is maximized. You just gave us the missing piece of the puzzle, congratulations. I'm not suggesting you solved the puzzle, mind!"

And before I can counter that I wasn't trying to solve any puzzle, all I did was report on my exchange with a policeman downtown, he dismisses us abruptly, mumbling something about posting on a chatroom.

Out in the street, it all happens very fast between me and Sophie.

What I knew for sure, later that afternoon, and I knew it right away, was that Sophie's company didn't give me stomach cramps.

For a moment I also thought I had found myself a new girlfriend.

Sophie's words taught me better.

Daniel is the only man with whom I can share any secret. He smiles and never objects to my words. But there are times when he helps me sweep away the emptiness I feel in anything I do.

It's hard to struggle against your heart's desires, Anton. Anything it wants, the heart gets it at the expense of the soul.

Bitcoin and the Ritual of Kyudo Archery

Love interested me briefly in the past and the recollection of that brief and perfect relationship makes any replacement vulgar and insignificant. But you must not think of me as a broken heart.

Out in the street, Sophie looks at me in a different way. Is it a condescending look I see in her eyes? An appreciative look? "You don't blow smoke when you talk, huh?" she says with a strange music in her voice. My heart overflows with an urge of spontaneity, and I'm on the verge of replying that all I did was to report on my exchange with a policeman. Even before I open my mouth, though, I realize that I'd be telling her only a partial truth. Fact is, I had put my feelers out as soon as the policeman started talking of risk containment. Something told me that he'd soon utter the word *trust*. The awareness that I can't lie and tell the truth at once, unless both me and Sophie undertake a huge effort in mutual comprehension – words, words, words – holds me back. To compensate, I try to inject the music I heard in her words into my gaze. I remind myself that the nose is Arabian and the red hair and freckled skin pure Norman.

Her bewitching eyes must be from an undisclosed land of sortilege.

At this point, we usually part ways and walk home in opposite directions. But this time Sophie takes to walking by my side. Fine with me: I take a step, she takes a step, like we agreed about something. She just took a vow of silence?

"You have the power to silence even a bigmouth like me," she whispers, like she's read my mind.

Okay, whatever.

We cross paths with my friend the policeman and I see a look of wonder on his face: the first time he sees me in someone's company, it's with another archer wearing my same monkish outfit. His eyes grow positively larger when Sophie's face come into focus. He raises and lowers his eyebrows several times, a Morse code message I'm unsure how to interpret.

Whatever.

Step in and step out, we make it to Cowper Street and turn toward the left wing of the apartment building where I live. Sophie remarks laconically, "It always impressed me this horseshoe-shaped building. So, you live in here, behind these pink walls." I open my door and she follows me inside. In the vestibule, she adjusts her bow and quiver on the floor along the base of the wall. She does it with great care, like she's handling two precious objects. Then she takes off the leather shield on her right breast and her face comes closer to mine.

BRAIN WALLET # 13

Jesus doesn't recognize me as his friend and disciple Anton when I sit by his side on the bench. I contacted the competent authority to find out if they couldn't get him a better life somehow, but there is really nothing which can be done for now. "He has everything a brain-damaged person like him may wish for," they told me offhandedly – which is true, after all. A full-time segregation in some institution where they'd look after him would make things worse. There are many homeless people who live the way he does in Palo Alto, free to come and go, organize their meals as they wish, and wander when and where they want. Besides, he only seems to be homeless, but is nothing of the sort. He owns a beautiful apartment where he could spend his days, if he wanted to, and ample financial means to pay for care providers. And even if there existed an institution where they don't turn their mentally impaired guests into vegetables, coercive institutionalization would amount, for the time being, to a violation of his constitutional rights. Besides, I'm told, such an institution is nowhere to be found.

The best I could do for Daniel, this past year, was sit by his side for long idle hours, eavesdropping on his monologues.

His monologues didn't lead me to any firm conclusion as to the aggression he suffered or the reason why he was attacked. Daniel used to be super-secretive about his wealth in bitcoin, and regarding the keys controlling his bitcoin portfolios, I thought I was the only person who knew the *Open Sesame* was hidden in the Dublin map. Yet, what else could his assailants be after, if not arm-twisting him into the revelation of the passphrases? The day I found him lifeless in his apartment –

back from a trip to Reykjavìk, I was going to update him on the performance of our bitcoin mining plants – I noticed something different, something weird on his Dublin map, while I waited for the arrival of the police: a few headless nails had been hammered into the section of the harbor's bay. I expect those nails must be the same kind of the one stuck in Jesus's brain. The criminal investigation goes slowly and for now all material evidence is classified.

Daniel's Mac was gone too. But that was more in the natural order of things.

From time to time, on that bench, Jesus's monologues shift in tone, and for a few minutes his lips take to spelling long strings of words, always the same: it sounds like chance fragments from his secret passphrases are exhumed from some corner of his memory. Now and then, some passer-by pauses in their tracks to listen greedily. To the ears of any member of the crypto space, and Palo Alto is full of them, it's glaringly obvious what those words might amount to, coming as they do from Jesus's lips.

I recorded those strings of words on my iPhone on several occasions, together with the rest of his incoherent babblings. For a couple minutes, less than that maybe, it's like Jesus is itemizing, interspersed with short silences, entries from a dictionary – always the same, I checked against a dozen recordings made at different times. Assuming his assailants didn't steal most of his bitcoins, those strings of words could lead to Daniel's treasure map.

In the hands of a decent hacker, even a string's fragment may suffice to break the code. Within certain limits, one can even do with words in the wrong order: the machine's brute force will fix that.

The problem is that all those strings, with one exception, have turned out to be wrong, either too short, or too long, and anyway leading nowhere. Yet, there always comes that special moment, that one exception, when Jesus enunciates a list of eight words with great clarity, preceded and followed by a moment of silence. Eight words out of twelve reduce the passphrase's entropy by a good deal.

Taking off from there, my Mac discovered the four missing words — hey, any self-respecting hacker will tell you it's not as easy as I make it sound — and from that twelve-word passphrase, it generated the hexadecimal characters of a secret key with access to a few thousand bitcoins. I added them to my portfolio without hesitation: it's what Daniel would've wanted me to do.

If they assaulted him to steal his crypto wealth, they have been only partially successful, if at all.

BRAIN WALLET # 14

At the Stanford Theater in University Avenue they show only Hollywood classics. Me and Daniel spent many nights there.

I grew up thinking that movie theaters were a pretext to eat popcorns – I was a fan of *Star Trek*. It was at the Stanford Theater I convinced myself that the metrics of feminine beauty are set forth by the stars of black-and-white movies. Yet, the day of my exchange with the policeman in University Avenue, the evening of that day, I would face a wholly new metric, a kind of colored beauty that gave me a sinking feeling in the pit of the stomach and the need to weep.

Holding her chin in the palm of a hand and her elbow sunk in my mattress, Sophie was telling me of her reclusiveness, of her heart's selfishness and her soul's generosity, like she wanted me to grasp – or accept? – her disinterest in conventional love affairs. I stared at the ceiling as I listened to her. I was forgetting she was seven years older than me: her words sounded pretentious and I was determined not to take them seriously. Soon I would. From time to time, she forgot I don't smoke and offered me her cigarette for a puff. I shook my head and waited for her to keep talking.

Without a word, like by mutual agreement, we climbed off the bed and moved over to my kitchen, where we started eating, standing in front of the open door of the fridge. On the kitchen table there was an uncorked bottle of red wine. While she filled two glasses, Sophie told me something quite extraordinary:

Bitcoin and the Ritual of Kyudo Archery

"I must hurry. Tonight I meet my husband at the Opera House in San Francisco. I haven't seen him since…"

She paused to sip from her glass but then, instead of returning to the subject that had piqued my curiosity, she grabbed her iPhone, tapped a contact, and had a long conversation in a strange language – sounded like French to me. After she hung up, she gave me a radiant smile. "In a short while you'll meet demoiselle Dambreuil," she said. Her smile turned into a mischievous giggle, framed by her dimples. "I'm sure you two will like each other."

She got her kicks out of telling me of demoiselle Dambreuil's professional relation to her – like she hadn't just revealed to me the existence of a husband in her life.

I had a strong impression of unreality. *Demoiselle*, what word was that?

Sophie had moved to Palo Alto ten years earlier to study at Stanford. On the eve of her flight to California, her parents snatched demoiselle Dambreuil from a family of acquaintances in Alexandria, Egypt. Alexandria is where her family lived and Sophie herself had grown and been schooled till she attended prep school in the United Kingdom. On her ID papers, at the entry *profession*, demoiselle Dambreuil had written *lady-in-waiting*. She had moved to California with Sophie and helped her set up house. For the first two years of attendance at Stanford, it's mandatory to live in an expensive room on campus, which you share with a roommate. But Sophie owned her own house downtown Palo Alto and crossed paths with her roommate seldomly. After graduation, she had been admitted to the PhD program in computer science.

Beau de Rubempré

By the day of Sophie's wedding to Nessim, demoiselle Dambreuil had been chaperoning her for seven years.

"Nessim." Sophie repeated her husband's name in a hushed tone: intently, her brow furrowed, staring blankly into space. "Nessim," she sighed again, "black Turkish cigarettes and frosted-glass eyes."

My chance to find out more. "Frosted-glass eyes… He wears prescription lenses?"

"Eyes that cast a spell on you," she mumbled, her gaze still lost in that blank space, "eyes that take over your mind."

She bounced right back though, leaving me no time for further questions, and started talking again of the demoiselle who, it seemed, I'd meet soon. Demoiselle Dambreuil was irreplaceable when it came to solving everyday problems, so much so that Nessim had tried – "To no avail, for sure" – to appoint her as caretaker for his own house in San Francisco, where he lived intermittently.

While Sophie hastened into my shower and I put on my jeans and t-shirt, I thought with disappointment that no longer than two hours before I confided to her that my father made a living in a factory of razor blades.

At the thought of my father, I regretted having had unprotected sex with Sophie. I promised myself not to repeat the mistake. Son of a fallen wall, *my foot*!

The doorbell rang and Sophie preceded me to the door wrapped in my bathrobe. A moment later, I saw walk into my living room a middle-aged woman with sparkly eyes, blond, slim, and rather withered: demoiselle Dambreuil, without a doubt. She was followed by a dark-haired Japanese girl wearing a servant uniform. The two women carried an impressive number of garments and accessories, some folded on their arms, some still on their clothes hangers. With a prolonged glance, Dambreuil sized me up from head to foot, and then held out her hand for me.

"Demoiselle Dambreuil, I presume?"

As I shook her hand, I found myself rotating her limp wrist of a right angle till I realized, blushing, that she had expected a hand-kiss. The Japanese servant, who must have been my age and hadn't been introduced to me, raised and lowered her eyebrows with intention, Morse-like, just like my friend the policeman had done a few hours before. Sophie was busy making an inventory of the outfits at her disposal.

Sophie threw her selection on my couch, after which the three women, chatting non-stop in French, seemed to forget my presence altogether. When Sophie stripped out of my bathrobe, I realized, taken aback, that Dambreuil and the Japanese girl were about to dress her naked body. I withdrew to my study, but I'm not too sure my absence was even noticed.

When I came back to the living room, Sophie was sitting on a chair, inspecting her face in the screen of her iPhone, while Dambreuil touched up her upper lip with a fine brush.

"Anton!" I heard a thrill of joy in Sophie voice. She got up and executed three pirouettes in a row, and then stretched out her arms to me.

Up to that day, I had taken for granted that some American movie stars from black-and-white films, like Ava Gardner, say, or Ingrid Bergman, were unrivalled beauties in spite of or maybe even thanks to the absence of colors. But I was unprepared for the sight of the multi-colored creature standing in front of me, her arms reaching out to me: the pink, the light and dark blue of her evening dress were mirrored in the soft shades of her makeup and in the freckled paleness of her naked shoulders, while the gray of her eyes, sprinkled with gold, gave me that sinking feeling in the pit of the stomach. And her red hair was gathered up now, like a blazing pyre.

My chin contracted out of control like I was ready to weep.

Maybe it's the same for anybody when they fall in love. How would I know?

Do you?

Bitcoin and the Ritual of Kyudo Archery

BRAIN WALLET # 15
I print and paste an email from Dublin: October 31, 2018.

Dear Anton Gunzburg,

You do not know me. I am Kathleen, the older sister and legal guardian of your friend Daniel. For several months my attorney has collaborated with my brother's attorneys in California regarding the handling of the formalities pertinent to this new responsibility of mine. The financial aspects of my guardianship (and may I confess, the value of the assets involved) are far above my comprehension and bound to remain so. Some friends are seeking on my behalf a team of skilled and, above all, honest administrators willing to assist me and give me guidance in this thankless task.

I share all of this with you, a stranger, because, forgive the incongruence, Anton, I think I know you fairly well. Please don't be surprised by these words of mine. I've been told that you too, just as I did, and just as futilely, consulted with the Palo Alto competent officers in order to make provisions for better living conditions on behalf of the man whom they still identify legally as Daniel Dunne. On my latest visit to Palo Alto, which I made in the fruitless attempt to move Daniel back to Ireland with me, I found among his personal effects several red notebooks, one of which includes many journal entries that are, for the most part, affectionately devoted to your person. I ignore whether you ever fully grasped the almost paternal nature of the affection that my brother used to feel towards you. I learned from his journal that the two of you met shortly after the wreckage of Daniel's marriage to Mary-Louise, and my brother found in you the surrogate of an already grown-up son. The divorce from Mary-Louise was mainly owing to the panicky attacks that Daniel would suffer through at the prospect of becoming a father. Mary-Louise is a pearl of a woman, I know her well. Most of all from life, she wanted a child from Daniel. But he was literally frightened at the thought of becoming responsible of a newborn's life, the life of "an absolutely defenseless charge," as he writes. One may understand this fear of his very clearly from the reflections he devotes to the subject in many journal entries; he could only see fragility and powerlessness in the newborn's condition, and the opposite arguments from the many pediatricians consulted by Mary-Louise could not assuage his fear. Not even his evident awareness of the psychological nature of this impediment could help him overcome it. The relationship with Mary-Louise fell apart owing especially to this impediment of his; he considered it unforgivably grave and could not come to terms with it. And Mary-Louise's willingness to sacrifice to his love her own yearning for the maternal condition achieved the opposite effect of crushing him. I do not think that my brother's is a very unusual case: two excellent people who, albeit with the best intentions, cut off each other's vital sources till cohabitation becomes unsustainable.

You may find these considerations of mine rather abstract, based as they are on my reading of Daniel's journals and a complete lack of personal experience. I was never married. But truly, if my old mother, who is still in the dark as to the unfortunate fate suffered by her predilect son, Daniel, were not so frail here in Dublin, I would like nothing better than devoting the rest of my life to my brother's care in California. But that is not possible. While for the time being, he resists his transfer back home with animal-like obstinacy.

I have gone on long enough, please forgive me.

I am writing to you, as I said, in view of the deep affection that Daniel felt towards you. If Daniel's mental disability had not occurred in such a tragic and sudden way, I am certain that one day he would have shared with you some of his most cherished possessions. I would like to remedy by offering you Daniel's collection of bows and arrows. I am told – and if you

Bitcoin and the Ritual of Kyudo Archery

will ever feel so inclined, you are welcome to confirm it – that they are rare handcrafted items from Japan. I gave disposition to my attorney that the pavilion called "kyudojo" should be put at your disposal for you to preside over Daniel's archery club, if you will be so inclined. I have also come to the conclusion that none better than you could appreciate the pages from Daniel's journal that gave me the solace of making your indirect acquaintance. I hope therefore you will accept Daniel red notebook together with the rest. I took the liberty of having the notebook's contents xeroxed for myself.

Trusting that you will be pleased with my initiative and in the hope to meet one day the friend who cheered up many days and many evenings to my ill-fated brother,

Believe me, Yours truly,
Kathleen Dunne

CHAPTER EIGHT

It's past midnight when Anton and Sophie walk into the garden together. Michel and Ursula greet them gaudily, loaded already. Except for Michel's over-the-top drawl, the Dimwits are their regular, perfectly staged selves, from vintage costumes to hairdos to makeup to the straw between her lips.

Masao pops up out of nowhere, ready to shake his shaker, but Sophie stops him with a curt gesture of her hand. She sips from Ursula's glass as she declares, to everybody and nobody, that it's Thursday night and there isn't a minute to lose. Bashir comes forward from the shadows he was hiding in, but I can tell from his face that it's just pro forma. Sophie addresses him at once, *"Non, merci,* Bashir. It's Thursday night."

On Thursday night, Anton surmises, she and the Dimwits use another mode of transportation.

When they are out in the street, followed by Dambreuil's petulant promise to stay awake waiting for madame, and Anton sees Michel insert the key into the door of a huge vintage Citroen parked in front of the house, he gets cold feet. Is he really going to put his life in the hands of a dead-drunk driver? He gives a glance at Sophie, but she doesn't bat an eyelid. Clearly, their Thursday nights are too special to give a thought to details like that. He can't bail out, he won't leave her alone again with those two.

Before igniting the engine, Michel turns on a music reproduction system that Anton is not familiar with. It works, he is told, with magnetic tapes. The car's cabin is filled with Brel's voice, the same familiar song. Sophie, Michel and Ursula sing in unison. *Grin and bear it.* Anton joins them in a phonetic imitation of Brel's words. ... *ne me quitte pas, ne me quitte pas, ne me quitte pas...* The music of this fellow Brel sounds a bit grandiose to Anton's ears, especially in this enclosed space, but there must be something good to him if Sophie cares so much about it.

Meanwhile, Michel turns around with the expression of someone who is sharing a secret. "Listen, Anton... Brel isn't dead... It's not true he died..."

Anton can't restrain himself: "Three days ago I hadn't even ever heard of this Brel of yours."

The three of them burst out laughing. Michel goes on, "Everybody thinks he died forty years ago, but he hides here in Paris."

He starts the car and announces their destination in an exalted voice: "Rue Vignon!"

The Citroen's cabin is flooded with an unbreathable stink of gasoline. A selection of Brel's songs plays on. Sophie and Ursula sing along. They must know all of Brel's songs by heart. Michel handles the steering wheel, so much larger than that of a normal car, as though he was at the helm of a boat. They cruise with large swerves, but the roads are almost empty.

They double park on rue Vignon and walk into a corner café. It's ten past one but the café is chock full of customers. All the tables are taken and many customers have to stand. Michel and his friends are welcomed with comradely waves and warm shouts. Their small group is evidently at home here. Anton and Sophie are the only customers who don't wear vintage clothes. Sophie, seriously disheveled, wears an expansive vagrant look: the women sitting near the entrance dart their eyes at her.

Several groups at the tables are made up of older people. From the loudspeakers in the café resounds, wouldn't you know it: ... *ne me quitte pas, ne me quitte pas, ne me quitte pas*... A group of boys and girls give up their table to Michel, who enjoys, it's evident, a special reputation in this milieu. He accepts the offer loftily and then pirouettes towards Ursula with a chair in his hands. How do you do that? Is Anton supposed to offer a chair to Sophie? Sophie saves him from embarrassment by sitting down at their table even before Ursula lowers herself onto her chair.

The clock at the wall above the counter reads 1:23 AM. It's a good fifteen minutes early over Anton's Apple watch.

"The ride always starts between 1:15 and 1:30 AM," Ursula tells Anton pointing a finger at the clock. "Sharp."

He nods. Whatever the ride she's talking about is, it already happened then.

"If you see a white Lancia Flaminia out there ..." she adds, pointing her finger to the glass window near the table.

Lancia Flaminia ... It sounds like an Italian car. Anton has never seen one in his life.

Sophie comes back from the counter holding a packet of Gauloise and a lethal-looking drink.

"It's Pernod," she tells Anton. "Want some?"

Pernod... Godot...

He touches the yellow liquid with the tip of his tongue and pulls back with an unintentional frown. It's a super strong essence of licorice.

"You ought to eat something instead," he tells her, pointing at the sandwich display. "When's the last time you had real food?"

Bitcoin and the Ritual of Kyudo Archery

She shrugs and takes a sip from her Pernod. He must not insist: the fumes of alcohol push her away from him.

Michel works the party with ease, playing the benevolent host at each table. Anton follows his performance. He tries to see him through the eyes of his admirers of both sexes, some of them quite older than him. Up to now, he has been reducing Michel to an indeterminate equation with too many bad solutions, nothing but a whimsically made-up cryptographer, but once again Parisian reality smuggles in its detours and convolutions.

Anton must be mistaken: a minute ago Sophie's drink was pearl-yellow and now it's pearl-pink. Did she get a new one while he was distracted with Michel?

He is bracing himself up, eager to reproach her – well knowing it's no use – when they hear several voices screaming: "It's him! It's him!" A white car is double parked just in front of the glass window. The driver wears a beige trench coat with the collar turned up.

Sophie gulps down her drink, Michel grabs Anton by the arm, and they hurry to their Citroen in the melee. Everybody else is out in the street, climbing in their cars. No sooner are they installed in the Citroen than Michel presses a finger against the music player and Brel starts again with his eternal *ne me quitte pas*.

"See, Anton," he says, "now he stands there for a while."

They are parked a few yards from the white Lancia Flaminia. The car they are double-parked by is filling with passengers too. Anton wants to take a good look at the driver of the Lancia Flaminia but can't see a thing: the taillights of all the cars parked and double-parked in front of the Lancia Flaminia make his eyes throb.

"Nobody knows why he waits so long there," Michel goes on. "Once he picked up a girl who came out of the café."

Sophie and Ursula keep silent, as though it was Michel's designated task to acquaint Anton with the state of affairs. Sophie must be working off her Pernod. Inebriation doesn't suit her talkative self.

Three young women who were working the street a block away come closer to the white Lancia Flaminia and mock up a languid ring-around-the-rosie over it.

"But you never get close enough to talk to him?" Anton asks.

"Never," Michel answers.

"Why?"

"Because!" he cuts him short.

"So, all we do now is wait?" Anton is talking too much. He has no idea why he is asking Michel these inane questions, as though he was trying to provoke him. Sophie and Ursula gaze at the Lancia Flaminia, smoking silently. Sophie is sitting in front in the passenger's seat, Ursula is behind by Anton's side. Anton lower the cars' window for some fresh air.

"Yes, all we do is wait," Michel says in a sulky voice.

The three young women give up on the Lancia Flaminia.

"Here we go… he starts the car…"

Anton tells himself that, after all, there is a trace of generosity in Michel's efforts to let him in on this strange nightly expedition. The driver of the Lancia Flaminia, then, would be the famous French singer who passed away forty years ago?

Bitcoin and the Ritual of Kyudo Archery

The Lancia Flaminia begins to roll, the Citroen is first in line behind it, and as they go forward along rue Vignon, more and more cars join in. The Lancia Flaminia runs at reduced speed.

They make s fairly long motorcade.

"There are times when he barely moves forward," Michel explains. "Then we pass him and wait for him further up the street."

"No risk of losing him?" Anton says.

"No, we know the itinerary by heart," Michel replies. "The traffic lights aren't a problem either. You always find him again, sooner or later."

In front of them is the Arch of Triumph.

The motorcade drives around it behind the Lancia Flaminia.

"It takes some patience here. One night, he made us do fourteen loops."

The motorcade is so long by now that after one loop it forms a perfect circle, so much so that the Lancia Flaminia could be taken for the tail of it. Anton can't stifle a giggle.

"Did you just giggle?" Ursula asks him.

"Me?" he shrugs. "Not at all."

"We are lucky," Michel says when the Lancia Flaminia exits the circle on the third loop. They follow in its wake.

The Lancia Flaminia moves forward at a slow speed in the middle of the street, swerving to the left side from time to time. But there is no traffic coming from the other direction, only their long slow motorcade. Compared with the driver of the Lancia Flaminia, Michel drives almost cautiously: he sobered up fast. Anton wonders how Sophie is doing.

Now they make a stop on the side of the street, and the rest of the motorcade does the same. The Lancia Flaminia drives forward.

"We lose him," Anton says.

"No, in a short while he'll come down avenue Montaigne in the opposite direction," Michel explains. "We just wait here." He lights himself a cigarette and Sophie and Ursula do the same. They smoke silently. Anton tries to make eye contact with Sophie, but she gives off hurtful vibes.

"There he comes!" Michel cries out.

When the Lancia Flaminia passes them by, Anton takes a close look at the man behind the wheel. He holds his arms rigidly on the wheel and has a woody sort of posture, like a marionette. His long, hanging-down hair reminds him of Jesus. The coat's turned-up collar covers a good deal of his face.

They make a U-turn to follow him.

There must be an implicit hierarchy among the members of this Parisian cult: regardless of the time it takes Michel to roll, the Citroen is still second in the motorcade, right behind the Lancia Flaminia. They keep going for a while.

"Pont Alexandre Trois," Michel announces in a concluding tone, parking the Citroen by the railing of the bridge.

The Lancia Flaminia drives on and its white outline vanishes at the first turn. The rest of the motorcade is parked behind the Citroen. Some of the cars are already making a U-turn, presumably to go back home.

"We are done for tonight," Ursula says.

"You don't follow him any farther?" Anton asks.

"It isn't worth it," Michel says. "Now he takes the beltway. He could drive around Paris for hours."

"But do you know where he lives?"

"Nobody does. He always manages to give the slip to those who follow him till dawn. There isn't a lot we can do."

"Let's get a little fresh air, okay?" Sophie says with a drowsy voice.

They step out on the bridge. Most passengers from the remaining cars have done the same. The general mood is the opposite of the thrill Anton felt in the café on rue Vignon. Nobody talks, everybody smokes silently with a withdrawn expression on their face. Not a star in the sky. The Seine flowing underneath gives a sorrowful reflection of the windows lighting up, one after the next, apartment building after apartment building, to greet the new day.

The stopover on the bridge, shortly before dawn, doesn't bring their roaming to an end. Before climbing back into his car, Michel declares he is tired of driving. As he parks the Citroen near the bridge, Sophie gives a call to Bashir. Bashir is there in a wink, like he never went to bed in anticipation of her call. Anton takes the front seat and questions him with his eyes: Bashir's eyes tell him that he is used to being on call in the wee hours of the night.

Under the pretext of showing their American mate certain joints, where, Ursula says, you can make special encounters, they take a tour of a few shady establishments. At each stopover, Bashir waits for them aboard the SUV. These special encounters result in long argumentations with sketchy-looking strangers who speak no English. Ursula acts as interpreter while she sucks her drinks from a straw, a small insolent smile on her lips.

"Why do you drink your cocktail out of a straw," one of these fellows, Jacques, asks Ursula.

"So my lipstick won't wear off," she replies, her lipstick-stained straw between her teeth.

Anton's nationality having been revealed, Jacques and his friends are adamant in their defense of the superiority of French cognac and French champagne over any American whisky. They give a demonstration of their patriotism by gulping down huge doses of the debated spirits. Sophie seems to derive a glum satisfaction from Anton's reluctant defense of USA alcoholic pride, but then insists on paying the bill.

Anton's heart lifts later on when, dropping into bed, she says in a pause of exalted lucidity, "You know, Anton, the Dimwits believe it for real that Brel isn't dead."

She doesn't leave him the time to reply that she drifts off to sleep.

Bitcoin and the Ritual of Kyudo Archery

CHAPTER NINE

Anton has breakfast in his kitchen at four PM. Downstairs, Elvis watches over Sophie's sleep.

He spends about an hour in the kyudojo to regain his balance after last night's long squalid vigil.

Back in the study of his apartment, he fishes a cable out of a pocket of his backpack and plugs the iPhone to his Mac to get data connection: he isn't planning to have any WiFi or even just wireless visibility while the Dimwits are around. He goes through some of the usual routines. The latest report from the mining plants in Iceland is about average. He browses through a couple of articles from *Hacker Quarterly*. He kills another half an hour toying around the giant curved monitor on the desk: for this size, it gives a fantastic resolution. It's hackable, but Nessim did not leave behind any obvious trace, except some inconsequential visits to sites devoted to the dark arts.

A fan of Harry Potter? "Dark Lodge of Malta," what's that site all about?

It's getting dark outside.

When Anton hears Michel and Ursula's voices in the garden, muffled by the steady buzz of the patio heaters, he opens his Dell, logs on Kali Linux, and sticks the suction cup of the USB wireless card to the outer glass of the window looking straight down on the garden. On the screen of the Kali window, he assesses the state of affairs down in the garden.

He looks out the same window into the garden, inhales, counts to three – One: *calm*. Two: *elegance*. Three: *flow* – and then screams Michel's name at the top of his lungs.

Michel tilts his head back looking up while his fingers dance a frantic dance on the keys of his Compaq. There is an expression of fear on his face.

"Michel," Anton says, "how tall is the Eiffel Tower?"

"Three hundred twenty-four meters included the tip," Michel answers in a vicious tone that gives him the finger. Then he lowers his head even before Anton pulls his own back from the window.

Social engineering is a pretentious label for a plain scream, in Anton's humble opinion. Tell that to hackers, though.

Anton comes back to the Kali screen. Michel was using the TOR browser, with no more precautions than most people adopt, and, as was to be expected, he blindly killed anything he was doing in there at the first sign of trouble. Hence, the last leg of his internet traffic is wholly unencrypted. It's not so much the contents Anton is after as the final server in the chain. A chain of this sort, not impossible to decode: Michel whispers in Mr. X's ear who whispers in Mr. Y's ear who whisper's in Mr. Z's ear who whispers in Mr. Banker-Monk's ear. Not all pseudonyms are created equal.

Hard to believe that at first Anton took Michel for the anti-Sherlock-Holmes…

Now Anton dissects the evidence, draws the predictable conclusions, turns off the Dell, and writes an email on his Mac.

Dear Nessim,
Your Michel and Ursula are the Scum of the Hacks. They aren't totally inept, though: slowly but steadily, they lead Sophie on the path to self-destruction.
Your call.

Bitcoin and the Ritual of Kyudo Archery

By the way, that Bentley of yours is a fine piece of steel. I've been enjoying it.
Ton ami,
Anton

Ton ami…

As a child, Anton used to think that the unequaled detective was his English instructor Basil, the mouse detective of Walt Disney, and the human version named Sherlock Holmes was an imitation gone wrong. He also used to think that colored movies had come before black-and-white movies: his mother Varvara was a fan of some new German movie maker who shot in black-and-white, as he recalls.

Daniel was seriously intrigued by these quid-pro-quos of Anton's. In the last ten years, the Stanford movie theater showed more than once the entire series of Sherlock Holmes' black-and-white versions, played on screen by Basil Rathbone, and Anton and Daniel didn't miss a single show. It's Daniel who taught Anton that side by side with the original Sherlock Holmes, the one authored by Conan Doyle, there sprouted out a thousand derivative versions. He also taught him that most adults are like the child he was: they confuse the derivative for the original, the character that reminds them of a previous character for the previous character itself.

Well, a little humility will do no harm. Especially in victory. Michel may have rodent-like attributes, like Disney's mouse detective, but that doesn't make Anton into the real Sherlock. He is just starting out, after all.

He doesn't have to wait long before his Mac loads a new email.

Cher Anton,
I could not expect any less from the worthy pupil of the Grand Master, Daniel Dunne.
Scum of the Hacks, I like that.
One of these days I'll pay you a visit.
Amitiés,
Nessim

Anton Google Searches *amitiés* out of scruple, even if it's easy to guess that Nessim keeps treating him like a great friend of his.

What will it be: undeclared war or indifferent unconcern?

Bitcoin and the Ritual of Kyudo Archery

BRAIN WALLET # 16

It was the day after Halloween 2008. After practice, we took the kiza posture in a circle in the middle of the arrow pathway, and Daniel taught us a very unusual lesson: it marked a crucial turning point in the arrangements of our standard practice, which later on we came to name the crypto-Zen turn. Daniel started off with an explication as to why we could never aim at the status of real samurai, even if the kyudo tradition had sprouted out of martial arts in Japan.

"The archery ritual was born out of the lack of external enemies. Around the year 1500, the samurai gave up on their fighting skills and started competing with one another in shooting competitions," he said. "In the beginning, the original belligerence was preserved in a sort of competition where the archer's combativeness was as indispensable as his ability. The most celebrated archer of the time, Wasa Daihachiro, shot thirteen thousand arrows in an uninterrupted session lasting twenty-four hours, and hit the target eight thousand times from a distance of four hundred feet. Later on, new Zen-educated archers distinguished themselves. Alien to the warriors' families, they restrained the belligerence and the display of technical skills in favor of a ritual based on the harmony of form and the gracefulness of motion. We are the heirs to this tradition."

The kyudo ritual limits the number of arrows at the archer's disposal to two, Daniel went on. This way, it distributes lethal force equally among the members of the kyudojo. But Daniel had come to the conclusion that the archers' single line formation on the shooting platform was misconceived, since each archer's back was left in a condition of utter vulnerability. This arrangement was based on the absurd premise of a blind trust among peers. From now on, Daniel said, we would place ourselves in a radial pattern on the shooting platform, so as to balance the mutual risk entailed by the presence of weapons: in a circle, everybody can be the target of everybody else.

"Do you recall your policeman, Anton?" he asked me. "The less I risk, the more I trust."

"If we shoot at one another, the kyudojo is *fucked*," Sophie burst out without waiting for her turn to speak. She put her hand in front of her mouth even before four surprised eyes stared at her. "Sorry."

Daniel declared that from now on he would take part in each practice session. We would start practice by kneeling in a circle on the shooting platform, just the way we made a circle – a triangle, really – in the middle of the arrow pathway after practice. But since the ritual endows each archer with two arrows, his participation wasn't enough: the only way to contain risk effectively was to find at least one new member for the kyudojo. Otherwise, with two arrows at his or her disposal, any archer could comfortably wipe out our three-member kyudojo.

When it was her turn to speak, Sophie said, "We could decrease the number of allotted arrows to one."

"I don't think it's a good idea," Daniel replied. "One of the legacies of the warrior traditions is that an archer carrying a single arrow on the battlefield is a dead archer, Sophie." He continued, "And now I come to the last reform of the day."

A second flaw in the received kyudo tradition pertains to the lack of incentives. He had noticed, for instance, that there were days when she, Sophie, for reasons unknown to him, seemed to be determined not to outclass me, Anton, even if her shooting skills were better by far. Daniel wanted to make sure that each archer would be constantly incentivized to excel: from now on, the archer to shoot the first arrow would be the archer who had outclassed everybody else in the last session by general consensus. And he or she would be the kyudojo's leader for the day. "This way, each of us will be incentivized to be at the top of their game."

Sophie had raised her hand again and was waiting to speak.

"The target's bull's-eye," Daniel concluded, "becomes the origin of the authority exercised over the kyudojo, as it's only right it should be in an archery ritual."

He gave the floor to Sophie.

"You are our leader and it should always be your right to shoot the first arrow," she objected. "The hierarchy of the kyudojo can't be changed."

Daniel burst out laughing. "I expected you to say that the hierarchy of the kyudojo can't be *fucked*." Then he went on. "I'm still the leader and in fact, as you see, I am changing the rules of my own volition. The hierarchy of the kyudojo must evolve. Leadership will be always assigned to the best archer among us."

He detected a trace of irony in my eyes and replied, "I wouldn't be too sure, Anton, that I'll always be the best archer of this kyudojo."

Then, magically, he added a detail bound to play a major role in our future lives. The day before, somebody using the pseudonym Satoshi Nakamoto had sketched out a sort of ritual not dissimilar from our new set of rules: competition, incentive, radial decentralization... His white paper, published online, labeled such ritual a *blockchain*. Nakamoto is an ancient surname made up of two Japanese words: *origin* and *center*. For the last few months, Daniel had been chatting online with this Satoshi Nakamoto about a number of issues: trust, risk, incentive, consensus – the same issues that had inspired today's reform of our kyudojo. (It'll do no harm if I share with you that Daniel alternated between two crypto-identities in his chats with Satoshi: Beau de Rubempré and Zero Cash.)

"Do we know who this Satoshi Nakamoto is?" asked Sophie.

Daniel: "His real identity is impossible to trace."

Sophie: "How about *hers*?"

Daniel: "Satoshi could be a woman, why not?"

Satoshi's genius, he was telling us a bit later, consisted in that he found a way for machines to verify uncontroversially whole blocks of information pertaining to human interactions. Those blocks, linked to one another, make up the blockchain. "Satoshi solved a problem that's been troubling humankind for centuries," he went on. "How can a group of strangers reach a riskless sort of agreement about reality? An agreement, more precisely, about the record which the machine of one of them provides of a situation of mutual concern? Thanks to blockchain technology, each of these strangers identifies deception of the group with the least profitable option."

This was my introduction to Satoshi's blockchain and to the cryptocurrency that fuels it: bitcoin.

Bitcoin and the Ritual of Kyudo Archery

BRAIN WALLET # 17
To grasp what Satoshi's blockchain is all about, think of a Trust Machine.

The blockchain is made up of a chain of blocks. A block is like a box, a container. Or like a newspaper, filled with all the info printed on its pages. Inside each block there is information about some state of affairs in the real world: about a transaction, for instance, which occurred between two strangers, but also, more generally, about any event which someone cares to permanently archive for posterity: my birthday, the US women soccer team's latest lineup, the murder of Jamal Khashoggi, a contested election... New information flows to the blockchain uninterruptedly.

This new information fills new blocks, one at a time – think of a box filled to capacity – and each additional block is appended to the chain, making it longer. At each given moment, the result is an immutable ledger, that is, a registry of occurrences among humans. And at each given moment, this ever longer ledger is condensed into a hash, a string of characters and numbers, just like the one generated by the twelve-word string of my *Open Sesame*. On the long run, decades from now, the hash of the blockchain will be the condensed expression of a good chunk of human history.

It is the hash that makes a Trust Machine of the blockchain. If a cheater ever attempted to falsify even the tiniest detail recorded in anyone of the blocks – claiming I was born on a different day, or the US soccer team lines a different goalie, or there is an extra comma in the American Declaration of

Independence – it would be immediately evident that the hash of the tainted blockchain, as broadcasted by the cheater, diverges from the true one, which is known to all miners. In sum, you can always trust the consensus reached on the truthfulness of the blockchain.

The amount of new information flowing toward the blockchain is more than a single block can contain. Each miner selects a chunk of new information, in the order it's received, and creates a new block. Of all these new potential blocks, the one that's appended to the chain is the block assembled by the miner whose machine is the first to solve the so-called mining puzzle. Satoshi's mining procedures are hinged on this competitive game.

On January 3, 2009 Satoshi Nakamoto mined block zero of the bitcoin blockchain and compensated the computational work which took his machine to solve the mining puzzle with freshly minted bitcoins. The new block was worth fifty bitcoins back then. The creation of block zero started the competition for the solution of the mining puzzle and the creation of block one. Satoshi didn't claim any special priority rights for himself, he remained on the fringes instead. From that moment onward, the right to create the next block depended on the solution of the mining puzzle.

Our mining plants in Iceland, of which Daniel's sister Kathleen is now majority stockholder (me being the entire minority), win often the contest to solve the puzzle. The contest is decentralized, a race of every miner against every other miner, and there is no arbiter of the result but the consensus among the miners themselves, who verify that the hash broadcasted by the winning miner is the correct representation of the new blockchain.

BRAIN WALLET # 18

It took me a couple years at least before I became aware of the full extent of Daniel's commitment to the convergence of our kyudo discipline with blockchain technology. It took me quite a while, in fact, before I quit my job at Google and entered the crypto space for real, joining Daniel in the mining of bitcoin, securing the blockchain, and improving its cryptography. There was an immense amount of work to be done, unfinished to this day.

It was only after I devoted all of my time to blockchain technology that I grasped the inner logic of the crypto-Zen kyudojo. The archers' initial disposition in a radial pattern, evocative of the decentralized competition among blockchain miners, brought about a balance of forces. Kneeling in a circle, everybody faced everybody else, and nobody had enough arrows to wipe out a kyudojo counting four or more members. This decentralized disposition made irrelevant this or that archer's individual predisposition or lack thereof to comply with the rule of mutual safety: attack against the kyudojo meant suicide, so, mutual trust resulted in the kyudojo from a network effect, regardless of individual will or whim.

Meanwhile, the kyudojo had grown to five members: Carlo and Margherita, two Italians from Turin introduced by Daniel himself, joined in.

Thanks to the blockchain, one day we'll build machines capable of turning themselves into the nodes of the network with no need for human intervention. That day, we'll have attained an incorruptible system of shared consensus about the state of human affairs. Between now and then, we are tasked with the development of ever more complex cryptographic systems. Looking back to those beginnings, as I write these words, I realize how the optimism of blind faith prevailed over common sense: among the growing number of coders who dedicated themselves to the blockchain, no one grasped yet the complexity of the challenge, the quicksand of the math which, still now, threatens to engulf us.

Cryptography feeds off tight mental logics. I had explored its depths in my years at Google, in a defensive, anti-hack perspective, if you will. I was now practicing it as manifestation of our crypto-Zen discipline. I went through this transition with a spiritual independence that invigorated me both physically and mentally. It wasn't much of a surprise, even, when I realized I had become a match to Sophie's archery. Competitiveness was so foreign to her nature that she barely noticed. Earlier on she had even allowed me to outclass her from time to time, and it was me, then, who didn't notice she did it on purpose: it had taken Daniel to point that out.

I was beginning to detect an untiring sturdiness in Sophie's temperament. She worshipped Daniel, his opinions were Gospel truth to her, and she changed her behavior and lifestyle no less than me in the wake of the changes undergone by our crypto-Zen kyudojo. The innovations of blockchain technology had struck her to such an extent that she changed the subject of her doctoral dissertation altogether: she would now study, still advised by Daniel, an alternative to the mining procedures described in Satoshi's white paper. She wasn't the only cryptographer, at the time, wondering whether there wasn't an even more ingenious method for bitcoin mining. There isn't, apparently.

"I simply traded Holy Script with Satoshi's script," she joked with me, like she was trying to brush aside objections I didn't dream of raising.

Script, I learned from her that day, is not spelled with a *y*. Not even cryptographic script, it isn't.

"Holy Scripts of all persuasions, Christian, Jews, Muslim, must be protected from impurity," she said. "The crypt, written with a y, is where you hide the truth of Holy Script, written with an i, from the eyes of the uninitiated."

Крипта, Kripta.

"You believe in that sort of stuff?" I asked.

"What stuff?"

"Impurity... the truth of Holy Script... the uninitiated..."

"Belief... What's the matter with you, Anton? You sound like Nessim, who obsesses about black Madonnas and all sorts of cult. Holy script is there to be decrypted, not believed in. What I was studying for my first project was the Koran's poetics of encryption, algorithms of sorts."

Rather like a Russian doll, I thought to myself. You open the crypt, pull out the secret script hidden inside, and, holy or not, decode it to find the secret hidden within the secret. As long as the regression from secret to inner secret leads you to the breaking point of utter clarity, you are facing what's truth to the believer.

"Ever heard of Edgar Allan Poe?" she said.

"Who is he?"

"A cryptographer from way back. A writer too. He is the one who discovered that the best crypt for a secret script is no crypt at all. He left his most secret documents before everybody's eyes."

Bitcoin and the Ritual of Kyudo Archery

"It worked?"

"No one noticed."

Sophie didn't keep her studies of bitcoin's script hidden in some secret crypt, yet she kept them disconnected from any reality check. She didn't wonder whether bitcoins would become legal tender one day. She didn't wonder whether the blockchain would one day contribute to the progress of American democracy. She didn't wonder whether the technology of the blockchain would one day provide the impoverished masses with direct access to the planet's resources. She didn't wonder whether it was more responsible to be a *hodler*, like blockchainers call those who hoard bitcoins regardless of the market price, or a *trader* who speculates on price changes. And least of all, owing to her family wealth, did she wonder whether she'd ever make a living out of her studies of the blockchain. She contributed to the progress of blockchain-related cryptography like it consisted of an exercise in logics detached from the real world: an ethereal proof of concept she repeated every day in some new guise in homage to our kyudojo.

Hence, we two progressed in parallel, at a different pace and with different goals. Both furiously fast, if I may say so myself.

The day of her dissertation defense, Sophie was highly praised by professor Boneh, Stanford's Cryptographer-in-Chief, who suggested she should look into the academic job market. The day of the PhD award ceremony, Daniel gave her two red Moleskine notebooks and a Pelikan fountainpen. (I taught her how to change the ink cartridge.) Sophie never pursued that academic career suggested by Boneh. She wanted to stay in the swing of things with me and Daniel, she told me.

I was rather under the impression that applying for a job was frowned upon in her family.

Daniel had fully committed to the future of the blockchain. To him, the social and commercial success of the blockchain was on a par with a mission of civic responsibility. That's what it'd become to me too, in time, cementing our collaboration.

"At long last, I found my categorical imperative!" he would tell me, plunging into a discussion of the intersection between a German philosopher named Kant and his own Catholic faith. German philosophy, he didn't make it any easier for me to grasp by using and abusing of long and obscure German words. Catholic theology, he kept comparing it with math, an inferior sort of math, regardless of my complaint that the math he talked about wasn't the math I called math.

He had discontinued all his previous projects and obligations, and was among the first three or four bitcoin miners. At first, his Mac's CPU sufficed to the task. Soon it turned out that even an Arduino or Raspberry Pi board was enough to mine, and he installed in his garage a rig made up of several dozens of cheap boards and old Macs. Admittedly, it was a large garage. Later on, there came the transitions to more and more complex processing units and integrated circuits. By then, I had joined him in the supervision of his mining plants in Iceland.

In the time before I made my choice between Google's generous salary and the prospect of this technological adventure by Daniel's side, he piled up a fortune in bitcoins. Daniel had a head for business which I lacked. Around the year 2000 already, when the dot-com bubble burst, he had grabbed a large quantity of prime real estate in Palo Alto. Now he was doing the same with bitcoins. But Daniel was not a greedy person. Strike that: Daniel *is not* a greedy person. The creation of new bitcoins plays an essential role in the upkeep and update of the blockchain, and he considered this task, as I said, his own personal mission. After all, one bitcoin was close to worthless in those early days: with ten thousand of them, you could barely buy yourself a pizza or two. Bitcoin's price peaked on December 2017, but Daniel didn't feel like making a profit even then. And a few weeks after Bitcoin's price peaked, he was turned into a zombie by the nail lodged in his skull.

Now we are going through the so-called Crypto Winter and bitcoin's price is crashing through the floor. Who knows what's going on with his bitcoins?

BRAIN WALLET # 19

In 2010 I had to learn to drive. Daniel bought himself a Ferrari 599XX a few months before this model reached the market, and he got into his head to give me his old F430. It couldn't be helped: I speeded up the process and got my driver's license. So, one afternoon Daniel drove me to the Ferrari dealership in Redwood City on the F430, stepped out of the driver's seat, threw me the keychain, and hopped aboard his new 599XX – Ferrari red, of course.

Vroom-vroom. If there was a guy in Silicon Valley who could afford to shrug off paperwork minutiae...

Vroom-vroom: the dealership's accountant was waving a sheaf of papers in my rear-view mirror. Back to Palo Alto on two thundering fireballs.

The red Ferrari was not Daniel's most generous gift to me. The portfolios of cryptocurrencies buried in my Michelin street map, it's Daniel who created them for me out of nowhere. Those rare times I checked the balance, I always found it had increased since last time. All I had to do was draw new geometries with colored ribbons on my Michelin map, and bury new secret passphrases under the flags.

One day, Daniel even presented me with a minority stake of his bitcoin mining plants in Iceland. That took some notary work and paper signing. In case he was ever hit with some unforeseen emergency, he told me that day, it'd be my appointed task to carry on his vision of the blockchain, and his bitcoins and the rest of the mining plants should be mine. I've archived an old email where he writes that he *scrypted* (yes, with a y) his last wills and secured them in a secret partition of his Mac.

That was meant as Daniel's ultimate challenge for me: his *Kripta*. Even he could forget what's the first breaking point in the chain of secrets.

Your Kripta is gone with your Mac, Daniel.

However, the red Ferrari was never totally mine: year in and year out, Daniel's accountants still paid my registration fee and insurance. I'll have it delivered to Kathleen Dunne's legal representatives when I leave for Paris.

Come springtime, me and Sophie would often take a trip to the ocean on weekday mornings – when there were no Sunday crowds out there, no sunbathers, no kids building castles in the sand. Sophie didn't know how to drive a car, she had *owned* her own chauffeur, as she put it, since she was a kid, and besides, she'd never stoop to setting foot in my red Ferrari.

"It's a gross car," she said, "a toy for Arab playboys."

I didn't take it the wrong way. I thought of the face my father would make if he saw me in the driver' seat of my red fireball. *How many cocktails would the price tag buy you, Dad?* I was learning from Sophie's company that some of the people who are born into wealth, a minority of them, share a rare gift: they drink it with their mother's milk and call it *sprezzatura*. Me, I had been infected with Daniel's passion for a color, Ferrari red. Was it vulgar in her eyes? Couldn't help myself.

And after all, I didn't like the prospect of lodging Sophie's hound dog, Elvis into the F430's cockpit.

Can you be loved with sprezzatura? Sophie reciprocated my love in an offhand, noncommittal way that confirmed me in the hypothesis that you can. It's not everybody who, entitled by birth to first-choice pick, would pick for herself a three-legged dog like her beloved Elvis. Wasn't that proof enough she had her heart in the right place? It just wasn't the place where ordinary people keep theirs.

Sophie's chauffeur Bashir was a mustached Arab with a military bearing, tasked with driving her everywhere she went and, I suspected, act as her security detail as well. To Bashir's chagrin, we two commandeered his SUV on those springtime mornings, leaving him, steaming yet obsequious, on the sidewalk by my apartment building. The funny thing is that when we got back, several hours later, he was still there waiting for us.

For how long had Bashir been *owned* by Sophie? Longer than Elvis, I reckoned.

Me and Sophie would always take the same road to Half Moon Bay, then we would race along the ocean on Route 1 till we reached the San Gregorio nudist beach. It was Sophie who had guided me there the first time. We parked on high ground, not far from the beach, and Sophie was topless even before Elvis had jumped out of the trunk. I took off my t-shirt as well, determined to shrug off the bite of the wind blowing from the waves. Then I shielded my eyes from the sun and gazed in the distance. Sophie mocked me gently whenever I proudly declared that I just spotted the blow of a whale. Meanwhile, Elvis ran up and down the water's edge with his uneven stride.

The sandy beach kept going for miles and miles, but to reach it we had to walk through the narrow passage between the waves and the promontory on top of which we had parked. Later in the day, the high tide would flood the base of the promontory: we had to be back earlier than then, or we would be at the mercy of the elements. Far away, the beach ended at the feet of another promontory, fronted by tall sea stacks. Near the water's edge, the sand was clean and smooth, but a hundred feet or so to our right, at the feet of a vertical cliff of porous rock, there were heaps of driftwood carried there by the ocean, trunks smooth and white like cuttle-bones. We walked barefoot. Usually there wasn't a soul, except some occasional, unresponsive angler, outfitted in rubber from head to foot like a deep-sea diver, or some equally unresponsive gay man in the nude, who kept busy building a sort of giant honeycomb structure with that driftwood. The remains of similar honeycomb structures were spread here and there along the beach. The previous summer they had belonged to nudist colonies, Sophie explained, spacious beach cabins that were abandoned with the bad season.

The sun was almost warm but the wind from the ocean studded her breasts with goose bumps. We moved forward at a fast pace toward the far-away sea stacks, our feet in the backwash, now hand in hand, now forerunning each other in a slow jog. Elvis pounced on some seagulls, busy pecking on wet sand, or he ventured into the taller waves and an instant later he became a tiny black buoy in a wreath of white foam.

I was twenty. I was in love with an older woman who loved me back in her own lofty way, surrounded herself with obedient and devoted servants, was inseparable from a dog missing a foreleg, and was disclosing to me a whole new world of wonders.

Oftentimes, we found a seal's carcass on the foreshore. The first time I saw one, Sophie reacted to my exclamations of wonder with a perfunctory chin jut pointing to the right. I looked that way and saw, perched on the edge of the cliff, a dozen or so vultures. Still as statues. Only the feathers at the base of their necks shook, stirred by the breeze. No clarification needed, and in fact Sophie gave me none. Those vultures were waiting for their turn, patient like kyudo archers: no sooner would the intruders, and especially the strapping, three-legged black one, move away, then they would pick up their meal where it had been interrupted.

That day the sun was unusually warm. On our way back, we stepped into one of those ruined honeycomb structures, sheltered from the wind. Sophie was leaning against the lukewarm white trunks, Elvis curled up at her feet, and I held her in my arms. The memory of the docile way she lifted her skirt still moves me. Afterwards, we walked back to the SUV without a word.

I was irked at myself for doing it unprotected. And irked for spoiling the occasion by being irked.

The moment I took the steering wheel in my hands, her docility was a faraway echo already. In our affair, for sure, she kept the driver seat.

Bitcoin and the Ritual of Kyudo Archery

BRAIN WALLET # 20

An arrow shot with true precision is a rare invisible bird. All that one sees is the tremor of the bowstring that makes it fly.
With kyudo, one can't go deeper than a certain depth. Beneath it, one must live it to comprehend it. It flows from the conceptual nugget to the heartbeat.

Eyes like Anton's eyes are an open book, a teardrop is worth a whole chapter. Sophie is teaching him to speak in words, too late for the one who managed to read the chapter in that teardrop beforehand.

Eyes like Nessim's eyes are a blank page. The solitude of the arrow shot with absolute precision. The invisible ink of the incest between two continents.

The entries on Daniel's red Moleskine are not dated, but the excerpts I just transcribed must go back to a day of 2015, because Daniel met Nessim only once, and it was in May of that year. Judging by the words he devotes to Nessim, Daniel must've known much more of Sophie's husband than I had imagined. More than me for sure, even if I met Nessim several times, and on one occasion I was his guest for a whole weekend in San Francisco.

Daniel defines Nessim the *banker-monk*.

It's a fact that Sophie confided in Daniel more frequently and sincerely than I was aware of. *Daniel is the only man with whom I can share any secret. He smiles and never objects to my words. But there are times when he helps me sweep away the emptiness I feel in anything I do.* She didn't tell him everything, though: for a long time, till a day in May 2015 in fact, Daniel was in the dark regarding our affair. And when he caught on to it, he came to the conclusion that Sophie had found in me something she hadn't found elsewhere yet. Of her too, no doubt, he knew more than I did.

Beau de Rubempré

Even though I slept with her, I had no idea about Sophie's sexual promiscuities and bipolar disorder. I'm learning of them from Daniel's red Moleskine, as I write these words.

Regarding Nessim, Sophie spoke to me in ciphers: *Frosted-glass eyes that cast a spell on you.* And how would I know that some of her impenetrable maxims were about him? *As to love, Anton, it interested me briefly in the past and the recollection of that brief and perfect relationship makes any replacement vulgar and insignificant.* She never hinted that the irreplaceable love she alluded to had come to her from Nessim, who was about twenty years older than her. This too I've learned from Daniel's red Moleskine, precisely from the entry devoted to the party he gave in his own apartment to celebrate the baptism of Andrea, Carlo and Margherita's newborn.

The dynasties that had given birth to both Sophie and Nessim had sprouted out of the graft of hostile continents and equally hostile religious persuasions. Nessim's lineage was related to the Reza Pahlavi for the Persian branch, but he was half-German too. And Sophie's lineage was related to the Renault carmakers for the French branch, but she was Egyptian. I was taking their age difference into account when I assumed, mistakenly, that Sophie's must've been an arranged marriage, Arabic-style. But it was a totally different story. To begin with, Sophie was only half-Arab. As to Nessim, "Nobody is less Arab than a Persian," she told me more than once.

"In meeting Nessim, Sophie had come across her own mirrored image," Daniel writes. "Two creatures of absolute privilege, exempt from obligations toward their fellow human beings. The solitude of two perfectly flying arrows, impervious to the obstacles in their path." Nessim's magnetism had lasted a short interval for Sophie, nourished by the charm of a banker-monk used to beguiling men and women alike by trade. It had faded away by the day of their wedding. "From the spoilt brat she used to be, Sophie became the dynastic wife, a future mother, the second buttress, together with financial assets, of their two inextinguishable families. In the conception of his son and heir, Nessim played his part with the same impersonal diligence he devoted to high finance. The more Sophie understood her husband's attitude, the more determined was she to boycott, to hinder the natural course of events." The randomly picked lovers, the white nights, the private jet, the seclusion of the ashram or the Bedouin camp or the inaccessible mountain hut in the Alps, and eventually, the compromise of separate lives – no extreme behavior had the power to undermine Nessim's stolid self-denial in his dedication to perpetuate their lineage. What troubled Sophie the most was the suspicion that her own body was not cut out for the natural course of events. "I'm a pretty empty shell, she tells me," Daniel writes, "destined to remain so." Would her marriage to Nessim turn out to be a repetition of Soraya's fate? Behind her refusal of the maternal role she was predestined to, Sophie was gnawed by the doubt that she would never measure up to it.

I'm learning from a Google search that beautiful Soraya was repudiated for infertility by the Shah of Persia and became an actress in Rome, Italy.

Sophie found rare intervals of peace in the kyudojo or at the keyboard of her Mac, Daniel writes.

Beau de Rubempré

She didn't betray her restlessness either during the long hours she spent in bed by my side, but the day Daniel wrote the pages I'm drawing from, he couldn't be aware of it.

Daniel's red Moleskine gives me the measure of my lack of imagination. I doted on Sophie, I've been in love with her for years. She loved me back in that non-committal attitude of hers, which I ascribed to the special prerogatives of old money with its innate sprezzatura. But in her absence, I was unable to assign her an autonomous existence from the one she shared with me. Sophie would suddenly vanish for weeks on end, but no sooner did she show up again at the kyudojo and we picked up our affair where we left it, than I showed no signs of curiosity. She could come back darkly suntanned or white as a ghost, and I asked no questions. She knew I'm a guy of few words and was unsurprised, I guess, by my attitude. When she vanished that way, I consoled myself with the discipline of practice at the kyudojo, the rigor of coding on my Mac, and the nights I spent at the movies with Daniel. I've never been less in love with Daniel than with Sophie, to be honest. The lonely rituals of food preparation and consumption, of hiking among the sequoias of Wunderlich Park, of meditation in the kiza posture: it's all stuff I learned from him. Sophie resurfaced in the same unannounced way she had disappeared from my life, a whiter shade of pale or a darker shade of tan, in either case, to me, more beautiful than before, and my food, my power walks, my meditation, my frugal life turned into a ritual for two without much change. What did change were my heartbeats. What made me think that Sophie's heartbeats were attuned to mine? She didn't need to enquire with me how I spent my days in her absence: she knew I spent my days doing what I would usually do in her company or in Daniel's. I took for granted – but the truth is that I never asked myself in a conscious manner – that the new version of Sophie standing in front of me, unresisting the second I lifted her skirt, had come out of the same, unalterable mold of the previous one.

I didn't have Daniel's inquisitive mind. On me, he had the lead of a bachelor's degree and two PhDs.

BRAIN WALLET # 21
I print and paste a snapshot from Daniel's red Notebook.

May 14, 2015.

Eyes like Anton's eyes are an open book, a teardrop is worth a whole chapter. Sophie is teaching him to speak in words, too late for the one who read the chapter in that teardrop beforehand. That hesitant teardrop hanging from Anton's eyelashes revealed to me his secret affair with Sophie. For how long has it been going on? She looked perfectly at ease in their fiction before Nessim's eyes. Which can only mean that Sophie's fragility finds in Anton the scaffold that no other lover ever gave her. That teardrop that couldn't bring itself to sliding away from Anton's eye kept telling me the same story of repressed jealousy. Anton doesn't believe his love is requited. He sees in Sophie an older woman, much too wealthy to take him seriously. If he was as acquainted with her soul as I am (the heart lies in certain predicaments, and in fact, surprisingly, Sophie's heart never let me in on her affair with Anton), Anton would be aware that, of the two of them, she's the one who acts childishly (yet isn't childish), frailly (yet isn't fragile), obtusely (yet isn't stupid), and inconsistently (yet is one of the most logical minds I've ever seen at work). Anton's worship cuts her loose from the role of reproductive shell, imposed on her by her family origin and her marriage to Nessim. The "pretty empty shell," so obviously unfair to the banker-monk's patient devotion, changes herself into the vamp, the femme fatale – or so she fears. Sophie will be the last to notice the reversal of priorities that is already in progress within her soul. A woman on the verge. Anton will grasp the miracle before she does.

Bitcoin and the Ritual of Kyudo Archery

Yesterday at the party, I thought for a moment that Nessim had figured out what's to come, and joined us here at my place to meet the rival destined to take Sophie away from him. I wondered whether a banker in his league and with his ancestral family (the invisible ink of the incest between two continents) is expected to keep up a pretense of marital bliss even when it comes at the cost of love itself. Nessim wandered from room to room with the unostentatious curiosity of an old-world gentleman visiting the stable of a dear friend. He chain-smoked thin black cigarettes with a golden filter, which gave him a thick halo of pungent smoke. Of the two presumed horses racing for his wife's heart (so I thought), most of Nessim's courteous attentions were for me, but Anton too was an object of constant scrutiny by those two glossy, piercing eyes, that peer out of an unusually oval face. Try hard as he might, Anton could not pull himself out of Sophie's orbit; his efforts not to get too close to her were conspicuous in their pointlessness. He reminded me of an addict going through some serious withdrawal. I had to do something before that teardrop shining by his right eye would tell everybody present the story of his jealousy for someone else's wife. I grabbed Nessim's elbow and steered him toward my study. After all, I thought (how wrong was I!), he was mostly interested in appraising the favorite rival, and that was I.

The study is the largest room in my apartment. There was nobody there, except Margherita who was changing Andrea's diaper on the couch. While I introduced her to Nessim, she thanked me again for volunteering the apartment for her child's party, and the apple-red spots on her cheeks were the best testimony to her genuine gratitude. We left her to her maternal duty and moved to the room's opposite side, by my desk.

Nessim noticed right away the map of Dublin hanging from the wall, and asked me the reason of all those colored flags connected with colored ribbons. I was beating my brains out to entertain this stranger, while keeping him in the dark as to my diversionary move. Hence, based on chaos theory, I could argue that it's Anton's teardrop that made me fall into Nessim's trap. Dismissing his question as the frivolous curiosity of a money man wholly incompetent of the blockchain, I told him in a low voice (I didn't want to be heard by Margherita, who watched us from the couch) that the Dublin street map provides me with mementos of my cryptographic keys. That's it. But it was enough. Right away, Nessim embarked on a learned disquisition about the mnemonic procedures adopted by Hugh of St. Victor and Albertus Magnus. 'De arcae description per crucis figuram, et agnum in centro ejous stantem, et columnam in altum erectam,' he quoted. He was citing by heart from Hugh of St. Victor's De arca Noe Mystica. And in Latin, no less! An homage to my doctorate in theology? Then he told me that last January he utilized Ingres's Grande Odalisque for the mementos of his talking points in Davos. He pulled out his iPhone and showed me the picture.

Each word he uttered pushed toward me a tiny puff of cigarette smoke out of the permanent halo around his head. The burning in my eyes was becoming unbearable.

'The odalisque's body is too smooth and uniform to provide a large number of stable reminders,' I observed.

He contradicted me, adducing the evidence of St. Augustine's theories on the interplay of erotic and mnemonic stimuli. He cited some other passages in Latin. And then he complimented the stratagem of my Dublin map. 'Stratagem,' he called it.

'My collaborators sifted through some analogous cartographic solutions to passphrase obfuscation,' he said.

The moment I heard him talk of passphrase obfuscation, my surviving hope that he was talking frivolous gibberish faded away. He seemed to be knowing what he was talking about.

'Passphrase obfuscation?' I echoed him in an inquisitive tone, to gauge the damage done.

Bitcoin and the Ritual of Kyudo Archery

'Please, don't ask me what it means, Dr. Dunne. I'm the layman who pays the bills. My collaborators handle the nitty-gritty.'

But he kept going about it, after that pretense of candor, probing me so shrewdly that I had to play along:

'Indeed,' I volunteered, 'most digital systems of key storage are still vulnerable to hacking.'

'Unless you write down your passphrase on a plain piece of paper and keep it in a safe,' he replied with a chuckle.

He kept chatting and probing, chatting and probing with those piercing eyes of his, as though he had a whole laundry list to test me by. Again, I couldn't dodge all of his shoves at once:

'Indeed,' I heard myself say, 'the hierarchical deterministic keys used by hardware wallets such as Trezor are not that bad of an idea.'

To that he replied, 'Obviously, when one handles a crypto capital as huge as yours, Dr. Dunne, one must tread carefully.'

Our conversation was becoming more personal than I cared for. What did he mean, I asked, and his answer left me speechless.

'My collaborators have done a few dusting attacks on your known bitcoin portfolios,' he explained.

'Dusting attacks?' I echoed him in the same inquisitive tone as before, feeling foolish.

'I hope you know what they are, Dr. Dunne, because I for one haven't the slightest idea. My collaborators tell me it's fair play in crypto, that's why I mention it. According to their calculations, there are no more than two or three bitcoin portfolios greater than yours on the planet.' Then he put his hand on my arm as if to take me into his confidence. 'Unless you are Satoshi, the one and only. In this case, you'd have the pole position. And I'll lobby for your nomination to the Nobel prize.'

'I'm not Satoshi,' I whispered in a hissing tone.

Beau de Rubempré

Dusting attacks! I couldn't fathom by what oversight had I left exposed that flank. And it was hard to take that of all people, it had been this international banker to strike it. I am not Satoshi, but it's a fact that my bitcoin stash is not much smaller than his. This was not what I bargained for when I took the initiative to shield Anton from Nessim's closer scrutiny.

I wanted to know where Nessim had found his collaborators and whether they were truly blockchain competent. I was inclined to rule it out. We blockchainers are still a decentralized collection of small local tribes. But he mentioned the names of a few doctoral candidates in cryptography, all of them from our own here at Stanford – the same names about whom rumors had circulated recently of clandestine initiatives and first-class flights to Riyadh, Tel Aviv, and Moscow. It so happens that one by one, all of these fellows have made themselves scarce from their departments, to the puzzlement of their academic advisors.

However unpalatable, I had to admit to myself that I had recklessly betrayed the secret of my Dublin street map to an insider.

To crown it all, I revised the immodest opinion I used to have of my own psychological insightfulness. It wasn't true at all, as I had assumed, that Nessim came to the party to meet the sentimental rival close to prevailing over him. Why should he? In the dimension of romantic behavior, the banker-monk sees himself as a saint. His face outlines the oval of a Renaissance Madonna and he recites by heart the writings of the Fathers of a Church that isn't his. He puts up with Sophie's frequent fits of temper and inconsequential adulteries, as though they barely entailed a harmless pruning of a genealogical tree bound to prevail over all obstacles. Nessim's unostentatious curiosity was a purposeful booby trap, and I fell into it.

I had not been taken in because of Anton's teardrop, after all. Even before Nessim took leave of me, disappearing behind a thicker cloud of

Bitcoin and the Ritual of Kyudo Archery

smoke, the doubt entered my mind that I had been taken in by a con man. Nessim had come to meet me on purpose, to lure me into revealing the way I hide my passphrases. The secret of what they protect, he knew beforehand.

BRAIN WALLET # 22

Sophie's outfit in the kyudojo was not too dissimilar from mine, with the exception of the leather shield that constricted her right breast, sheltering it from the lash of the bowstring when it releases the arrow.

After Carlo and Margherita joined the kyudojo, Sophie made me suffer through many exhausting discussions on the relationship between archery and the female body. There was the problem of Margherita's advanced stage of pregnancy. Sophie couldn't let it go. Never ever should Daniel admit a pregnant woman to kyudo practice! After practice, we two walked as usual to my apartment, but the peace of our intimacy was gone. It was hopeless. To the knowing nod of my friend the policeman at the corner of University Avenue, I could only respond with a sad smile.

I didn't dare ask Sophie how much had she read up on the subject. Her leather shield, we both knew, does figure among the traditional components of a woman's outfit in the kyudojo. Was she spurred by rivalry against the newcomer, when she opposed her admission to the kyudojo? It was evident that Sophie didn't dare challenge Daniel's decision openly. At the time of the crypto-Zen turn, it's she who claimed that Daniel should never give up his leadership. It didn't make things any easier that Margherita had proven herself almost as skilled an archer as Daniel. Sophie didn't breathe a word the day that Daniel introduced the two new members of the kyudojo, and day in and day out, she kept hiding effortlessly her discontent during practice. She treated Margherita like the dearest of friends and never forgot to enquire about the progress of her pregnancy.

Once again, I had the opportunity to gauge the special advantages bought you by wealth and an elite education.

Was I the only one who heard the strident sound coming from Sophie's bowstring? Maybe the sound was the same as always, but it gave me a foretaste of the sharp tone of voice she'd talk in later that day, at my place, when she would let out all of her indignation. The sight of Margherita maddened her, accordingly it wore me out. I even found myself wondering if Sophie's attitude was driven, to an extent, by some obscure envy for the soon-to-be Mom.

Margherita was even taller than Sophie and obviously more athletic. Quite your dark-haired Amazon, a bit on the butch side. Carlo, very lean, his hair dyed blue, was the tiniest and shortest of our group.

It had never occurred to me, before the two Italians joined our kyudojo, to indulge in this sort of physical comparisons. But I found myself doing it now, and that's how I became aware that I had finally grown as tall as Sophie. I was now more than half an inch taller than Daniel. It was different back when I first joined the kyudojo: at the time, the tallest of us three was Sophie, then came Daniel, and the shortest one was me, still in the long tail of growth spurt.

After an impartial analysis, I came to the conclusion that I couldn't disagree with Sophie: it's evident that a pregnant belly prevents the archer from assuming several of the prescribed kyudo positions. One day, at my place, Sophie tried to prove it to me by handling her bow after stuffing a pillow under her dress. There was no need for it, and jokingly I stroked her dummy belly.

"So, it's decided already?"

"What are you talking about?" she asked.

"Our baby. How are we going to call him?"

I shouldn't have said it. She slapped me. "Thanks to your unlimited supply of condoms, baby, we are not at risk."

To notch and then shoot the arrow, no doubt, Margherita had to go through several unbalanced positions, an unforgivable transgression in kyudo. If Daniel overlooked it, I told myself, he must have his own reasons. But I wouldn't dare say that to Sophie. She would've come after me: how did I dare question Daniel's integrity! I was growing painfully aware of two things: one, Sophie had put Daniel on such a tall pedestal that one of these days she would succumb to the impulse to take him down, and two, even if she slept with me, Sophie didn't ascribe to me the same stature she ascribed to Daniel. I wished I could grow in her esteem. Did she share her rage with me and nobody else because the other members of our kyudojo deserved more deference?

I learned later on – Daniel himself told me so – that at first he didn't have any especially good reason, nor any especially bad one, to overlook Margherita's pregnancy.

The blockchain's grapevine had given advance notice to Daniel of the young Italian couple moving to Palo Alto. Margherita had been awarded a postdoctoral fellowship at SLAC, the Stanford lab for particle acceleration. Carlo was an initiate of the blockchain, a voluntarily unemployed with a master's in computer science. Shortly after their arrival in California, Margherita threatened to divorce Carlo if he didn't find himself a coding job, now that she had brought him to Silicon Valley and besides, they were going to have a child. Carlo was taking his time. He believed that the blockchain would create fabulous opportunity for first comers. Years earlier, Margherita had won an Olympic medal in archery. On their honeymoon to Japan, she and Carlo had discovered the yumi bow, which has little to share with the bows used in Olympic competitions.

Under pressure from that same blockchain's grapevine, Daniel had consented to using his good offices to save Carlo's marriage from divorce. Frequent practice at the kyudojo distracted Margherita from her husband's ineptness. Events would prove her wrong, eventually: soon, Carlo would create Futura, the crypto company whose funding, wholly shouldered by the crypto community, started one of the first token sales in the crypto space and the most memorable by far.

The initial token sale was an experiment in fundraising, born with the creation of a new blockchain called *ethereum*: it consisted of the sale of tokens that entitled the buyer to use the blockchain of the company doing the sale. Under certain conditions, these tokens were the equivalent of conventional securities. In my opinion, it's Futura's initial token sale that gave birth to the world's crypto-economy.

So, Daniel's reasons for overlooking Margherita's pregnant condition turned out to be justifiable in the long run, and even advantageous to everyone involved – inclusive of the couple Sophie-Nessim, as it'd turn out to my total sorrow. Margherita would eventually give up on her scientific work at SLAC to take over the management of Futura's fast growing personnel.

But Daniel's slight to our kyudojo came at a high price. He experienced it under a cloud of shame, made more oppressive by Sophie's disdain, which didn't go unnoticed. All along, and especially after Sophie's defection from the kyudojo, Daniel was tormented by the doubt of having made an unforgivable mistake. He had debased the sacred bond among me, him, and Sophie – and bowing to whose pressure? Six months after Futura's initial token sale, the same grapevine that pushed Daniel to take that perilous step turned itself into an oligarchy of coders, committed to diverting Satoshi's original protocol onto dubious tracks. Daniel consoled himself with the thought that he had prevented the wreckage of Carlo's marriage. Me and Daniel agreed that, except for Margherita's over-the-top temperament, she and Carlo sparkled with kindness and good intentions. It depended on idealists like Carlo if the future of the blockchain would not be ruled by blind faith in unregulated profit, as advocated by the anarcho-capitalists, or by unbounded digital anonymity, as advocated by the crypto-anarchists, two large tribes in the crypto space.

"With fellows like Carlo," Daniel argued, "one can work well." Regarding which, he added, "Bitcoin was not invented to subvert the established order, as many blockchainers think. It was invented to make sure that the principles informing established order don't go unheeded. Too many bankers, lawyers, notaries, accountants, middlemen of all kinds abuse the law at the expense of the helpless, the uneducated, the destitute, the unbanked. Bitcoin will end this vampirism. This is something Carlo understands well."

Bitcoin and the Ritual of Kyudo Archery

BRAIN WALLET # 23

In the Sixties there was an American singer called Bob Dylan who had formidable charisma. Daniel told me about him one Sunday afternoon, after a Meet Up we both attended downtown at the Institute for the Future.

The Meet Up's organizers had invited a zit-faced kid five years my junior, named Vitalik Buterin, born in Russia like me, about whom there was a great deal of talk in the crypto space. Not long before, with the first initial token sale in the crypto space, Vitalik had created ethereum, an allegedly more flexible blockchain than bitcoin. He was being accused of recycling previous ideas, but that was the same charge leveled at Satoshi every other day.

Carlo too had come to the Meet Up. Only absent were Sophie and Margherita. Sophie and demoiselle Dambreuil were spending the weekend in San Francisco at Nessim's place. As to Margherita, she was still hostile to her husband's *ravings*, as she called his crypto ambitions.

After the Meet Up, as we left the Institute for the Future, both me and Daniel were dazed and astonished. It was around the end of September, so the Indian Summer had filled downtown Palo Alto with young engineers of both genders: Far Easterners, Middle Easterners, Africans, Latin-Americans, and what's not. A few white youths too. We were looking half-heartedly for a free table at a restaurant when Daniel, annoyed by the crowds, sat down on a bench – the same bench in front of the J. P. Morgan's offices that would become the daily stopping place for his future incarnation as Jesus – and started telling me of the trip that his father Gerald took to the Island of Wight in 1969 to attend concert.

At the concert, Gerald saw Bob Dylan and many others perform. Dylan was recovering from a motorcycle crash. But the memorable impression from Dylan came after the concert, the day of Gerald's flight back home, when he found himself sitting side by side with Dylan on the shuttle to the airport. Dylan was traveling with Sarah, his wife. Gerald had smiled to Dylan and Dylan had said, "Howdy." Gerald barely managed to emit a groan. Daniel was very young when his father told him of this episode. Gerald was still struggling to explain the paralyzing effect which the mere proximity of Bob Dylan had on his tongue.

A gangly boy with zits all over his face, Vitalik Buterin arrived at the Institute for the Future carrying a backpack. While an organizer introduced him, Vitalik waited by the side of the auditorium, making weird, spell-like gestures with his hands and body. He looked like the most insecure of teenagers. When at last we had him in front of us, I noticed the pants of his track suit were faded and so short that the rim hovered way above the ankles. I found myself thinking that there weren't too many restaurants downtown that would appreciate the patronage of such a character. But the moment he opened his mouth to speak, I felt the same sinking feeling in the pit of the stomach that I got at the sight of Sophie on that first late afternoon, after Dambreuil and the Japanese girl had dressed her up for a night at the Opera.

Sitting on that bench, Daniel was wondering whether our astonishment on leaving the Meet Up wasn't, after all, precisely what you are supposed to feel when you are in the presence of genius. I was thinking of that sinking feeling in the pit of my stomach, but couldn't find the right words to express it. It was something more, or different, I felt, than being in the presence of genius — not that I've met many geniuses... But when I looked for the words to say it, all that came to mind was a scent of incense and the vague memory of a bearded man, dressed in black from head to foot, shaking a censer in front of a golden crypt.

Darkness and silence.

Where that came from, I've no idea.

BRAIN WALLET # 24

After the next practice at the kyudojo, Carlo monopolized the group discussion with the description of his new blockchain-based project. He had been thinking for a while on the potentials of an algorithm designed to predict the future. He got the idea from an American economist, a Something Robinson, notorious for certain delirious writings about large-scale duplication of elephants' brains. In youth, before going off the deep end, this Robinson was highly regarded for the invention of a mathematical scheme for prediction markets. This scheme was deemed unrealizable, owing to the limited power of available technologies. Inspired by Vitalik Buterin, Carlo was persuaded that the blockchain would afford him the technological leap needed to develop a prediction market based on Robinson's scheme.

"My company will trade a special commodity," Carlo declared, "a priceless commodity: knowledge of the future. I'll call it Futura!"

"Knowledge of the future is the same as finding the philosopher's stone fabled by the alchemists," Daniel remarked.

Carlo nodded enthusiastically, even if I'm sure he knew as much as I did, namely zero, about the philosopher's stone.

"How are you going to fund Futura?" I asked.

In such cases, by then, the obligatory follow-up question was: "Are you thinking of an initial token sale?" Sophie asked it.

Bitcoin and the Ritual of Kyudo Archery

Three years later, Futura's initial token sale would raise twelve million dollars in less than twelve minutes – one million a minute. But the number of would-be contributors was much larger than the number of those who managed to grab the tokens they wished to buy before the sale was over. Although followed by harsh polemics, this result triggered a new phenomenon, the *Fear of Missing Out*, or FOMO. The fear of being locked out of token sales, as experienced by Futura's would-be contributors, made a huge success of most subsequent initial token sales, in 2017 and 2018. A large number of those token sales were plain frauds, and it was just a matter of time before many contributors would be left to foot the bill.

Carlo answered that he had been planning Futura's token sale for a while. That day he showed a solid understanding, better than any of us at the kyudojo could claim at the time, of both the flaws and the promises of this new funding source. He worried about the possible intrusion of the US Internal Revenue Service or some regulatory commission. Maybe he should make his initial token sale from abroad rather than from here in California, he brooded. The tokens sold by Futura would be called FTR, he explained. The token holders would be entitled to use Futura's prediction-market application, based on Robinson's scheme. By trading on prediction markets, monetary gain being their incentive, the token holders would obtain reliable forecasts on a virtually boundless variety of future events.

For the next several weeks, our discussions after kyudo practice became a workshop on the nature of the initial token sale. The only member of the kyudojo who objected to these discussions was Margherita, who couldn't foresee or imagine, at the time, that one day Carlo's intuitions would bring her to a drastic career change.

"Palo Alto is not Turin. My babysitter costs me fifty thousand dollars a year," she burst out one day, laughing bitterly, "because my out-of-work husband can't find the time to look after our child." Margherita had her own special way of speaking English, which grew sharper whenever she was absent-minded or annoyed by something: she would start moving her lips a few seconds before any sound came out of them, and from time to time she'd utter almost inaudible syllables.

Sophie: "You just roll with the punches, Carlo?"

His eyes down, Carlo scratched his blue-hair. "I guess I roll with the punches." Then, looking up with a hangdog expression on his face, "Else, Margherita won't code me the truly hard algorithms."

Just like the field of cryptographic security, this new fundraising concept of the initial token sale was hindered by a complexity of challenges that went far beyond our limited foresight. All sorts of challenges, from legal to fiscal and even monetary, owing to the volatility of the tokens' price. At first, most people in the crypto space, me included, thought these obstacles could be dealt with head-on. We were wrong.

Above it all, Carlo predicted, there hovered the menace of governmental regulations. In hindsight, it's easy to argue that those dreaded regulations were destined not so much to break the golden egg as to grab a piece of it through taxation. But in

Bitcoin and the Ritual of Kyudo Archery

2016 and 2017, eight years after the birth of bitcoin, the whole picture was fuzzy.
Terra Incognita.

BRAIN WALLET # 25

"Why do I waste my time arguing with you, Margherita! You don't know *a fuck* of crypto!"

The truce between Sophie and Margherita couldn't last. It ended the day Carlo gave us a presentation of his egalitarian theory of the initial token sale.

From the outset, Carlo had given me the impression of an excessively romantic soul. In the workshops we devoted to the notion of the token sale at the kyudojo, he went so far as identifying the mining puzzle with an egalitarian principle. Competition didn't fit his temperament – a trait he shared with Sophie, the only one, I reckon. In his view, all interested parties should be given the same opportunity to contribute to the token sale of his company Futura. Even the price of FTR, the tokens sold by Futura, would have to be fixed by the consensus of all concerned. He was planning to model his token sale on a procedure of price-finding called Dutch Auction.

As I recall, it was the first or second week of 2017. After five long years of draught, it was often rainy that January. Each rainfall turned grass and leaves an emerald green we hadn't seen in about four years. Our wet shoes were aligned by the door of the kyudojo.

Carlo introduced his presentation with a question. "Why should it be me who decides the initial price of Futura's tokens?"

Margherita crossed her eyes. "Because they are yours, it's you who are selling them, and if you are lucky, they'll pay for our babysitter," she said.

Bitcoin and the Ritual of Kyudo Archery

I was thinking that if Carlo was ever to be turned into an angel, Margherita would be sure to clip his wings.

Carlo didn't respond, and asked another question instead. "Why should the wealthiest investors prevail over the least affluent ones?"

I kept my eyes down to avoid Margherita's predictable wink.

Carlo's scheme wasn't that bad. That day I learned from him that the Dutch auction is used for the sale of goods whose fair price is hard to define: the auction lowers the price till buyers are found, and that's the fair price. That's why it's called *price-finding*. Carlo's token sale would start from a very high price and lower it by degrees. Contributors would make their offer only when the token price reached a level they considered fair, and the auction would be closed the moment a ceiling of twelve million dollars had been sold. The magic of this Dutch auction was that every contributor would pay the same price for an individual token, and that price would be the lowest one offered by the last contributor before closure. All earlier contributors, who had made their investment at a higher price, would invest the pledged sum but get more tokens than originally expected.

Sophie livened up. "Carlo," she asked, "did you ever study financial math? Has anybody here ever traded on financial derivatives?"

Carlo shook his head, and me and Daniel followed suit. Margherita shrugged her shoulders.

"Just as I thought," Sophie said.

In front of us was the wife of the international banker now. None of us knew much of finance. Since I started handling the mining plants' payroll in Iceland, I had become a decent trader on crypto exchanges, but that could be hardly passed off as financial expertise. Even before her marriage to Nessim, Sophie had grown up with the *Wall Street Journal* on her family's breakfast table, open to the pages of stock quotes. I was surprised though that she had become animated about a money-related subject that she would normally brush off.

"It so happens that I know a thing or two about Dutch auctions," she said. "They were a favorite expedient of a fellow named Muammar Ghaddafi, may hell swallow him. At first blush, they appear to be an innocent financial operation. Truth is, they facilitate collusions that would be impossible out in the open," she said. "If you mean to obstruct egalitarian competition among the contributors to your initial token sale, Carlo, go ahead and do a Dutch auction."

"Well," Carlo objected, "in my case…"

"In your case…" Sophie interrupted him. "Collusion is the enemy of decentralization, Carlo. Do we agree on that?"

"Sure, that's why Satoshi hedged bitcoin from a majority collusion among miners."

"Well," Sophie continues, "give me a sheet of paper and I'll sketch you the algorithm that a collusion of large contributors will use to grab as much as they like from your auction. So much for, what did you call them, the least affluent contributors. I could do it blindfolded."

Then she added something that blew my mind. "Just like you and Margherita, you are husband and wife, right? A collusion between you two makes a total of four arrows, and four arrows are enough to wipe out this kyudojo."

Bitcoin and the Ritual of Kyudo Archery

How could I miss it! It had been before our eyes all this time! The flaw in our crypto-Zen kyudojo was that it left the door open to collusion among archers. One archer with two arrows could never wipe out a kyudojo with five members kneeling in a circle, but two colluding archers could. How could Daniel miss it!

I was going to throw an alarmed look at Daniel when something unexpected happened, something that had never occurred before in the kyudojo and would never occur again: Margherita spoke up for Carlo. No sooner did she utter a few words than I knew she had no valid arguments against Sophie's. But she wasn't pregnant anymore. While her and Sophie's voice grew to a feverish pitch, I was telling myself that Sophie's lady-like enquiries about the progress of Margherita's pregnancy must've taken their toll on the latter's credulity. The usual apple-red spots on Margherita's cheeks had turned ashen, signaling the end of truce.

It was an awful session. Margherita's voice, worked up by vexation, interposed deafening high notes with feeble, almost inaudible syllables. Sophie hissed, with the fierce coolness of a gangster, about financial doctrines which she must've been as well acquainted with as indifferent to – only to round them off with her poison pill: "Why do I waste my time arguing with you, Margherita! You don't know *a fuck* of crypto!"

Daniel had kept quiet throughout the quarrel and now dismissed all of us unceremoniously. He was well aware that me and Sophie would spend the rest of the afternoon at my place, so he limited himself to addressing me a knowing nod, the message that we two needed to talk. After Sophie's angry outburst, I wouldn't have minded the opportunity to spare myself her rage for the next few hours. Besides, her brutal unveiling of the breaking point in our crypto-Zen kyudojo called for advice.

So, my Sophie's brain had an extra gear even over Daniel's?

Later that afternoon I buzzed at Daniel's door. He welcomed me wearing one of his Japanese kimonos and wooden sandals. His apartment had been renovated in the style of a Mexican architect he admired. The walls were painted primary colors, red, blue, and yellow, and the angular sunrays from the large windows crossed diagonally the walls' vertical edges. The sparse furniture was Scandinavian minimalist, as he put it.

Every time I set foot in his apartment, I got the same protective, cloistered feeling.

"Sophie is right on both counts," he told me right away, implying that was the reason why he wanted to see me. "As to the obvious truth that a collusion between two archers is enough to undo our kyudojo, what can I say? I erred, Anton. Big time. Sophie applied Satoshi's consensus principles to my crypto-Zen turn and found it lacking." He gave me a dismal smile.

"What can we do?" I asked point-blank. This emergency didn't lend itself to the cozy vibes of our telepathy.

"Nothing for now. Something for sure later on." He cut it short. "But as to the second count…"

"Carlo's initial token sale."

"Right. I think that initial token sales of the sort Carlo has in mind will bring about the ascendancy of an oligarchy of coders in the crypto space. That was Sophie's first point. We need to see it first-hand."

Bitcoin and the Ritual of Kyudo Archery

He opened a red Moleskine where he had jotted down a longish algorithm. He explained its principles to me, and I was soon able to decode it by myself. As I perused it line by line, he set by my side a steaming cup of his famous Kenyan tea. Daniel's algorithm modeled the predominance of collusive groups of investors in an auction of the sort favored by Carlo.

"The premises for the collusion are all in place," he concluded when I lifted my head from his red Moleskine. And he suggested we invest into Carlo's token sale together.

Our contribution to the token sale gave exactly the expected result. I'll come back to it. After skyrocketing for several months, however, the value of Futura's tokens fell like a ton of bricks. In hindsight (I'm writing these words on January 23, 2018, the day of my thirtieth birthday, in full Crypto Winter), I can say we ought to have sold our tokens around the end of 2017, making a huge profit. Yet, at the time of the aggression against Daniel, a couple months later, the fate of initial token sales of the sort of Futura's was yet undecided. Besides, it's not that we contributed to Carlo's token sale as a form of speculation. We just wanted to test the algorithm which had been inspired to Daniel, that afternoon, by Sophie's lethal objection to Carlo's ideas.

CHAPTER TEN

Dambreuil bursts into Anton's apartment and rushes on to hug him. She gives him a sonorous kiss on each cheek.

"They are gone! They are gone!" she exclaims, her broad white teeth radiant with joy.

Anton feigns ignorance. "Who's gone? Where to?"

"But the two Characters! Of a sudden, *boom*, they are gone!"

It seems that Dambreuil bumped into Ursula in the vestibule while the young woman was about to leave the house. Michel was waiting for her outside with their Citroen. Questioned by Dambreuil, Ursula had mumbled something about an old Belgian grandmother on her deathbed, and snuck out instantly.

"I had a hunch, really a hunch, monsieur Anton, that monsieur would fix everything in no time!" Dambreuil is breathless, Anton doesn't recall ever seeing anyone talk and inhale at once like she does.

"But I didn't do a thing," he objects. *Am I pushing it too far?*

Even more out of breath than a minute ago, she plants two more sonorous kisses on his cheeks, turns around and is out the door.

Now comes the tough part.

He just walked into Sophie's bedroom carrying the usual tray when she says in a carefree voice, stepping out of the shower: "Alone at last, Anton!" Who told her that the Dimwits left? Her own inference from the gravel that nobody has thrown against her shutters yet?

Anton puts the tray down on the table. He grabs the sealed whisky bottle and goes throw it into the garbage can in the kitchen.

"How funny! Ursula thinks she is a born-again Amy Winehouse." She bursts out laughing. "One night she wanted at all costs to sing with a gypsy who played the accordion in a joint. I wish you could hear her, couldn't carry a tune if you gave her a bucket!"

"They were in the garden a while ago and left in a hurry," Anton says.

Her answer knocks him out. "They work for Nessim. Nessim surrounds himself with spies and informers." She reads the objection in his eyes. "Who cares, they keep me company. Masao too is in Nessim's pocket."

He is about to tell her that the Dimwits won't come back to keep her company, but he doesn't. "Michel is a hacker," he says instead.

"One must make a living," she replies with a snarky laugh.

"So, he doesn't go to school at Oxford, you think?" he asks.

"What the *fuck* do I know?"

Her profanity tells him the matter is closed.

"Starting today," she goes on, "I want to do regular sessions in our kyudojo, just like the old days with Daniel."

He nods.

"Every day, one hour a day at least! Agreed?"

"Agreed," he says. "That's why I'm here."

"Today we start a new life in the kyudojo! Enough, I'm done with those idiotic funerals behind that idiotic white hearse! And I will start working again on TEXOR! Are you going to help me with TEXOR?"

"That's why I'm here," he repeats.

She drops her bathrobe on the floor to get dressed.

Only now does he become aware that the loudspeakers play music that sounds Arabic: a woman's resounding voice.

Sophie notices that he noticed. "Umm Kulthum," she says.

It's the first time Anton hears Sophie speak Arabic. He mimics her talk, "Umm Kulthum?"

"It means 'Mother of Kulthum.' It's the name of this Egyptian singer, she was a good friend of my grandmother in Alexandria."

He thinks he hears similarities between the musical grandness of this Arabic music and some of Brel's songs. But what does he know? He is a stranger thrown into a strange world.

Sophie has put on her lingerie and hums to herself from the walk-in closet: *Inta omri illi ibtada bnurak sabahu…*

It occurs to him that she can understand both the words sung by this Umm Kulthum and those sung by Jacques Brel. *What's in the head of a woman like Sophie that's not in mine?* When she listens to Brel singing *ne me quitte pas, ne me quitte pas, ne me quitte pas*, what does she hear that he doesn't? Those days when Daniel drove him southbound on his red Ferrari toward Big Sur, did they see the same things, did they feel his same emotions at the sight of the icy color of the ocean? What's in someone's head that's not in someone else's? In Anton's head there are mathematical functions and elliptic curves, the *Open Sesame* of his bitcoin portfolio, his several crypto identities, the characters from Belmondo's books, the weirdest hypotheses on the backgrounds to his own birth… Let's see: his love of Sophie… If he thinks hard enough, he gets a glimpse of the girl

Bitcoin and the Ritual of Kyudo Archery

from Pittsburgh whom he didn't phone to after that last binge together, and even a glimpse of his interpreter in Reykjavik, a young woman who's too attractive for her own good – she must think her customer Anton is gay... The list never ends: archery, molecular cooking, the reason that brought him to Paris. Strike that, the *two* reasons that brought him to Paris: Daniel's revenge and Sophie's love. In whichever order.

Thirty years on this planet have piled up all sorts of things into his head, but it's a pell-mell matrix, self-made, with little or no formal structure behind. And not much parenting behind it either, from when he was little. No wonder he never finds much to talk or sing about.

Yet, thrust a nail into your skull or a high alcohol content into your blood, and that unique matrix that turns this world into your world, breaks up in a jiffy.

Sophie devotes longer than usual to the choice of her outfit. She keeps humming in Arabic to herself: *Ibtadait bilwakti bas ahib omri, ibtadait bilwakti akhaf la ilomri yiri*. Her animation gives Anton an optimism he hasn't had in a while, but it feels over-the-top, groundless: it reminds him of his father's occasional, contagious optimism, and what came in the aftermath.

He eats a tramezzino sandwich.

Sophie walks out of the walk-in closet wearing her expansive vagrant look, totally disheveled. She pretends not to notice that, his mouth full, Anton gestures at her to join him in front of the tray. She swings the French window wide open like someone eager for the blaze of the sunrays, but facing her she finds Masao and his shaker, haloed by the buzzing glare of the patio heaters. Anton drops his half-eaten sandwich, reaches her on the threshold, and, with one abrupt gesture, ships Masao back to his kitchens.

Sophie stands still for at least ten seconds, staring at him with a sneer on her face, her garrulousness all but gone. A few drops of sweat bead her forehead. She takes hold of his hand: it's as though she wanted to keep him here by her side, or let him know he shouldn't mind, it's only her body's fierceness that's raging against him. Or reassure him that as long as she keeps his hand in both of hers, she won't claw at his eyes.

How could I do different, my love? He is even ready to find beautiful the dark shades spreading under her eyes, like two half-moons rising out of a mud puddle. He feels the contrast Umm Kulthum's voice makes with the two of them. He has a clue that Umm Kulthum sings of a simpler passion fueled up by its own heat. He wishes he knew of a short cut out of the night facing Sophie, but there isn't one.

If all you've done wrong to me and Mom taught me how to handle this, Dad, it was worth it.

He gives up on his unfinished meal and drags Sophie out in the street for a walk. Dambreuil and Bashir have the presence of mind to leave them alone.

It's the time of night when there is no traffic and the traffic lights switch their colors for nobody and nothing. Just them two. They walk holding hands on a long tree-lined lawn by the river. A scent of wet soil comes to Anton's nostrils. They turn around, come all the way back, and cross place de l'Alma. The Seine on their left looks like a smooth slab of black marble. Sophie doesn't speak. Anton wishes he could make her speak, but of what? Some rare birds chirp when they are almost by the Eiffel Tower, on the other side of the river, while a pale blade of light, low on the buildings behind them, gives him a deceptive expectation of sunrise. They step into a café but Sophie won't have any food, just a glass of tap water. He drinks an espresso.

They go back home, but it's unrealistic to bring her back to bed already. She just got up. Her face is totally upset now, her fingers are shaking, and the half-moons under her eyes have grown darker. He drags her to the Bentley, and no sooner does he manage to lift the top than they are out of the garage. The GPS retraces his first Parisian itinerary: avenue du president Kennedy, avenue de Versailles, boulevard Exelmans, porte d'Auteuil, boulevard Suchet. He cruises confidently through the roundabouts on the square of porte Maillot and park the Bentley on the spot in Bois de Boulogne where he parked it the other day, astride some railroad tracks. He hadn't noticed these tracks that first time, and now he sees again, briefly, in a different light, the inquisitive gaze that the officer driving the police car gave him. He leans over Sophie, reclining her seat and lifting her skirt, and she whispers her docile reply to the silent question he just asked himself: "We are parked across the miniature railway, baby."

Then they are both silent.

They get back home after dawn, not a cloud in the sky, and he persuades her to undress and get into bed. No use trying to make her eat something. While they were gone, the food tray was taken away from the bedroom. Anton too hasn't eaten a real meal or drunk any water for he doesn't know how long, but there's no time. Sophie needs him, she needs him *now*. He undresses, pulls all the curtains, and lies down by her side. He doesn't feel sleepy even if he ought to sleep some. He lost count how many times he rose late in the afternoon and went to bed after dawn since he is in Paris.

Sophie clings to him silently and he holds her in his arms. He feels the pounding of her heart against the palms of his hands. They stand like this a while as he braces himself for the long vigil he has in front of him. Her heart keeps pounding like mad. He is overwhelmed by tenderness, as though he was holding that small heart of hers in his hands: it's pounding, if not *for* him, because of the ordeal she submits at his behest. Their breaths are made burning hot by the closeness of their lips. "Anton," she says with a wisp of voice as though she was trying to kiss him, "Anton… baby…" Then she turns around and with feverish motions pushes her back against his belly. He holds her in his arms again. The pressure from her buttocks drags him into a mortifying state of arousal. His eyes hurt like when he sits too long in front of his Mac. The breast he holds in his hand is in a cold sweat.

He flinches when he opens his eyes after blacking out for what feels like the shortest nap. He is parched, his tongue as dry as a bone. His brain feels as though it was scrambled. Not a shred of light creeps by the sides of the curtains. Which is impossible: how long did he sleep? The bedsheet is soaked with sweat and Sophie's buttocks are still pressed against his belly. Her neck shakes intermittently as though she couldn't keep her teeth from chattering. But he is not totally sure of what's going on around him because his eyes pound when he tries to open them up. Is he smelling puke? Did he just hear someone call his name: Anton… baby…? *Just wait till I get my bearings.* He instructs himself to scour the room as though blindfolded. This is his old room after all, he has known it inside out for so long.

Bitcoin and the Ritual of Kyudo Archery

A short inspection is enough to reassure him – it's only logical after all – that a bright daylight is creeping by the sides of the curtains. In a bit he'll open up his eyes and see its shine for himself. He is stricken by the slightest anomaly the instant he feels that his body is still totally naked. Why would that be? But there's no time to lose, he just saw Margherita aiming her arrow at Sophie. All he has to do is keep hiding in this shadow till the right moment, and nobody will notice his arousal. Sophie plays smart by sneaking behind the target of the kyudojo, but she doesn't suspect Margherita only pretends not to notice her move. Now he is aware he is actually dozing under a bedsheet, so Margherita could not notice his arousal even if she looked this way. *Look if you must, Margherita, but watch out.* He is of a mind to replace Sophie behind the target with a rag doll that looks just like her. All chips are down. Margherita shoots her arrow while the target revolves about itself. But on the other side his rag doll is gone already, there is a woody marionette with its chest to the target instead, and the arrow hits it on the scruff of the neck.

BRAIN WALLET # 26
I print and paste an email from Paris: January 23, 2019.

Dear Anton,

Happy Birthday from your Sophie. Thirty years old! You are becoming an adult and I'm almost an old lady. I can't wait to have you here by my side.

I started writing this email telling myself that if I hurried, you'd be reading it this morning on your way to the kyudojo. But then I thought that perhaps the kyudojo is no more, just like our Daniel is no more. So, I tell myself that perhaps you are reading it while sitting on that bench, side by side with Jesus. Even if I refuse to think that our kyudojo is no more. Or perhaps you are reading me while flying to Iceland, as you are wont to do in this season so awful to travel. My husband Nessim collects information with the automatism of a robot. If I asked him, I'm sure he would tell me where you are right his moment and what you are doing. Don't fear, I ask him nothing!

Nessim knows everything. It's from him I heard of that nickname they gave Daniel: Jesus. How can people be so cruel? And he told me of that bench facing J. P. Morgan too, where Jesus sits all day long.

There were two kyudojos in our life together, Anton. One was the pavilion near Whole Foods, Ideo, and Palantir, where Daniel taught us kyudo archery and so much more. The other kyudojo was in the mood of concentration we reached before going to your pink-walled palace to have sex. The first kyudojo, I made it anew, from scratch, its spitting image, here in this house in Paris. But the first without the second, what's the point of it, I ask you.

I tell myself that you must have found a way to preserve the kyudojo in Palo Alto. Tell me that my Anton never stopped practicing kyudo

Bitcoin and the Ritual of Kyudo Archery

archery! Daniel must have some heirs, does he? They wouldn't tell no to you. Nobody ever could tell you no. When I met you, I wondered whether your introversion was a pose, a trick. It was sincere, your innocence was sincere, but it took me a while to get it.

How was it possible for you not to feel any jealousy? I deserted you for weeks and you wouldn't ask a single question. Did you care about me only when I was there in your bed? That doubt gnawed at me, so it was me who became jealous of you. Jealous of Daniel, of your tender telepathic duo, but also of Daniel in the sense that when you joined the kyudojo, you stole him (my advisor, my mentor, my kyudo instructor, I loved him so much!) from me. Later, that viper of Margherita showed up and you both were unrecognizable. I'm jealous like a tiger but can hide it well. I bet you never even suspected it, huh? Since I was a child, jealousy bites me here in between the highbrows and gives me a sick feeling. I hide it well and don't think that Nessim either, who always knows everything and in fact he made me fall in love with him twice, ever figured it out. So many days of practice in the kyudojo were ruined by the bite between the highbrows I felt whenever Daniel answered questions you had not even asked and I felt cut off from your tender telepathic duo. I didn't even know exactly if I was jealous of you or of him. Or both. Now Nessim accuses me of jealousy because I refuse to collaborate with him and his sex slave, poor dear.

Demoiselle Dambreuil told me you bring with you a whole collection of bows, so you already answered my question. Our new kyudojo is waiting for you.

Where was I? Later, Margherita shows up and you and Daniel bowed down to that viper and snubbed me and treated me like a hysteric. How could I not be jealous of the way she kept you both wrapped around her pinky. Of course I lost control! But I was also furious because you were both blinded by something that was so clear to me. Did you eventually figure it out, who that woman is?

Beau de Rubempré

It took me a long time but in the end I figured out how much you suffered from jealousy because of me. I figured it out in a dream. Weird, huh? I dream of you often, of the kid you were when we first met. The trick with dreams is that as a girl, you tell any guy you dreamt of him and he falls for you. I learned it since my early teens. A teenager's wet dream, who can resist it? I used that trick left and right, so much that when I dreamt of some guy for real, I felt ashamed and didn't tell him. Well, there is nothing to hide in the dreams of a thirty-five-year-old woman. A scrap of a woman, an 'old biddy,' as Nessim calls me, ill-suited to cohabit with the see-through veils and gold anklets of my substitute, his Yemenite sex slave.

I'm digressing but perhaps that's the point if this never-ending email, huh?

I'm feeling a little tipsy.

In my dream you and I were lying on beach chairs by my family's pool in Alexandria, but I was you, I was Anton, and there was nobody from my family around. I looked at the blue of the pool's water, the green of the palms' leaves, a servant in high uniform wearing a red fez walking toward me, carrying a silver tray with a tiny espresso cup on it. I couldn't hear any of the city noises at the foot of the hill, no cars, no traffic. I was in the world of your silence. Do you know that silence is the highest expression of cryptic mysticism? I was going to write about it in my dissertation, the first of the two subjects I dropped. The most cryptic secret is the untold one. Contrary to you, though, the ancient theologians of silence were awfully chatty, the opposite of cryptic. So, I was this Russian kid with teary eyes while you, you were me, you were Sophie the-spoilt-brat, working on her tan, her eyes closed, indifferent to Anton's solitude. Wasn't that the way I hurt you? It took me that dream to get it.

But perhaps I'm talking nonsense and now you think I'm going crazy.

Our initial token sale went the way Daniel had predicted but this everybody in crypto knows already. TEXOR sold a huge number of

Bitcoin and the Ritual of Kyudo Archery

tokens, we cashed almost thirty times as much as Margherita's company did, you know this as well. When our tokens will go to market, they'll be worth close to nothing. There are too many of them! At first I wondered why Nessim didn't foresee it. Then I told myself that he did foresee it to a T. He grabbed as much money as he could, using me as an accomplice. Our TEXOR company ended up being the fraud predicted by Daniel, there are plenty of people who think of it like that. I accepted Nessim's condition of an uncapped token sale that would go on for an unlimited time, because in return he accepted my condition, my dream: I wanted to create a blockchain where human beings will execute algorithms instead of machines, at close-to-zero energy costs. Besides, Nessim was willing to put me in charge of everything, included his army of coders. Well, he kept his promise. I head DRS, the company tasked with writing the code, but the ultimate irony is that DRS is incorporated in Delaware, USA, while the TEXOR Foundation's registered offices are in Switzerland. And Nessim nominated himself president of the TEXOR Foundation, of course. So, his proxy in Switzerland controls the capitals and I can't even pay the coders' salary without approval from the Foundation. The hardest part to swallow in all of this, Anton, is that the software I had in mind, which enables humans to execute algorithms, is much more complex than Satoshi's bitcoin script and it takes forever to write. If I think that I gave up an academic career for this!

After we conceived the TEXOR project, Nessim and I came to Paris on a second honeymoon. Will you ever forgive me, baby? Once in Paris, we decided to organize the initial token sale from here and set up home. Paris is the most romantic city in the world, you'll see for yourself. I was totally in love with Nessim. A lame excuse for my behavior, I know. I was totally under his spell, the spell of those frosted-glass eyes of his (just like the first time, unexplainable as it is). I told myself I was the first Hosnani woman who turned her back on the role of reproductive vessel. Silly me, I even believed it! My illusion lasted a few months, long enough to discover that meanwhile Nessim was buying himself a progeny with that substitute mother he imported from Yemen. And now he accuses me of boycotting him ("If you are not part of the solution, you are part of my problems," he says) because I refuse to live under the same roof with his sex slave. The niqab she wears on her face is so thin she looks naked. So last Spring I kicked him out of here.

Can I keep my TEXOR *dream alive all by myself? I think so, but only every other day.*

In a few weeks I'll have you here by my side again. That's what matters!

XOXO
Sophie

BRAIN WALLET # 27

The news from Sophie's email makes my self-assigned mission harder. I had no idea she and Nessim were living apart in Paris too. I had counted on breaking into Nessim's Mac and iPhone while living under the same roof and using his same WiFi. I can't get it out of my head that Nessim is behind Daniel's aggression: Daniel's Moleskine speaks plainly.

There is no limit to what you can achieve when you penetrate your target's WiFi traffic while he types in his passwords. Not to mention the quick-and-dirty slights of hand like peeking at the target's screen from above his shoulders or rummaging through his wastepaper basket. Or picking his pockets, even. For lack of a better name, hackers call all of that social engineering. You must've heard of it. Who hasn't ever been a victim to social engineering, raise your hand.

If it was up to me, I'd call it stalking, pure and simple. I can't stalk Nessim if he is not there.

But I'm lying through my teeth. It's not true that I'm disappointed with the news. The warmth and eagerness transpiring from Sophie's words filled me with a sort of euphoria I won't try to name, not to jinx it. I'm not totally sure I'm going to France just to investigate the aggression against Daniel.

BRAIN WALLET # 28

Sophie: *The software I had in mind, which enables humans to execute algorithms, is much more complex than Satoshi's bitcoin script and it takes forever to write.*

One of the biggest controversies around the crypto-economy concerns the waste of energy of proof-of-work: the amount of electric power used up by hundreds of powerful competing machines in the solution of the mining puzzle is humongous – that's why my mining plants are in Iceland, where energy is cheap. Vitalik Buterin was among the many endorsers of the less energy-intensive alternative called proof-of-stake. In proof-of-stake, the blocks of the blockchain are created and attached to the blockchain by human validators, who are compensated for the time they put into the process and the work of their smaller machines. To earn the rights and compensations of the validator, you must stake a substantial amount of your own money, which you lose by expropriation whenever you validate unkosher states of affair. Your stake's expropriation signals that your decisions differ from the majority consensus reached by the other validators.

I don't forget, how could I, the day at the kyudojo when Sophie came forward with her proof-of-stake project: it's the last time I saw her. The whole vibe in the crypto space was weird those first few months of 2017. You felt the foretaste of an imminent breakthrough: something was close to reaching boiling point, something huge. In my opinion, it's Futura's initial token sale, in April 2017, that gave a face to our expectations.

Bitcoin and the Ritual of Kyudo Archery

By April 2017, Carlo had discontinued his attendance of the kyudojo. He managed his initial token sale entirely from San Francisco, where he moved together with a bunch of coders from Turin he had relocated to California for that purpose. (At first, Carlo wanted to incorporate Futura in Gibraltar, but eventually he chose Delaware for expediency.) Meanwhile, Margherita kept working at her job at SLAC and living in Palo Alto with their child, Andrea.

But Carlo was still with us the day Sophie announced that she and Nessim were planning to create a new blockchain: it was to be called TEXOR, and fueled by tokens to be identified with the acronym TXR. The novelty of her approach was that their tokens would be mined by proof-of-stake. Sophie seemed uneasy with herself as she spoke to us. A fitful wind, unseasonably warm and blowing in strong gusts, shook noisily the walls of the pavilion that day, which didn't help her delivery. Carlo and Margherita were kind of half-listening.

Sophie's self-impose benchmark was a consensus reached by human validators yet as rigorous as machine-made consensus. To attain that goal, the low-energy proof-of-stake advocated by Vitalik would have to be complemented with self-governance algorithms.

Daniel's eyes met mine and he made a remark which he had shared with me more than once. "Satoshi Nakamoto's innovation is that the machine makes human mediation obsolete. One day there will be machines able to turn themselves into network nodes without human intervention or decision. That way we'll have obtained an incorruptible system of collective consensus."

He broke her heart: that's the first thought that came to my mind when Sophie's face dropped.

"But we can coordinate humans to reach that same kind of consensus…?" The tone of her reply, midway between surrendering and beseeching, crushed my own heart as well.

And what about us two, Sophie?

In the last few seconds, I had realized that this TEXOR project would bring her collaboration with me and Daniel to an end. No more staying in the swing of things with us.

And what about us two, Sophie? I was desperately trying not to face the music.

This TEXOR project had already brought her dispute with Nessim to an end, or so it sounded like. No, my own heart wouldn't be doing too well either by the end of that windy day. For the first time in eight years, suddenly, I pictured Nessim, her husband, like a rival.

"I don't think you can coordinate humans to reach the same kind of machine-driven consensus," Daniel was saying. "You will put together a kind of theocracy charged with block creation. A priestly cast with executive power, supervised by another priestly cast with normative power. Just think of what happened to the Catholic church."

"What happened to the Catholic church… ?"

"I mean, just think of any theocracy. Nessim's part of the world isn't lacking in that department, right? Does it ever work?"

"What?"

"Theocracy."

"But this is different, Daniel! This is a business proposition. The validators of my blockchain must stake real security… ?"

Bitcoin and the Ritual of Kyudo Archery

Same crushing tone, midway between surrendering and beseeching.

Daniel was strangely uncompromising. "Before abusing children and nuns, Catholic priests stake their eternal life. How do you beat that?" And here he rubbed it in her face. "Sophie, all I'm saying I learned from you: collusion, collusion, collusion. Remember the day you pointed out that a collusion between two archers could wipe out our crypto-Zen kyudojo. You were right. We simply can't program humans not to cheat the way Satoshi programmed machines. A 100% safe kyudojo won't ever exist, nor a 100% human-powered blockchain."

Sophie hadn't yet recovered from that blow when Margherita took the occasion to speak her mind. "This is pure ignorance, coming from you, Sophie. In Italy we still have some respect for history, you know. Ever heard of ancient history?" She crossed her eyes. "Satoshi puts an end to centuries of iniquities and deception, brings us to the egalitarianism of Carlo's forthcoming initial token sale, and what do you do? You bring the conversation back to prehistory!"

Why was she talking like that? Out of spite? I went back to asking myself this question several times, especially after Margherita started managing Futura's personnel. After all, Carlo too adheres to Vitalik's project to substitute machines' computational work with human time. As I write, Futura's blockchain is still struggling to transition to a human-powered regime. Proof-of-stake, Vitalik's pet project, has become a utopia shared by a majority in the crypto space.

So, why all the fuss, Margherita?

An embarrassed silence followed Margherita's outburst. Sophie's face had turned a bright red, I couldn't tell if out of anger or shame. Should I have spoken, should I have said something? But what? And how, since I agreed with Daniel's views? In a situation like that, one word weighs like a boulder.

Silence may weigh like a boulder too. On your conscience.

Sophie stared at Daniel, her eyes two burning coals. Had the white of her eyes turned red too, or was it a reflection of her cheekbones? The balance of my kiza posture was collapsing: the fire in her eyes wiped out an invisible halo around the idol she had worshipped till a moment ago. The death blow had come to her from a woman who should never have been a member of *our* kyudojo! When she jumped up abruptly to her feet, picked up her bow and arrows, and left the pavilion without a word, the wind gust that blew through the door threw me off-balance. I had to support my weight with the left arm not to fall sideways. With the same arm I pushed myself up to my feet, but before running after her, turned my gaze at Daniel. The way he shook his head, calmly as he stared back at me, a resigned expression on his face, dissuaded me from the pursuit.

That was a Sophie I had never known yet.

BRAIN WALLET # 29

That month of April 2017, Futura's initial token sale raised twelve million dollars in an auction that lasted less than twelve minutes. Carlo and his backers sold 90% of available tokens. They promised that the remaining 10% in their hands would be frozen in a digital vault for the next several years. A few weeks later, Margherita gave up her job at SLAC, she and Carlo took leave from the two remaining members of the kyudojo with a small party in Daniel's apartment, and flew back to Turin. Soon, Margherita would take charge of Futura's personnel.

I took it upon myself to test Daniel's algorithm. In agreement with Sophie's ideas about Dutch auctions, Daniel wanted to prove that Carlo's token sale had led to token concentration in a few hands – the opposite, that is, of the egalitarian result aimed at by our Italian friend. It didn't take me much effort to crunch the data.

All the contributors who took the concept of Dutch auction at face value, waiting for the tokens to reach a fair price before making their bid, were left in the cold. Almost the entire supply of Futura's tokens was grabbed by a so-called *Whale*, probably a super-wealthy coalition of crypto investors.

All by itself, the Whale owned now more than 50% of the tokens' total supply. If this had been an IPO, a public offering of ordinary voting shares, now the Whale would be Futura's undisputed majority owner. The rest of the tokens had gone to no more than a dozen contributors, all coalitions of investors as well, clearly. With 6% of the total supply stored in our two wallets – 3% each – me and Daniel were the seventh of those coalitions in order of magnitude.

In sum, Daniel's prediction turned out correct, even if neither of us had foreseen the greed of the investors he called *crypto oligarchs*: expert cryptographers who leveraged technological lead to push out competition and amass equity.

We very much thought that the investors who had prevailed over the rest were Carlo's initial backers.

A few weeks later, it turned out that the time stamps of the Whale's purchases were a few minutes ahead of everybody else, signaling a suspicious technological lead. Rumors of a fishy collusion started making the rounds of the crypto space. The Whale was none other than Carlo's sponsors, and they had pumped the token price by buying from themselves. Futura's promise to freeze 10% of the tokens was a diversion good for suckers.

There was a major flaw in this accusation, to me, and it was that I couldn't picture Carlo being involved in such a scam.

Before leaving for my usual trip to Reykjavìk, I sent a circular email to Carlo, Margherita, and Sophie, highlighting my results . In the couple weeks I spent in Iceland, I didn't hear from the Italian couple. It was understandable. Nobody likes it when, data on hand, they show you were wrong. Not even later on did Carlo and Margherita write back to me, which is stranger, given what happened to Daniel in the meanwhile. But I'll hand it to Carlo and Margherita that they are on a mission to pave the way for the blockchain revolution, and besides, they have a little child, Andrea, to care for. Like everybody else in the crypto space this Crypto Winter, they are probably staring into the huge gap between the dream and its fulfillment. The rumors of collusion have been muffled, but not invalidated, by the repeated occurrence of the same scenario in countless initial token sales throughout the rest of 2017. And anyway, as I said, I never gave credit to Carlo's alleged complicity with the Whale.

Sophie replied promptly and warmly to my email. She missed me and she missed our kyudojo. The TEXOR crypto company she was setting up with Nessim promised to fulfill her dream of a less energy intensive blockchain, wholly decentralized via protocol-embedded governance. She asked me to please apologize to Daniel on her behalf for her violation of the kyudojo's rules, that last time she was there. She wanted to know if Daniel would be willing to correspond with her: she needed to consult him on the exact dimensions of a kyudojo, and the best materials for setting one up in Paris. As to the results of Futura's initial token sale, which had been the subject of my email to her, she dismissed them with a plain, "Didn't I tell you from the start?"

Which she had.

What she hadn't told me then, and wasn't telling me even now, was if it was really over between us two.

It's from this email, which I opened in Reykjavik not long before the lethal attack against Daniel, that I came to know at long last where Sophie had ended up. Up to then, my Google searches had given no results. For the duration of her company's initial token sale, the location of the founders had not been disclosed. I had no idea she had moved to Paris with Nessim.

BRAIN WALLET # 30

Today is the last time I write on this black notebook. Page after page, you have deciphered my scrawls and scribbles. Thanks for that. My solitude ends today, with this page, and so does our association. I don't need to tell you how precious your company has been to me through all this. Tomorrow I'm off to Paris.

CHAPTER ELEVEN

Anton and Sophie go through the next several days like recovering patients at a spa, and practice in the kyudojo is their constant focal point. In her fight against relapse, Sophie confirms the unstinting sturdiness she gave proof of for the last ten years or so in Palo Alto. They work together at the algorithms demanded by her TEXOR coders. Gradually, their lives set up back on the solar cycle rather than the moon's. Masao is fired. On Anton's request, Dambreuil adds a list of organic foods to the groceries that are delivered daily at the door. In an excess of zeal, Jacques Brel's songs are blacklisted. They listen to Arabic music a lot, especially Umm Kulthum.

Anton regrets he is not much help to Sophie with her algorithms. At the end of the day, he is a college dropout, a *gun for hire*: good at some things, better at them than most hackers in fact, but he has got no chops to deal with the complex network architectures Sophie handles. A self-governing blockchain where humans take to themselves the roles that bitcoin assigns to machines, that's no small feat. For sure, nobody's been totally successful at doing such a thing so far. So, Sophie submits a batch of new algorithms to her coders, they find the breaking point in no time, and she must start all over again from scratch. Anton help as he can with logical transitions, Boolean loops, brutal coding, such sort of basic stuff. All of Sophie's exchanges with her coders have been long distance so far, connecting place de l'Alma with rue Blanche by teleconference.

The other day, he barely managed to keep his appointment on rue Blanche 38 with the Airbnb guy who gave him the keys to the third-floor apartment. Then he left his new video camera and tripod, still boxed up, on the premises. His investigation lags behind, but there isn't much he can do about it right now. Sophie is top priority.

The container of his Michelin map was delivered from the airport after Bashir dealt with some unforeseen custom formalities. He took it upon himself to pry it open, and then helped Anton fix the map to a wall in his study. Once they were done, Bashir lingered in front of the map and then said with a faint note of sarcasm in his voice, "Monsieur joined the Yellow Vests?" Anton shrugged: it's like they have been trading jokes for a lifetime. These days, it makes sense that to a Parisian this map looks like a coordinated plan of roadblocks. But back when Anton started sticking flag pushpins into it, the Yellow Vest movement didn't exist in France yet. Daniel joked often that their maps of Paris and Dublin could be taken for the coordinated locations of some secret society. Or a terrorists' plan to take over the city.

Masao's departure is having zero impact on their small community. It turns out that Masao cooked only for madame. Dambreuil and Bashir cook their meals in their own separate kitchens on the second floor. In an attempt to further normalize life in the homestead, Anton asked Dambreuil why couldn't the four of them cook and dine together, but she gave it the thumbs down.

"Moi, j'sais pas, monsieur… it would lessen madame Sophie in Bashir's eyes," was her surprising objection, "and therefore he would feel lessened in hers."

Bitcoin and the Ritual of Kyudo Archery

Something tells Anton that if he asked Bashir's opinion, he'd give him the same answer, but replacing Dambreuil's name with his own.

Later that night, as he was preparing some of his molecular foods for Sophie, he asked her who did she share her meals with, after Nessim moved out.

"Nobody," she said. "Not that with Nessim either…"

She didn't finish the sentence.

"But I thought you had your meals with demoiselle Dambreuil at home in Palo Alto?" he said.

"I wouldn't have minded, but she has her professional pride, you know. She keeps her distance, you know. A lady-in-waiting is not a dining companion and all that."

This exchange helped him better understand why Sophie was such a pushover for the Dimwits. Thanks to this *most romantic city in the world* – is it really? – she'd fallen a second time under the spell of Nessim's frosted-glass eyes. As a result, she'd fallen in thrall again to the mandate to perpetuate her dynasty. So, it's only natural she sought shelter in getting plastered in the company of the Dimwits.

If love makes me blind, so be it. I'll never judge you, my love.

It's since the night Sophie went through withdrawal that they don't have sex. From the home speakers nested in every other room, Umm Kulthum's voice reminds Anton of uncomplicated passions endowed with spontaneous combustion, ignited by their own heat. But since that night, their alternation of kyudo practice and algorithmic composition adds up to a plain sort of brotherly camaraderie. The unprompted dash of Sophie's body seeking his in the dark of night, that's the dismal memory that lulls him to sleep every night.

CHAPTER TWELVE

While he compiled his black Moleskine in the solitude of Palo Alto, Anton assumed, like the confident child prodigy he had been, that his Parisian mission would surely come to fruition. The black Moleskine was to be a navigation logbook of sort: in it, he listed the supporting facts pointing to his European target, as well as the pre-emptive, exculpatory evidence for whatever shape his revenge would finally take. For the time being, his mission unaccomplished, that Moleskine is meaningless, utterly irrelevant to anybody but him. Like that American fellow named Poe that Sophie told him about in Palo Alto, he keeps the secrets inscribed within it before everybody's eyes, on his desk.

A pair of eyes noticed it, though.

"Is that a war novel you're writing on the notebook you keep on your desk?" Sophie asks him today. "I want to read it."

"Me, write a novel! What made you think of it?" he replies. In the space of an instant, all the bitter musings on frustrated love scattered through the pages of the black Moleskine flash before his eyes. Add to it the pages he devoted to Sophie's offhand way to love him back, which she'd be sure to argue that he plucked out of thin air.

"The map taped to the cover, the same you keep on the wall in the study, looks like a color-coded war plan."

"That black notebook is just my journal, Sophie. And the map… I had a lot of time in my hands after you disappeared from Palo Alto. The map traces the episodes of most of Belmondo's novels, that's all."

"No war novel, then?"

"If I was a novelist, you know what I'd write about now?" he says.

"What?"

"A couple walks alongside the ocean on a sunny and breezy day. They see a seal's carcass surrounded by vultures and her dog scares the bird away, then they step into a honeycomb structure made up of dead tree trunks, smooth and white like cuttle-bones, she rests her back against those lukewarm trunks, her dog curls up at her feet, and he holds her in his arms."

She casts him a troubled glance and then keeps her eyes down for a long moment. It's since the night of her withdrawal that he is waiting for the miracle. She must've sensed a sour note in his voice.

"Yet, you acted vexed afterwards…?" she says in a tone, halfway between surrendering and beseeching, which reminds him of something.

"I was vexed because we did it unprotected. And vexed at myself for spoiling the moment by being vexed."

"Your ubiquitous condoms," she says enigmatically as she brings the espresso cup to the sink.

Ubiquitous…? The noise that the espresso cup makes against the steel of the sink tells Anton it's not the moment to learn the meaning of a new word.

CHAPTER THIRTEEN

Dambreuil walks anxiously into his kitchen. "Monsieur Anton, monsieur Anton!" she pleads with him, "Monsieur Nessim came visit with his *fille fertile*!" She widens her eyes the lecherous way she did the first time she told him of the girl from Yemen.

"They are in the house?"

"I diverted them up to my apartment," she explains. "Madame Sophie refuses to receive them. She's furious!"

He gazes at Dambreuil, lost in thought.

"They are waiting in my living room, monsieur Anton."

He weighs up the best course of action. He is wearing his cooking apron. He was in the middle of something.

At the sight of his hesitation, she grows even more anxious. "I must go back down!"

Does she leave him a choice? "Okay, I'll come down right away."

She shoots him a curt, childish nod of her chin, and runs to the stairs.

He climbs down the two flights of stairs between his apartment and Dambreuil's. He knocks at the door and she is there in a wink. Her eyes are as wide as before, but he can tell they're widened by terror now. As she guides him to her living room, she takes him by the hand, which gives him a stronger sense of the seriousness of the situation. She isn't speaking, but it's as though she was yelling it from the rooftops, that only Monsieur Anton can fix this, etc. Monsieur Anton would be only too glad to do without her blind trust in his magician's powers.

Beau de Rubempré

They step into a bright room furnished with singular care: the parlor of a cuckoo clock. The first thing he notices, in the corner by the window, is a tailor's dress form with a yellow tape measure draped around the neck. Nessim moves a few steps toward him in a cloud of cigarette smoke. He sticks out his hand. Without a word, Nessim bores his frosted-glass eyes into his, a moment too long, and then hugs him the Arabian way with two kisses on the cheeks, the way he used to do with him in California. Anton's eyes are burning from the smoke of the black cigarette. He feels the trace of saliva that Nessim's thick lips leave on his skin. He wonders should he reciprocate and brush Nessim's oval face with his lips. As he reclines his head, sort of chastely, he brings out instead the same priggish smile this slush used to force out of him in Palo Alto. Nessim doesn't give him time to raise his eyes again and pushes him away to the left. Through the smoke, his eyes fasten on a pair of black feet with purple-painted toenails, and he hears Nessim utter one word, a name: "Gala."

"Anton," he introduces himself raising his eyes on the girl facing him. He sticks out his hand instinctively, and just as instinctively he pulls it back.

Gala is the blackest creature he ever set eyes on. She's dressed in layers of pale-green, see-through veils. One of these veils covers her face and hair, yet it doesn't hide the slightest feature. Sophie's words flash through Anton's mind: *The niqab she wears on her face is so thin she looks naked.* She's worse than naked, he thinks, and the absurdity of this thought makes him dizzy. She can't be older than seventeen. He can't take his eyes off the brazen face behind that veil. Actually, he sends her a Morse-code message with his eyebrows before he is even aware of what he is doing. He just stands there, frozen at the sight of her fleshy lips beneath two large eyes made even larger by thick lines of mascara. These are the eyes, he muses, the very thought of which makes Dambreuil widen her own like a tramp. They are green and staring into his. At the bottom of the pupils glimmers a fantastic promise: he sinks into that depths. There's a part of him wondering if the clock is ticking at a slower pace in Dambreuil's parlor, or else, is he embarrassing himself in front of this girl? He recalls faintly that somewhere in this room there's Nessim: the strange idea comes to him that it's his puffs of smoke that feed this mirage of a girl. One of the girl's nostrils is pierced by a diamond whose light shines even through the pale-green veil that covers it. But the dark lips behind the veil release a shine of their own too, and the white of her eyes is like glow-in-the-dark against its thick frame of mascara. He comes to his senses with a jolting shake of the head. And he lowers his eyes, not too early though not to get a glimpse of the scornful smile that surfaces on the girl's lips: this time he can't hide his arousal behind a bedsheet. He reclines his head, chastely, like he did in Nessim's arms, but it's a new trap. At first, he had thought the girl walked barefoot. Now he sees leather strings of sandals thinner than tissue paper. Shod that way, her black feet look even more naked than before. Never in his life has he seen such sexually alluring feet. Several gold anklets circle her ankles. His hands shake, he can't stop them. He doesn't dare raise anymore his eyes into those of the girl's, but he feels he must take them off the sight of her feet at the soonest. It feels as though he has been standing frozen here before her for an eternity. Where's Dambreuil, why doesn't she come to his rescue, why doesn't she say something? He turns on his heels, groans some indistinct words, and rushes out the door.

He is up the stairs to his apartment three steps at a time. He locks the door and, beside himself with shame, drops to his knees, doubled over his hard-on. He sobs, feels like weeping but can't. And he sees again the girl's fleshy lips. How is this possible! Can this possibly be happening to him! The scornful smile on the girl's lips comes back to mind. That open-eyed smile, that's the reason of it all. He buries his head in his hands. They keep shaking. If they could have it their way, these hands of his, they'd be tearing those thin veils off her body. Right now.

He pulls himself up with a huge effort, goes to the bedroom, steps into the walk-in closet, strips naked and puts on his kyudojo outfit. The elevator carries him down to the kyudojo. He strings Daniel's bow. He kneels down in the kiza posture, the bow in the left hand, two arrows in the right, and remains still like that for a long time, half an hour at least, his eyes on the target. He empties his mind of thoughts, aligns head neck and spine vertically, relaxes his chest and shoulders, and slides gradually the body's center of gravity toward the lower abdomen. He becomes one with his heartbeats. He stands up and takes the shooting position: his collarbone orthogonal to the target, his bare feet glued to the wooden platform, his legs apart, his arrow notched to the bowstring, his naked left arm stretched out and motionless. Then he shoots. His left arm is motionless while the bow in his hand turns slightly leftwards and the bowstring brushes his elbow's inside. He hears the familiar, steady note in the air. As his bowstring's vibration dies down, he keeps both arms stretched out in a straight line, an extension of his collarbone: the left hand holding the bow and pointed at the target, the right hand, gloved, pointed in the opposite direction: as though he was bracing himself to hug the specter called to his rescue by the sound of Daniel's bow. He does it all over again a second time.

He hears the swish of the door opening and closing again. Dambreuil on recon mission. Elvis crosses the shooting platform and goes curl up in his corner.

He kneels down again in the kiza posture. Like a long litany, he tells the specter in the room of the randomized set of events that led him to this kyudojo in Paris, starting from his unsubstantiated birthplace in Petersburg – *the son of a fallen wall,* in his father's remote words – and then getting through the day Daniel taught him that coding on Mac is like shooting arrows from a yumi bow, the day he taught him how to bury his *Open Sesame* into a Michelin street map, the day he gave him his red Ferrari, the day he fell into Nessim's trap to protect him from it, and on and on, ending with his encounter with the green vaporous genie wafted out of Nessim's black cigarette a short while ago. Except for the vision of Gala, he recites, page by page, the contents of his black Moleskine.

When he relinquishes the kiza posture to stand up, it's all over: all's been contained, forgotten. Forgiven. He knows perfectly well what's left for him to do. He snaps his fingers at Elvis and they go back up to his apartment.

CHAPTER FOURTEEN

Dambreuil is waiting in his living room.

She gives him a puzzled look. "What went on down in my flat?" she says. "I saw you in the kyudojo a while ago but didn't want to interrupt."

"I felt unwell all of a sudden, sorry," he answers.

"That's what I thought," she says.

"Should I apologize to Nessim?" he asks.

"Oh, no need for that! Monsieur Nessim is a real gentleman! You know what he said when you left abruptly?"

He projects a hint of curiosity in his gaze.

"He said, 'I always envied the inspired fellows my wife surrounds herself with. I'm a grey accountant by comparison.' That's what he said: 'A grey accountant'! ... Inspired fellows!' isn't it adorable?"

Adorable...

"Indeed," he says.

Dambreuil goes on. "And then he said, 'Anton enters stage-left, hugs me, casts a glance at Gala, turns around, and exists stage-left without speaking a word. A one-act play worthy of Artaud! How do you beat that?' And having said that, he added with a shrug that he could only follow suit. So they left, just like that! Gone!"

"Is that so? He compared me with Artaud!" he says, mimicking cheerfully the sound of the name mentioned by Dambreuil. This Artot – or Artod, like Pernod, whatever – must've something to do with the Godot of his gaffe a few days ago. He won't put the foot in it again.

Bitcoin and the Ritual of Kyudo Archery

Weird, the mere effort of pretending cheerfulness in response to Nessim's indifferent unconcern puts him in a good mood. Somehow, the emergency of Nessim's unannounced visit to madame's house was patched up thanks to Anton's indecorous exit? So it seems.

Dambreuil is positively galvanized by their narrow escape. At his reference to Artot, or Artod, she indulges in a no-comment stare: a short one, it tells him nonetheless that only her steely professionalism keeps her from calling his bluff.

"… and madame Sophie?" he asks.

"Madame didn't show up. Monsieur Nessim left her a business card with a corner turned down. The right-hand upper corner, of course."

"Of course."

This time his bluff goes unnoticed. Dambreuil is in top conversational mode. "He may be a grey accountant," she says, "but there's a subtle irony to all he does."

In so many years, it occurs to him, he never had a chance to find out if Nessim kisses Dambreuil's hand when they meet. Something in Dambreuil's attitude tells him he does.

"What about Gala, how did she take my exit from stage?" he asks.

"Gala! *La fille fertile*? But she can't even speak!" Dambreuil bursts out with an inevitable widening of the eyes. "That girl is a beast, a wild beast!"

They are both euphoric and she seems ready to go back to her ordinary duties. Before getting out of his kyudo outfit, there's a first step he can take in the execution of the plan he concocted with the assistance of the specter in the kyudojo. He asks Dambreuil if he can borrow a sewing pin. She pulls a yellow tape out of her pockets, sinks her hand in again, and pulls out a fist of pins of all sizes. One is enough, he tells her as he picks the size he needs.

No need to walk her to the door. Like a Byzantine general in her encampment, she comes and goes as she pleases anyway.

With Dambreuil's pin and a tiny piece of paper, he makes a rough-and-ready white flag and plants it on the Michelin map, at the intersection of boulevard de Montparnasse with rue de Chevreuse: in celebration of the night he made his acquaintance with Paris, facing the Tschann bookstore in Sophie's arms. He walks to the bedroom and opens the bedside table's drawer where he keeps his stash of condoms. He walks to the kitchen and throws all of them in the garbage can.

Next, he must go to the Tschann bookstore.

Bitcoin and the Ritual of Kyudo Archery

CHAPTER FIFTEEN
Anton is reading from Belmondo's *Weekdays of Summer:*

It was a very warm summer and they were certain that nobody would ever find them here in Nice. They had never been so happy as in the days at the beach, mixed among people lying on the sand who smelled like suntan lotion. The kids build sandcastles and there were peddlers hawking sodas and ice cream. They blended with the rest of the bathers on those weekdays of summer.

Belmondo's novels end well even when they end badly. Anton can't explain why, it's an impression he has every time he gets to the end of one of Belmondo's novels. Daniel told him once that that sort of impression has a Greek name, *catharsis*.

Bad is not the right word, though, to define the end of most of Belmondo's novels. *Dreary*, maybe? There are dreary endings in Belmondo's books that don't make you sad at all.

Daniel had never read Belmondo. Once, Anton found himself telling him that he couldn't recall a single happy ending in Belmondo.

"This means you admire a true writer. Happy endings don't work well in literature." That's when Daniel told him of *catharsis*. "You rejoice because the unhappy ending is someone else's lot in life."

Why shouldn't you rejoice, though, that someone else's happy ending could be yours too? Or even rejoice that, inspired by the happy ending, you find out you have it in you to make that ending yours? It was seldom the case that Anton disagreed with Daniel, but this time he did, and vehemently. Maybe that's why he now remembers that Greek word so well: *catharsis*.

He closes *Weekdays of Summer* and opens the last page of *Youngsters*:

A whole fortnight in Nice! Cruising on a large American convertible that could bring them anywhere on the French Riviera in no time! One morning they were driving along the Corniche toward Villefranche. Jean felt strangely languid and careless at the sight of a piece of rock that, falling slowly into the sea, disappeared in a wreath of white foam. It was the burden of his youth breaking off him because its time had come.

Now he reads one last passage, from *In the Environs*:

His old dream was coming true at long last. He would soon be the owner of the villa in Nice that had belonged to baroness Orczy, whose books he had loved fondly in his youth, long before he became the best-selling author Guy de Guise.

Belmondo's versions of the city of Nice, so frequent in his novels, has been on Anton's mind lately. And today his intuition… Strike *intuition*. Today an irrational hunch started him out on a Google search of Nice's real estate market, and here is what he found:

For Sale – Villa Baroness Orczy
Private estate with large garden facing the sea
19, avenue de la Costa, Nice
Owner: *Guy de Guise*
PRICE UPON REQUEST

Bitcoin and the Ritual of Kyudo Archery

Guy de Guise. How many pseudonyms does Patrick Belmondo have? De *Guise* is not a bad one, for a Frenchman disguised as a British author. Most of Belmondo's novels are encrypted autobiographies, if you know how to break the code.

Anton toys around with a blank Trezor hardware wallet, the time it takes him to initialize it, then he transfers a bunch of bitcoins to a wallet on his iPhone. Now he wipes the Trezor clean and slips it into a pocket of his jeans. He grabs his Mac, slips the iPhone into another pocket, puts Elvis on his leash, and off they go toward the Tschann Bookstore.

He clicks on the iPhone's GPS. They keep a brisk pace as they cross pont de l'Alma in the direction of place de l'École Militaire, reach boulevard des Invalides, and from there get into boulevard de Montparnasse till they are facing the bookstore's green front. The front door between the bookstore's two separate entries is open. They enter the building, climb to the second floor, and on the landing he rings the bell of the right-side door.

A white-haired man comes to the door. He must be around six feet and a half.

"Mister Guy de Guise, I presume?" Anton says.

"You have read *In the Environs*. That's something," Belmondo replies in a Frenchified English. "*Alè!*" He gestures at Anton to follow him inside.

They walk through a room in total darkness, and Belmondo steers Anton by the shoulder. Elvis synchronizes his steps with theirs. Anton feels like a blind dwarf in the hands of a giant. Belmondo opens a door and they step into a living room filled with blinding sunlight. Two French windows look onto the boulevard. The walls are white, except for a long and narrow painting above a very long couch covered with a green blanket that reminds Anton of a pool table. Belmondo gestures at him to take a seat at the right corner of the couch and he does the same at the opposite side. Elvis curls up near Anton's feet.

To look at each other, they both must rest one knee on the couch.

As an icebreaker, Anton asks Belmondo if he's aware of the three roundabouts they're building on the square of porte Maillot. He hasn't passed through that area since years ago, Belmondo says. Anton tells him of his drive on the trail of his two characters, Jean and Jacqueline, and how his car fell into orbit around those roundabouts, in the vicinities of his destination in the Bois de Boulogne. No sooner did he crawl out of one of the roundabouts than he found himself caught up in the next one, and kept going in circles.

"Did you reach destination eventually?"

"Did I? Of course. To celebrate, I even parked on the side of the street near the station of the miniature railway." Anton decides Belmondo doesn't need to know about his second nocturnal visit there in the company of Sophie.

"In your shoes, I would have driven to the square of Porte-de-Saint-Cloud."

At first Belmondo's words take Anton back.

He speaks without thinking. He remembers well, he says, that the square of Porte-de-Saint-Cloud appears on the last page of the novel. The day after Jean and Jacqueline go to the Bois de Boulogne and clump together in her car, Jean walks back to the building where they met, to retrieve his rental car. The night before, on being told that Jean had his own car,

Bitcoin and the Ritual of Kyudo Archery

Jacqueline insisted on giving him a ride: she found it hard to believe that the Jean she had known long ago could actually drive a car. Jean is now ready to climb into his rental car when he sees Darius, the host of yesterday's party, on the sidewalk. They exchange a few words. Darius tells Jean that, in the morning, Thérèse and her husband (to him, Jacqueline is Thérèse) left suddenly for Majorca. Jean takes leave of Darius and drives awkwardly his car through a sun-scorched, deserted city. He's filled with a strange premonition, which gains definition as soon as his car enters the square of Porte-de-Saint-Cloud. Having come back to Paris in 1964, after Jacqueline disappeared from their London flat without a word of explication, Jean had a frequent dream of taking a walk with her just here, in this square, on a little street behind the church.

Belmondo brings Anton's summary to a close. "That is the point, give or take, don't you see? Jean knows they had never taken that walk together. Consequently, *voilà*, he tells himself it must have been in another life."

Since the moment he walked into this room, actually, Anton has been feeling that he himself swerved into some alternative reality. Sitting on a couch side by side with the great Patrick Belmondo, Anton Gunzburg busies himself with telling him the ending of one of his novels. He may as well throw a Hail Mary: "The conformity of the street map with urban fabrics is not subject to causality," he says, citing himself, the first sentence he ever wrote, and then crossed out, on his black Moleskine.

"That's another way of making the same point," Belmondo answers with a shake of his head. "*Mais, alè*, I still have to meet the person who would put it in such an affected way!"

Beau de Rubempré

Test positive: Anton himself had felt it could be put more plainly in his Moleskine, and so did he.

Anton decides the time has come to explain why he is here.

Belmondo listens with great attention and without interruptions. Then he says, "I am afraid the real estate agency in Nice won't like it."

As Belmondo speaks, it occurs to Anton that he hasn't asked him yet who is he and what's his name.

"They'll fine you for sure for breach of contract. If you allow me, I'll take care of it."

"But how does one arrange an agreement of the kind you have in mind?" Belmondo wonders, scratching his forehead. "The last time I dealt with a public notary, he defrauded me. *Voilà*, that's the way they operate!"

Anton tells him that he doesn't know either how you arrange an agreement of the kind he's proposing to him, and that's why he leaped over the middleman and came to see him in person. "I don't like notaries either, you know." Daniel had to deal with notaries on the occasions of his donations to Anton; it wasn't pleasant for either of them. Anton explains his plan as concisely as he can: all he suggests is a handshake and a Bitcoin payment with no written contract.

"This way," he adds to make himself totally clear, "you and your heirs will always have the option to claim the villa back, if you feel like that. Simply put, I trust you, monsieur Belmondo."

"And in return for a non-existent contract, I am paid with invisible money. Fantastic!" Belmondo replies, slapping high thighs and rolling with laughter.

Anton feels dismissed by that rolling laughter.

Bitcoin and the Ritual of Kyudo Archery

Belmondo slaps his thighs again a couple of times and brings his laughter to a close. "Fantastic, I like the idea! I like it very much! You are a true novelist, you know?"

Then he keeps silent, totally motionless, one bent knee still resting on the couch, his eyes on Anton. And little by little Anton transitions from dejection to euphoria. A certainty works its way into his mind: that last statement of Belmondo's, *You are a true novelist, you know*, was meant as praise, not blame. In sum, there's nothing more left to say.

Anton raises tentatively his right hand and, wholeheartedly, Belmondo raises his. Anton goes through a brief out-of-body experience, which he doesn't find all that extraordinary, given the situation: Anton Gunzburg, his torso bent sideways, extends his right arm above Belmondo's long couch as the writer extends his own. When the hands connect, the two men shake repeatedly each other's arm.

The price Anton pays for the villa in Nice is the price that Belmondo established with the real estate agency. The bitcoin's exchange rate is favorable to Belmondo today. Anton takes care of the whole transaction. Belmondo explains to him, his lips shaped into a bizarre pout, that he doesn't understand a thing about bitcoin – he pronounces it: *beet-cuan* – and keeps patting him on the back. Anton asks Belmondo to show him his smart phone. The gizmo he is shown, a bluish affair with a rotating lid, is hopeless. Anton plugs the blank Trezor to his Mac, initializes it from scratch, and transfers the bitcoin payment from the wallet on his iPhone to an address on this Trezor. He shows Belmondo the result on the Mac's monitor. This is his new Trezor wallet, those bitcoins belong to him, Anton explains Belmondo looks at the black-and-white figure and shrugs his shoulders, spreading his hands submissively like the statue of a Catholic saint.

There is a sheaf of white sheets of paper and poorly sharpened pencils on the floor in front of the couch. Anton takes one sheet, writes down the twelve-word passphrase of this Trezor on it, and give the list of words to Belmondo. It must be kept in a safe place, he explains, away from meddling eyes. In case the Trezor gets lost or misfunctions, this passphrase will retrieve Belmondo's bitcoins. Belmondo shrugs and spreads his hands like a saint again. But his face is good-humored, even merry, as though he was having fun. As a matter of fact, here Anton is too, doing his utmost to pay Belmondo the fairest of prices, even volunteering to subsidize the costs and penalties of the real estate agency, and having his own sort of fun in the process.

Anton feels briefly undermined when it comes out that Belmondo has never typed a password or a PIN on a keyboard, not even to open his email. Anton writes the PIN of the Trezor on another sheet of paper. He explains that this sheet must never fall in a stranger's hands either. By the way, where did Belmondo put that first sheet of paper? The old man starts fidgeting with his hands, searches his pockets, stands up to look through the folds of the green blanket, kneels down even, to look under the couch. Nothing doing. He looks at Anton with a hangdog expression on his face.

"Meanwhile, how about an orange soda?" he says.

While Belmondo disappears into his kitchen, Anton writes again the passphrase and PIN on two new sheets of paper. He takes their pictures with his iPhone. His iPhone is protected by software and physical keys, safe enough to protect Belmondo's secrets. On a third sheet of paper, he writes down his own phone number and email address. This is something he hadn't planned: for the foreseeable future, he'll be tied hand and foot with this French writer, technologically challenged, who is trusting him with a huge transaction and a totally virtual payment without even knowing his name yet.

And me: I just gave him a fortune in bitcoin, and don't even have a pair of keys to get into my new property yet, not to mention a sale contract.

Daniel, you wouldn't like this. Satoshi's riskless trust, my foot.

Belmondo comes back holding an orange bottle and a glass. He pulls one more glass out of a pocket. He sets this stuff down on the floor and goes back to the kitchen. He reappears again with a saucer and a bottle of milk. He sets the saucer in front of Elvis and pours some drops of milk in it, like you'd do with a cat. Elvis sizes him up with open interest. Before filling the two glasses, Belmondo crosses the room to a drop-leaf writing desk with thin, crane-like legs – legs so long that Anton wonders if Belmondo writes his novels standing in front of it. He just noticed that, except for the couch he is sitting in, the desk is the only other piece of furniture in this room. Belmondo lifts the leaf and, his back to Anton, begins to rummage through the drawers inside. Anton can't see his face, but from his muttering, it sounds as though he was going through unexpected surprises – one more search of the past, the materials for a new novel? At long last, he turns around shaking a bunch of keys, a jubilant expression on his face: the keys to Anton's new property!

As he hands Belmondo the sheets of paper with all the vital information, he stresses that now Belmondo has his contacts as well. "Any problem with your bitcoins, I'll fix it," Anton says. "It can be done from wherever, I don't even need to be on this continent to retrieve your crypto funds."

They toast to their deal with glasses filled with a sparkling orange liquid. Belmondo keeps asking Anton if he likes orange soda. The third time he does, Anton answers: "Not this one," and Belmondo almost splits his sides with laughter. Elvis looks up with renewed interest.

Time to unplug the Trezor from the Mac and hand it to Belmondo. Belmondo pockets it and asks, "You use this gadget like I use my checkbook, *hein*?"

"Yes," Anton says. It'd be a waste of breath – too many words – to try and explain why he doesn't, not really. He rarely needs a Trezor at hand. He needed one this morning, to transfer bitcoins into his iPhone wallet. So, what he did is, he stood in front of the lopsided triangle on the Michelin map whose sides are traced by red ribbon – the triangle, that is, that surrounds the neighborhood to the right side of the Bois de Boulogne – retrieved his twelve-word passphrase from its mnemonic pointers, used the passphrase to initialize a blank Trezor, transferred enough bitcoins to buy Belmondo's villa from the Trezor to the wallet app on his iPhone, and then wiped the Trezor clean to use it once more now with Belmondo. Normally, he would have smashed that Trezor to smithereens. He always keeps a stash of blank Trezors at hand. Call him paranoid, but new Trezors come cheap enough to be hyper-cautious.

A word to the wise: *Don't wipe, smash*. On one occasion, as an experiment, Anton managed to extract five of the twelve words of his own passphrase from a wiped Trezor.

Bitcoin and the Ritual of Kyudo Archery

It's when Anton and Elvis are back out in the street, in front of the bookstore, that he goes the closest to losing heart. If you try to pay your real estate tax in France, he wonders, shouldn't you first prove the real estate does belong to you? Wouldn't the same go for your electric power contract and the gas connection contract? How could he miss that? No sooner do you poke your nose out of the crypto space than trouble begins. Just like this city of Belmondo's: on the one side, the outlines of a map, smooth and linear, and on the other, everyday life with its detours and convolutions.

As they start toward home, Anton regrets not having shared these doubts of his with Belmondo: real estate tax, power contract... He pictures Belmondo splitting his sides with laughter all over again.

Smeyat'sya kak sumasshedshiy: laugh like crazy. Sounds about right.

Did he ask him his name, in the end? He can't seem to remember.

CHAPTER SIXTEEN

With the warmer season, the city area at the foot of the Eiffel Tower is crammed, day and night, with double-decker coaches. Between some shopping and many selfies, their passengers go visit the scorched remains of the newly gutted cathedral, a fifteen-minute walk from Sophie's mansion.

Anton and Sophie agree: Paris is the most romantic city, as long as you visit it in the off-season or in torrential weather. Otherwise, you must deal with the throngs of tourists disgorged from those double-deckers, who turn Paris into a theme park of sorts. When Anton gets caught in their midst, somehow he wouldn't be surprised to run into the parade of friends who taught him English from a TV screen: Captain Hook and his treasure map, Ali Baba and his *Open Sesame*, Aladdin and his Genie, Basil and his deductive logic, Scheherazade and her forever retold story.

Would those two-dimensional lecturers recognize their old friend Anton in this American in Paris?

Every time Sophie seeks Anton's bed or he seeks hers, she wants him to tell her once again how come he thought, as a child, that the matchless detective was Walt Disney's mouse, Basil, and Sherlock Holmes the cheap knockoff.

"Holmes of Baskerville versus Basil of Baker Street!" she says, and her laughter reminds Anton of her eyes' purposeful mirth back in Palo Alto. "I was born too early, Anton! I'm jealous of that upended world of yours!"

Since they started doing it unprotected, things are positively looking up between them. Anton doesn't know how to name this state of grace – unless he calls it *that*, a state of grace – but he is sure it streamed out of the plan he concocted a couple of weeks ago in the kyudojo, advised by Daniel's specter.

The first time he'll pat Sophie's pregnant belly, she won't feel like slapping him anymore, the way she did that day in Palo Alto, when she had stuffed a pillow under her clothes. It'll be her turn, rather, to wonder how should they name their baby.

The answer to that question is inevitable anyway.

Patrick Belmondo was born in Boulogne-Billancourt is written on the first page of most of Belmondo's books. You find yourself in the city of your birth, step into city hall, and when you step out of it, you hold in your pocket the piece of paper certifying that's the place where you saw the light on a certain day of a certain year. There! This sort of foothold, like a stony placeholder, is what Anton truly cares about, even more than the given name: origin and center, Nakamoto. You can go back to it whenever you like, and from there, if you feel like it, you watch the chain of your whole life unravel backwards in time, block after block, till it meets you right there, where you stand waiting.

It must feel something like that, Anton guesses.

Paris is the most romantic city he knows anyway – side by side with his Sophie.

Petersburg may have been the most romantic city for his parents, for all he knows.

Leningrad is an arithmetic accident – it was renamed Petersburg almost three years after Anton was born.

CHAPTER SEVENTEEN

TURIN, May 7, 2019

Dear Anton,

It feels like an eternity since we did archery together in Palo Alto! Carlo and I created Futura out of nothing meanwhile that our Andreino, whom you met a few times in Palo Alto, grows at breakneck pace. Now this Crypto Winter stands in our way. How do you say it: the spanner in the works, the fly in the ointment… We have a fifty full-timers' team, Futura can survive 5-7 more years in this crypto climate but no longer than that. In spite of it all, we decided to organize again the conference which was such a big success last summer.

This being told, what's the next step? I think that this June's conference would benefit very much from your views and experience, but I find it embarrassing to offer you the meager per-diem or the coach flight we give to our affiliates. You live by different standards in Palo Alto. If I think how much I had to pay my babysitter when we lived there!

So, this is what I suggest: if you feel like coming to our Futura conference, I'd be happy to send you an official invitation (actually, thinking of it, why would you need one, you work for no employer), and I'd cover your two nights at the hotel here in Torino.

I'm inviting Sophie too, who lives in Paris now. She's the Captain of TEXOR now! Who would have thought? If she comes, would you mind sharing the room with her. Crypto Winter budgeting, you know.

Did you ever try makiwara kyudojo? You know, here in Turin kyudo archery is not for everybody. Carlo and me, we adjusted well to shooting into the makiwara target. We'd love to do a makiwara kyudo session with you, and who knows, with Sophie too, God willing, here at our place.

Bitcoin and the Ritual of Kyudo Archery

Followed by an intimate dinner on our terrace overlooking the Po river, and talk of old times.
   Don't forget to bring bow and arrows! If you come, of course.
   Margherita

CHAPTER EIGHTEEN

Sophie receives the same email from Turin. She shows it to Anton on her Mac. He tells her he was invited to the conference too. He doesn't tell her that the two emails are basically the same, except for their two names swapping places and that poisonous allusion to her success with TEXOR's initial token sale. It'd be too much of a mark against her former enemy Margherita. They find it funny that Margherita has no idea Anton live in Paris now, nor – they are both sure of it – did she ever suspect of their relationship. It's weird to realize it, but it's not an eternity at all since the kyudojo in Palo Alto still counted five members, even if it feels that way: no longer than two years ago, Sophie hadn't even described her TEXOR project to the members of the kyudojo yet. Things in the crypto space go indeed at breakneck speed. Anton tells her of the wind gust that threw him off-balance that day, the moment she broke up with them – "… with me," he can't help adding with a sort of childish obstinacy, overthrown by the recollection. Her eyes, unsmiling, seem liquid too, for a moment. He tells her of the cloud of shame that weighed Daniel down for allowing Margherita, heavily pregnant at the time, hardly a tolerable archer, into the kyudojo. "Daniel feared he had debased the sacred bond among us three," he says. He walks her through some of the technical details of the study he made of Futura's initial token sale.

As to the prospect of shooting into the makiwara target, Sophie makes a funny allusion to Anton's hallucinations of a few days ago, in bed by her side. "If nothing else, Margherita's makiwara kyudojo will be too small a space for her to shoot at me unnoticed. I'm saved!" Then she kneels down by his armchair and puts her hand on the fly of his pants. "Just to think that you were trying to save me from her arrows but could not come out from behind the bedsheet, poor thing…"

After trying a couple of acrobatic positions, they give up the armchair for her couch. Such spontaneous episodes are more and more frequent, followed most of the time by a meal in the kitchen. Standing in front of an array of fruits, nuts, honey, cheese, yogurt, cucumber, and fresh bread, they agree that Margherita's conference is an excellent chance to visit a European city new to them both.

"To be honest," he says, "it's not that I've been in any other European city, except Paris."

"You are wrong, baby," she objects. "You were born in Saint Petersburg, which is in Europe too."

He is bitterly aware of how many wasted words it'd take him to object. He just smiles back. She isn't far of the mark, after all: he wasn't born in Petersburg, but was still around, apparently, when they renamed the city that way. Leningrad and Petersburg count for two European cities or just one?

Sophie writes a warm reply to Margherita, saying she'll be happy to join the conference. Of course she'll share her room with Anton! "Any sacrifice to save her some money!" she says in laughter as she clicks the Send button. They find the secrecy of their lovemaking so enormously amusing that hunger can hardly delay some more of it, in her bed this time.

Later in his apartment, Anton opens the private internet access app on his Mac and logs in from a server in Palo Alto

Beau de Rubempré

before confirming with Margherita that he'll go to Turin in June. The shared room with Sophie will be just fine.

CHAPTER NINETEEN

Anton is in the apartment of rue Blanche.

Early this morning he had an Uber driver leave him in the vicinities, then, the hood of his black hoodie low on his eyes, he reached number 38 and climbed here, third floor.

The plan was to set the video camera atop the tripod and then set the tripod behind one of the three windows, the bedroom's French window precisely, which is equipped with heavy curtains. The video camera is programmable, so, once its telephoto lens is hidden behind a small opening in the curtains, he will be able to film at predetermined times.

But he is stuck.

It's ten AM, the time of day when the average American coder gets going. And in fact, who does he see down on rue Blanche but a couple of the Stanford doctoral students that Nessim coopted on to his crypto projects: Nick and – Anton forgets the name of the second one. They are both sipping their coffee from a paper cup and chatting in the springtime sun as they approach number 21. They must sure be part of the team of coders which Nessim put under Sophie's direction for work on the TEXOR project. They don't seem in a hurry, and after all, why should they be? Sophie persists on consulting Anton on her algorithms when those two guys, who were enrolled in her same PhD program, know a lot more than him about crypto architecture. He wonders, what do they do at the office, when they're not busy destroying Sophie's latest bout of ingenuity? Nick and his colleague walk into the HOSNANI HOLDING building. The TEXOR coders under Sophie's direction have their offices on the first floor, in the French headquarter of Dynamic Registry Solution, or DRS. The rest of the building, Sophie told him, is occupied by Nessim's finance company.

The crux of the obstacle that keeps Anton from deploying his simple plan for the day is all there, before his eyes, in the gap between the DRS offices on the first floor and the rest of the building. The DRS windows are darkened. If he zooms his video camera on the right-hand lower corner of each window, he can see the low-frequency pulse emitter which shields the interiors from one-way laser microphones. Not for nothing those TEXOR coders were trained at Stanford. He would be highly surprised if the whole first floor was not a state-of-the-art fortress, unassailable by crypto espionage.

But that's where the shoe pinches. It's no less than a quarter of an hour that he zooms unimpeded his video camera on Nessim's fingers typing on his keyboard. The floors of Nessim's finance company seem to lack the most basic security measures. The windows are neither darkened nor shielded from microphones. Behind the largest one, opposite Anton's bedroom window on the third floor, is the oval of Nessim's face haloed with a sun-stricken cloud of cigarette smoke.

At the sight of this unexpected spectacle, Anton had felt a triumphant satisfaction, at first. The secrets of his target would be unveiled to him in not time: all he had to do was film the keys typed by Nessim on his keyboard, extract his passwords, and hunt for the proofs of his guilt among his files and folders, with the very deftness, not a moment too soon, of Sherlock Holmes. But a moment later, his triumphant satisfaction turned itself into a feeling of compassion – not too different from the feeling he has felt on rare occasions, as he was undermining the misdeeds of some black hat who was clearly too unwary not to end his days in some federal prison. Anton presumes that is the feeling felt by the cat playing with the mouse. And yet, before he could bring himself to position the tripod by the window, it's despondency that prevailed over both triumph and compassion. How can Nessim type on his keyboard in full daylight, before any hacker's eyes? Granted, the banker-monk may be partial to the old-fashioned ways of his elders, when it comes to managing the fortunes they hoarded before passing him the baton. No digital files, and pile after pile of paperwork are, after all, the best security against black hats: all you need, instead of the *Open Sesame* coveted by the hacker, is an army of blindly devoted accountants. Old World families like Nessim's may still keep artificial intelligence out of the equation of personal wealth; it's possible. As to his new venture into crypto, TEXOR's digital side is fully delegated to Sophie. *I'm the layman who pays the bills. My collaborators handle the nitty-gritty*, Nessim told Daniel on their fateful first and last meeting. But criminal deeds of the sort Daniel was a victim to are a different matter altogether. The more warm-bodies are interposed between the crime and its instigator, the more breaking points are made available to the investigators: the murder of Jamal Khashoggi, in the Saudi consulate of Istanbul last October, is a case in point. Anton knows Nessim well enough, he's too smart for that. He must've created some digital wall between himself, the warm-bodied executors, and the scene of the crime.

And here's the thing. The moment blood is shed on the other side of that digital wall, your keyboard becomes the smoking gun. You won't ever use it again in full daylight. Unless, that is, you are an exhibitionist of Michel's sort —

unworthy, even, of the improvised Sherlock Holmes on this side of the bedroom window. No, Anton can't put Nessim's savviness on a level with the Dimwits'.

He watches the play of light and shadow the sun makes on the oval face on the other side of the street, and a certainty crawl its way into his mind: that sun-kissed keyboard doesn't hide the Map of the Crime, pure and simple.

Is Anton dealing with a con man, super-savvy about computer technology, as Daniel suspected, or with your run-of-the-mill, Middle-Eastern billionaire, born with a golden spoon in his mouth?

Anton's heartbeat starts going faster and an instant later he knows why. Gala is coming from the same direction Nick and his colleague entered the scope of his vision a while ago. She's wearing a lobster-colored version of the niqab she had on the day he met her. She walks into the door to number 21. Anton waits a few minutes. Now a floating flash of lobster-colored veils appears behind Nessim's head, mingled with his sun-stricken, smoky halo. She walks around his desk, reaches the window, lays both hands on the glass like a child would, and raises her face, black like coal, at the sky. Anton's Apple watch shows 12:15 PM.

He gives up for today. He pulls the door shut and climbs down the stairways. He is so distracted with this state of affairs that he is out in the street before pulling his black hood. And of course, his luck, he finds himself face to face with Nick and the other doctoral candidate he saw walk into the TEXOR offices a couple of hours ago. They're having some argument. *Lunch break*! he thinks in terror. Nick opens up his arms in a vexed way, crosses to Anton's side of the street, and ask him a question in a dramatically Americanized French: something to do with *gilets jaunes* – yellow vests, Anton learned that much from Bashir. He looks Nick straight in the eyes, and Nick doesn't recognize him! He has taken Anton for a local. He picked him as a referee to settle some disagreement with his friend about the yellow vests.

"*J'sais pas,*" Anton utters, mimicking one of Dambreuil's recurring phrases, and wriggles away.

How many times did he cross paths with Nick in Palo Alto? Nick's face is stamped on his memory forever. Yet, to be fair, what's the chance that the face of a college dropout like Anton would register durably in the mind of a Stanford doctoral candidate in the pay of an international potentate?

CHAPTER TWENTY

Anton has two deputies in Iceland charged with the mining plants' daily management. The plants mine bitcoin 24-7. The personnel rotate on three eight-hour shifts. One of his deputies is in charge in the daytime shift, the other one works at night. Mostly, he hires his deputies among locals, so the turnover is not too frequent. When they hired his first two deputies, Daniel decided to do the search among managers of geothermal power stations, and most hires have come from that field since. The required hardware and software expertise in the mining plants is not greater than that of a good manager of geothermal power stations. Aside from the supervision of the personnel, who in turn control the machines, the electric circuits and the cooling systems, it's Anton's deputy's task to update the software and the hardware, get rid of obsolete machines, and reconfigure old ones. He pays salaries in American dollars, which he trades on a variety of bitcoin exchanges. Through the years, the volatility of bitcoin's exchange rate forced him to become a decently skilled trader: you never want to trade at current exchange rate, with that volatility making the price jump up and down all day long. Also, it's often lucrative to engage in arbitrage, juggling a couple of national currencies at once. Anton won't ever be one of those wizards who short and long bitcoin on a daily basis, but he knows the ropes.

You could say he heads a production system which reached its technological plateau with the procedure called proof-of-work. Day-to-day maintenance is the main objective. Compared with it, the algorithms of Sophie's proof-of-stake dream are still in diapers. In proof-of-work, it's machines that mine bitcoins, and their work, proof of which is in the results, is compensated with freshly minted bitcoins. In proof-of-stake, the mining is done by humans who give proof of their reliability by staking their own money in the process, and are compensated in turn with freshly minted tokens. Sophie's TEXOR tokens will be called TXR – if they'll ever be mined, that is.

Anton doesn't know who invented proof-of-stake. Whoever they were, he wonders if they thought carefully about the main implication of their idea. Turning humans into machines, or to put it more mildly, training humans to operate with the mechanic insensitivity of the mining machine, is a huge challenge.

It's not all that different from the predicament he faced the day that living in Palo Alto became unbearable to him and he embarked on this Parisian mission. A faceless stranger branded Daniel's skull with his own signature, and he has come to Paris to decode that signature. All he knows of the plot that led to it is the last page: a nail stuck in Daniel's brain, a stolen Mac, and, maybe, the theft of some hundreds of thousands of bitcoins. Sure, to become a perfectly calibrated revenge-machine, he ought to teach himself mechanic insensitivity: unlearn love and loss, and all that. But unseasoned with heart-felt emotions, what would his revenge taste like? No, thanks.

With her proof-of-stake, Sophie is facing an analogous obstacle. She must devise a human-driven system where individual and collective interests collude with each other. In the TEXOR blockchain, the ideal miner is a human motivated by self-interest, yet immune from greed and corruption. But you have to wonder: isn't that the definition of a well-programmed machine? How do you draw a line, in humans, between greed and self-interest?

Anton wouldn't be surprised if it turned out that on creating bitcoin, Satoshi Nakamoto tackled the issue of uncontrollable human passions from all imaginable sides, before concluding that proof-of-work was the only viable procedure to verify and extend the blockchain.

Be that as it may, the TEXOR project has made some headway since Sophie brought herself to do frequent brainstorming with her cryptographers of rue Blanche. Mostly, they do three-way video conferencing – place de l'Alma, rue Blanche, and Palo Alto – with Anton's Mac logged in on a Palo Alto server, and his camera off. Sophie agreed with the ruse of keeping his camera off after Anton told her, without entering into too many details, that one day he found himself face to face with Nick here in Paris. The sight of Anton's face might trigger Nick's memory of the shifty neighbor he consulted on rue Blanche about the Yellow Vests. And unavoidably, he'd come to the conclusion that of all places in the French capital, it was no coincidence that he crossed paths with Anton Gunzburg – hacker and former Google white hat – in front of the headquarters of the Hosnani Holdings LTD.

On their first video conference, Nick was totally at ease with the news that Anton Gunzburg – his "friend Anton," whose camera was kept eccentrically off – figures now as a special consultant of Sophie's. Nick asked Anton news of Jesus ("Same-o, same-o"), of the mining plants in Iceland ("Same-o, same-o"), then he welcomed him into the team of Mrs. Renault Hosnani's "very innovative project."

Bitcoin and the Ritual of Kyudo Archery

More than anything else, these brainstorming sessions help Anton gauge the gap between his self-taught know-how and the formal instruction the cryptographers on Sophie's payroll got at Stanford. They suffer from the one weak spot: if you show them an egg, all they see is the shell. Anton sees the shell as well, but assumes that if you showed him the whole egg, you meant to call his attention to yolk and white too. It's called survivor's primacy. Suppose we were all starving in the jungle and found an eagle's egg: guess who would've gobbled it up before the rest of the team had properly assessed its status vis-à-vis our collective predicament? That's what hackers do. But beyond that, Anton is no contender with any of these guys. Once you break the shell for them, so they can see the whole picture – shell, yolk, white – they're unstoppable. Just ask them, and they'll come out with algorithm after new algorithm to model the forces that were holding the shell's mineral structure in place before you broke it. Just ask them, and they'll apply some new gene editing technique to the yolk to raise healthier chickens or harvest more nutritional eggs. Just ask them, and they'd even contrive a way to fry yolk and white while keeping the egg hover between the frying pan and the coal fire. Good training is everything.

Back to the video conferencing...

Anton raised the issue of the unreliability of human nature in proof-of-stake. It was taken stock of, discussed at length, broken into smaller pieces, chopped up, and put to rest in no time. Amen.

They are instead devoting much attention to the issue of scalability.

"Time is life." Without fail, Daniel used to sum up his own views on scalability with this phrase, *time is life*. He was among the first to highlight that mainstream usage of the blockchain depends on speed. The blockchain is the latest and most powerful technology of communication among humans, but you can't tell humans, "Keep your communication with one another at a minimum, and make it slow." And yet, that was bitcoin's norm, it still is: like a highway with slow mandatory speed and very high tolls. The faster we communicate with one another, the less time we waste. The less time we waste, the more time we can spend on worthwhile endeavors. Put it another way, faster communication equals a longer and more fulfilling life.

But you need to operate at scale to speed up the operations of the blockchain, and larger scale calls for faster machines. The problem with the human validators of proof-of-stake is that they use domestic-sized, small machines – *slow* machines. Someone from the rue Blanche side of their brainstorming came out with the idea of *supernodes*. Why not have clusters of validators operate in concert with one another, using huge machines? Then economies of scale would be easily attainable, solving the problem that bitcoin hasn't solved yet. One crucial problem remains to be tackled with this idea: an out-of-control supernode might exercise dictatorial powers over the consensus attained by the rest of the blockchain, hence, some regulatory mechanism will have to be deployed within the TEXOR protocol.

That's the state of the art as of now.

CHAPTER TWENTY-ONE

Sophie bucks herself off of Anton and falls backwards onto the bed. "You outdid yourself!" Sophie teases him.

"It's you who outdid yourself!" he replies. He is not lying. To him, each time it's better than last. Each time she seems to find it in herself to be hotter, more intense, and of a steady, fiery docility.

Fiery docility... An expression that wouldn't have made much sense to him till not too long ago.

"At thirty-seven I can't outdo anybody anymore, not even myself," she mocks herself.

Does she say it to force once again out of Anton that she's but a girl? He couldn't say any different anyway, or feel any different.

Their favorite moment in bed comes after daily practice in the kyudojo. They get the elevator straight up to his bedroom: the body ready, the mind empty of its usual detours and convolutions.

Anton wonders if Sophie ever guessed how limited his range of sexual partners was before he met her: two drunk girls in Pittsburgh, that's pretty much it. Or was it the same one girl on a binge that lasted two days? He is not sure.

As a child, he was busy being a prodigy. Besides, children don't have sex, most don't. As a boy, he made love to his IBM PC, followed shortly later by his true love affair, a threesome with an Arduino and a Raspberry Pi board. Then came college life for, well not for that long, make it six to seven months before he dropped out. And while on campus, no sooner did he become partial to drinking girls in Pittsburgh than he discovered their company gave him a bellyache.

From time to time Anton leaves Sophie to her algorithms and goes back to his secret outpost on rue Blanche 38. He renewed the Airbnb contract for the next six months. In there, he has been gathering more and more pieces of spy tech, each less expensive than the next, as though this was his latest hobby. Still, he can't get anything done.

He walks in, doesn't even bother to lock up, puts packages and boxes full of new equipment down on the floor, and then sits down in the armchair in the bedroom, a few feet from the window. He watches Nessim in front of a screen, his fingers typing who knows what on the keyboard, a black cigarette between his lips, and he tells himself that, aside from the Hosnani family's wealth, the banker-monk must have no secret to hide. If Anton was a black hat, he would have cracked Nessim's *Open Sesame* long ago and run away, if not with the proof of the banker-monk's crime, with his gold ingots for sure. Or maybe not even that. Maybe Nessim is really an old-fashioned, Old-World operator, the master of a long progeny of trustworthy intermediaries – devoted, servile, sworn-to-loyalty accountants – and his treasure is safe from hackers like Anton. Be that as it may, some instinct, deep inside Anton, refuses to read the features of an assassin in that defenseless oval face kissed by the sun in the window.

Every time it's the same. It's as though Anton hypnotized himself into a stagnation of willpower, and this paralysis lasts till around noon, when the flutter of Gala's veils steers him away from it. She appears in the bluish haze of Nessim's smoky halo around lunchtime. Her arrival tells Anton it's time to go back home for a snack with Sophie.

Is he giving up on his revenge? Is his state of grace with Sophie a deterrent to the other mission that brought him to Paris?

He makes often a mental note that he must stop pestering Sophie for news about the prospects of her pregnancy. She may get really impatient: "When I'll get pregnant, baby, you'll be the first to know! What do you think?" But the mental note is soon forgotten. He asks again. She gets even more impatient. And he makes another useless mental note.

CHAPTER TWENTY-TWO

It's Saturday, late morning. In a week Anton and Sophie will drive down to Turin in the Bentley.

Sophie kneels down on the sidewalk in front of the Hosnani Holdings LTD to inventory the contents of her handbag. She finds her magnetic ID badge, opens the door, and they take the stairways to the third floor.

Strikingly fancy interiors. Not a soul in sight, being Saturday. Corporate culture, Anton ponders, will always be hampered because its personnel rests on weekends while hackers don't. Merci for that, though: on any regular workday, he would've refused to come meet Nessim in his fortress. Nick may not be much of a physiognomist, but Anton's face on the premises might strike the wrong cluster of synapses: how weird that not long ago Nick met, just across the street, the Parisian look-alike of her boss's consultant from Silicon Valley! It can't he helped, hard-earned or not, the hacker reputation makes one radioactive.

They knock at the door of Nessim's office.

"Come in."

Nessim is sitting at his desk reading a book in a cloud of smoke, a black cigarette hanging from his lips. The desk is totally uncluttered: not a pen, not a sheet of paper or a piece of correspondence on its surface, except for an ashtray full of cigarette butts, his desktop, a weird triangular book with a red cover on the left corner, and the book he's engrossed in. No sooner do they take a few steps forward than he starts reciting, his head down, in a foreign language which to Anton sounds like Mexican. "El universo se compone de un número indefinido, y tal vez infinito, de galerías hexagonales."

Sophie replies robotically, seemingly despite herself. "La distribución de las galerías es invariable." Then she gives a restive shrug.

Nessim raises his eyes on Anton. "Ever read Borges, Anton?" he says without even asking them to take a seat.

"If he writes in that strange tongue, I can't read him."

"He was Argentinian, wrote in Spanish," Nessim replies, pointing at the book in his hands. "It's not too different from the dialect spoken by your Mexicans in Palo Alto, you know." Then he lifts the book and shows Anton a powdery blue cover. "First edition, 1942. With this tiny book published in Buenos Aires, Borges wanted to write an infinite library."

Sophie intervenes in French. Anton can tell from her tone that she's angry. "Nessim, *je t'en prie*..." She takes a seat before the desk and lets her handbag fall heavily on the carpet.

Anton stands.

Nessim isn't done yet. "... a library made up of endless versions of the same few plots..."

"Did he manage it?" Anton asks.

"Manage, what?"

"To write this infinite library?"

Nessim bursts out laughing while he presses his half-smoked cigarette into the ashtray with cruel pleasure.

Anton must have fallen into some trap.

Without a word, Sophie gets up, picks up her bag from the floor, and leaves the room, shaking her red mane like a wild beast.

Beau de Rubempré

Nessim jumps to his feet knocking over the ashtray, catches up with her in the hall and, judging from what Anton overhears, throws himself into earnest apologies. When they come back, Nessim's contrite face tells Anton that the banker-monk may play cat and mouse with him all he wants, still, the lioness in the room will eat him up in one bite. Nessim goes sit back behind his desk after throwing a pained look at the cigarette ash spread on the carpet. Anton take advantage of his stooped posture to look at the windows of his apartment on the other side of the street.

Seen from here, his windows look quite dirty.

The meeting was called by Nessim a few days ago. Its agenda is full of revelation for Anton.

He used to think that the crypto space was the exclusive domain of brilliant coders and cryptographers, starting with Satoshi Nakamoto, the founding father, and moving on to the purists like Daniel (and Anton in his wake), the revisionists who diverted Satoshi's protocol onto dubious tracks, the brilliant idealists like Carlo, to end with the well-kept secret of Sophie's superior brainpower. But things don't stand exactly that way. It turns out that they all – hackers, cryptographers, computer scientists – are low men on the totem pole. Rather than their algorithms and network architectures, what really matters in the day-to-day management of the crypto space are patent rights and regulatory norms. Anton is learning, to his surprise, that Nessim is constantly on the TEXOR frontline, but he grasps close to nothing of the banker-monk's battlefield of choice. To the contrary, Sophie knows all there's to be known of it: it seems its name is corporate law. She must have learned about it as a toddler while riding her tricycle, or making herself a paper hat with the pages of the Wall Street Journal, but her body language tells Anton she would gladly do without hearing about it if she could help it.

This morning she can't.

"It's a lucky strike," Nessim begins, "I didn't incorporate TEXOR in the USA like that acquaintance of yours from Turin did with Futura. According to the Security and Exchange Commission in the States, Futura's tokens ought to have been traded only by accredited investors. They are securities, plain and simple voting shares. Futura muddled through with a heavy fine, but wait for their board of directors' next annual meeting. Futura is a regular American company, and they sold off all of the voting shares. The next board will have to be chaired by the tokens' majority holder. Your friend from Turin might find himself fired on the spot!"

"A Whale bought more than 50% of Futura's tokens," I say.

"Quid erat demonstrandum," Nessim replies.

For once, he used a foreign expression Anton is familiar with. He learned it in his child-prodigy days, from the math teacher.

Now, DRS, the software company headed by Sophie, whose parent company is the TEXOR Foundation, is incorporated in Delaware – same as Futura. Reliable informers leaked to Nessim that the Security and Exchange Commission will soon indict DRS for carrying out an unregistered sale of securities – same as Futura. Nessim's attorneys could easily prove to the regulators that the TEXOR tokens were never sold to American citizens. He and his legal team had taken precautionary measures. But those same reliable informers assured Nessim that the regulators would look favorably on

DRS coming spontaneously forward with a request for auditing.

"One hand washes the other, and…?" he says, addressing Sophie.

Sophie: "And?"

He repeats himself. "One hand washes the other, and…?"

"Nessim, *je t'en prie…*" Sophie replies. "You give me a headache."

"… and both hands wash the face," he says after a ferocious suck on his cigarette. "Sophie, really, you would take the air out of a Zeppelin."

"Back to business, would you mind?" she replies.

So, Nessim explains that all things considered, the best strategy for them is to go for a plea deal, pay a tolerably large fine – "We have cash galore from our initial token sale, that's for sure" – and leave the other financial ramifications of the TEXOR's Foundation out of it. As chief executive officer of DRS, Sophie must make the first move.

"I will," she says. Apparently she sees no alternative to Nessim's action plan.

The next part of their discussion is a tad too legalistic for Anton's taste. He half-listens, deep otherwise in his own thoughts. Nessim deals with plenty of confidential matters in his daily dealings, no doubt about that. *Nessim knows everything, Nessim collects information with the automatism of a robot.* Sophie's words. But it just occurred to Anton that in all the time he spent watching Nessim at work in this office, his fingertips nakedly exposed on his keyboard, the banker-monk was rarely visited by some collaborators, and rarely took a phone call. How does he operate, if his internet persona is totally see-through for a fact? How does he harvest classified information, how does he manage to have it leaked to him by such reliable sources as his SEC informer? How does he communicate with the staff of the Hosnani Holdings LTD? Anton has this faint recollection, from hacking into the giant curved monitor left on his former desk by Nessim, of a site named "Dark Lodge of Malta." Sophie and Nessim are absorbed in legalistic quibbles, so Anton can get away with a bit of Google search on the iPhone. There is a Sovereign Grand Lodge in Malta, but no Dark Lodge. He browses through the Wikipedia entry of this Sovereign Grand Lodge. Apparently, they have a myriad of secret societies in Malta, sources of the most occult know-how. So secretive that they won't even tell you what this know-how is all about, or what's to be used for. Could it be that Nessim's Dark Lodge of Malta is the most secret of them all, totally invisible? What the heck are occult societies anyway?

How did Sophie put it, again? *Eyes that cast a spell on you*, that's it.

Nessim's words cut short Anton's ruminations. "Second and last point on the agenda." This year, he goes on, there occurred a fast and historic change in the rules of the crypto game. "I don't know if you heard of an Aussie named Craig Wright who lives in London and was demonstrably the first bitcoin miner."

"You are telling us that this Craig Wright is Satoshi...?" Sophie asks.

"I never said that."

"Well," she objects, "you said that he was demonstrably the first bitcoin miner. If I put one and one together..."

"Look, Sophie, put one and one together, which makes two, if you feel like it, but not on my time, please," Nessim replies curtly.

"Point taken."

"As I was saying, Wright has been patenting every crypto scheme that can be possibly patented. He started a race that's spreading like oil on water. Downstairs in the DRS offices, the fellows think…"

How does Nessim know what Sophie's collaborators think that she doesn't? They think, it seems, that the idea of the supernode, which the other day we came out with after brainstorming on video conference, could solve for good the dilemma of scaling in proof-of-stake. "But time is of the essence." Nessim is coming to a closure. "You must patent all the math behind the supernode before someone else does. What's more, from now on you must patent every single innovation regarding our mining procedures." First thing first, Sophie ought to start an immediate search to hire a patent attorney or two.

"I will," is Sophie's dry reply. "First thing on Monday."

Of them two, clearly, Nessim is the unchallenged strategist in this course of actions. Anton leaves the meeting under the impression that Sophie's technological dreams would leave too many fronts unguarded without the contributions of a banker in Nessim's league. *He grabbed as much money as he could, using me as an accomplice*, Sophie wrote Anton regarding TEXOR's initial token sale. Nessim certainly did, and on purpose, if Sophie thinks so, but Anton is beginning to wonder if it's not all there, the gap between the man of finance and the scammer: scammers grab the money and run, bankers grab the money and hold on to it by fine-tuning the law? That must be the long and short of it, or Sophie wouldn't have agreed without a fight to all that her detested husband suggested this morning.

"It looks like you'll have to go to Turin by yourself," Sophie comments while Bashir drives them back home. "No way I can be done in time, too many loose ends."

"It's what I feared since Nessim started talking," Anton says.

"Not that I was too eager to meet Margherita on her home turf."

"It's what I feared since she invited you to Turin," he says.

"Nor was I too eager to figure as target for her arrows," she jokes, her right hand reaching out to him. And she adds under her breath, not to be overheard by Bashir, "Even if I wouldn't mind seeing you changed into a satyr again."

… *a satyr?* Does this word mean what Anton thinks it means? He is learning an average of a new word a day, here in Paris.

"If you're referring to those hallucinations of mine I told you about," he admonishes her under his breath, "watch out, I'll be a satyr again in no time if your hand doesn't stop doing what's doing."

"You're telling me!"

"Can I bring Elvis to Turin with me?" he asks.

"No."

CHAPTER TWENTY-THREE

It's the day before Anton's trip to Turin. *Torino*. He came to rue Blanche 38 determined to get something done, but here he is, sunk into the usual armchair in the bedroom, weighed down by the usual fatalism which overruns him whenever he is in sight of the banker-monk. It feels like sorcery. He gets up and walks up and down the room. He leans against the side of the French window just in time to see Gala move forward on the sidewalk in her fluttering green veils. She must have a different plan than usual today because once she's in front of number 21, she keeps going, crosses to Anton's side of the street, and disappears from sight.

Even Gala, the wild beast, is stirred to try something new from time to time. It must be this apartment that takes Anton's mojo away. At home with Sophie he feels alright.

He is ready to sink back into the armchair when he is hit with sudden fright. A moment later he hears the mechanical noise of a doorlock closing on itself. It comes from his door to the stairs. Of course he didn't lock it up, he never bothers. He tries to get his fear in check and forces himself to walk toward the vestibule. And the first thing he sees in there is Gala, wrapped in her green veils, vaporous and a tad blurry, as though Nessim's black cigarette hadn't totally released her ectoplasm yet. She watches the walls and furniture around them with impersonal interest. Then she walks beyond Anton as though she hadn't even noticed his presence. He follows her silently. In the bedroom she takes a disdainful look at the piles of boxes and packages on the floor, touches lightly the tripod with fingers full of golden rings, and giggles when she sees

Bitcoin and the Ritual of Kyudo Archery

Nessim at his desk on the opposite side of the street. She walks into a long hall. Anton never ventured into this section of the apartment yet. It turns out the master bedroom is not the one he has been using as his outpost, there is a larger one. Her face expressionless, Gala looks closely at an olive branch hanging above the double bed. Back in the hall, she opens a French window and the shutters behind it. There is a long narrow balcony running the length of the building, joining separate apartments, and looking on a wide private courtyard. Now Anton follow hers into the bathroom. She nods at the sight of the side-by-side sinks, like she expected to find them here, and gives another giggle. In the kitchen there is a Nespresso machine like the one Anton used at home in Palo Alto. Instinctively, for lack of better things to do, he presses a button and turns it on. Where could the coffee capsules be? It's the first time he sets foot in here too. Gala opens the fridge: a few bottles of mineral water, an open jar of jam, and a dried-up avocado. She grabs a stick of butter from a side compartment, turns toward him, acknowledging at long last his presence in the room, and shows the stick of butter to him without a word. It's true she can't even speak, then? He recognizes the scornful smile on her lips. Then she puts the butter back and shuts the door of the fridge.

Anton follows her back into the vestibule while he hears the wasteful gush of the Nespresso machine he turned stupidly on. She walks to the door, opens it, turns around, and speaks to him in uninflected English, a totally serious expression on her face. "Anton, I think you should know that Nessim knows you are here."

Beau de Rubempré

She turns around again, walks out, and shuts the door behind her. Dumbstruck, he can't take his eyes off the strip of green veil that got stuck between the door and the jamb. He is too stunned by Gala's words to care about the scene flashing in his mind: she's spinning in a whirlwind of smoke, stripping out of the veils that bridle her to the door, till, stark naked, is sucked in by the tip of Nessim's black cigarette. Meanwhile, the door opens back up a crack and an instant later the strip of green veil is gone too.

That leaves just him, plunged into a sea of perplexity.

CHAPTER TWENTY-FOUR

Anton is not used to long distance driving. Most of all, he finds it hard to believe what scatterbrained drivers you cross paths with on French expressways. They take it personally, as though, the moment they stumble upon you, they suddenly recalled some grievance they've been nursing against you since – since another life, you can only guess, or since being on the road in some parallel universe.

He drives for about six hours and spends the rest of the day in Lyon, not far from the Italian border. After he finds himself a hotel downtown, he WhatsApps Sophie. She isn't too hot about Lyon. Lyon is a frequent destination of Nessim, and not just now that he lives in Paris; he made regular visits to the city even at the time he made San Francisco his home.

"All I know of Lyon is that Nessim never misses a visit to the black Madonna in the cathedral and always dines at Pierre Orsi. He used to tell me of it, you know, way back when."

Should Anton drive the Bentley in town or use Uber?

"Uber. If you feel like walking, though, I understand it's a short hike up the hill to the cathedral."

He follows her advice, and later takes a short and pleasant walk uphill in the approaching sunset.

Gala's perfectly uninflected English keeps echoing in his mind while he stands facing a black Madonna in a white cape framed by golden statues. *Nessim knows you are here.*

Here. Is Lyon still here or already there?

The Madonnas in Russian icons are mostly white. Not that Anton has seen that many. This one's black. He wonders what does Nessim find in it.

Beau de Rubempré

At Pierre Orsi's they seat him in a quiet garden full of roses and chirping birds. He gives the waiter an elaborate order. But no sooner does he relax in front of a lobster salad than his brain starts bombarding him again with Gala's voice. *Nessim knows you are here.* He calls back the waiter, cancels his glass of red, and asks for a bottle of their best. The waiter brings him a rosé. Anton has never drunk a rosé before tonight. *Whatever*, he decides: it'll do.

It does. His brain's compulsions leave him finally alone. Alone for the rest of the night, that is, since the local food plus the rosé claim his digestive attentions till dawn. He manages a nap before getting up and start for Turin.

The route Lyon-Turin takes him hardly four hours. A large number of the Italian drivers he came across must have spent quite some time on the roads of that same parallel universe, where he rattled their cage too. He could have handled this leg of the trip even faster, but he paused a couple of times to admire the snowy peaks of the Alps, white from top to bottom against a perfectly blue sky. He was tempted to take some pictures to send to Sophie, but thought better of it: she's seen it all already.

The GPS navigates his Bentley through Turin to the Boston Hotel on Via Massena, where Margherita booked him a room. The hotel doesn't have private parking, and the streets in the neighborhood are lined with tight rows of tiny cars, glued to one another. What's more, there are no-parking signs everywhere. He resigns himself to some exorbitant fines and wedges the Bentley into the first open gap he can find. There must be parking garages somewhere around here. *Whatever.* He takes no comfort in the idea that the fines will be delivered to the address where Nessim registered the car.

The front of the Boston Hotel reminds him of the Hosnani Holding in Paris: it's even cuter. They give him a twin room wallpapered with huge black-and-white illustrations picturing some masked hero wearing a black spandex bodysuit that leaves only his eyes and eyebrows exposed. A brochure on the bedside table explains that it's a comic-strip character named Diabolik, an outlaw with a strict moral code. Anton takes the pillow off one of the two beds to make room for Daniel's bow and his *yazutsu* quiver. The bow is longer than the bed.

He WhatsApps Margherita that he has arrived. She writes back asking him to join them for dinner. "Sorry I forgot," she writes a moment later. "Come at least half an hour earlier and bring bow and arrows!"

Half an hour earlier – around six thirty? He WhatsApp Sophie for advice and she writes, "Show up around eight thirty."

What's dinner time in Italy?

He kills some time wandering around the hotel's neighborhood. He walks a couple of times by the Bentley; there's no parking fine yet. He goes back to his room to check *Google Earth* on the Mac: Carlo and Margherita's address shows a mansion downtown on the left bank of the Po river, not terribly far from here. He is not a real-estate expert, but it's an easy guess that their mansion can't be worth much less than the Villa Baroness Orczy he just bought from Belmondo. On the riverbank opposite their house there's a short pier. He clicks on the repertory photo of a rowing crew docking their shell to the pier.

When it's time to go, he has some problems with the Uber app. At the reception, a young man dressed up like a Wall Street tycoon tells him that in Turin they "uber" with regular taxi cabs. When Anton asks him if here in Turin they "taxi" with regular uber cars, the receptionist doesn't seem to get the joke. Instead, he launches on a long story about the collusion of the ministry of transport with the lobby of passenger-transport companies, facilitated by the recent collision between the ministry of transport with the ministry of the interior. Maybe it's Anton who is not getting the joke this time, but the receptionist's dead serious expression doesn't seem to call for laughter.

A white cab brings him to destination. Margherita welcomes him wearing her kyudo outfit. He won't imagine how happy she is that he came visit in Turin. As she says it, two apple-red spots light up appealingly on her cheeks. She takes him by the hand and walks him into the small room they use for archery.

"Any experience with makiwara?" she asks.

The target, a longish drum of straw, is a mere bow's length away from the shooting platform.

"I never shot so near the target," he replies.

"Well, you and I can't miss, that's for sure. It's the ritual that matters."

Carlo is finishing up his preparation to address tomorrow's conference and won't join them. They spend half an hour in absolute silence and perfect coordination.

CHAPTER TWENTY-FIVE

"Summertime, we live on our terrace from breakfast time to sleep time," Anton hears Margherita say.

Shortly before dinner, under a starry sky on the rooftop terrace, he finally meets Carlo. Carlo is teaching Andreino to shoot arrows from a tiny wooden bow. The arrows are made of some generic wood and end with a rubber suction cup which never sticks to the target, not even when it's Carlo that shoots. Carlo looks like his usual introverted self: they barely exchange a greeting as he stammers a few words, making it sound like he never spoke English before today. His hair is pink now.

The *Google Earth* app is a spoiler of surprises. The view of the river from this terrace is quite spectacular, but Anton saw most of it already on his Mac. On the opposite bank he recognizes the short pier protruding into slowly flowing waters. There are two rowing shells docked to it. It must be a rowing club.

Margherita was talking to Renzo, the second dinner guest: a skinny mathematician Anton's age with red curly hair. When Anton joins them, Margherita introduces Renzo as Anton's roommate at the Boston Hotel. He just arrived from Berlin, where he works in fintech, but is *Torinese*, he claims, born and bred. The two of them get along right away; it feels as though they had known each other in some previous life.

"I left my bag at the hotel on my way here," Renzo tells Anton as they shake hands. "I propped your bow against the wall behind the desk and put the quiver on the desk. I hope it's okay. So, you too shoot the bow, eh?"

"What can you tell me of that cartoon hero, Diabolik, on the wallpaper of our hotel room?" Anton asks.

"My granddad was a collector of those comic strips. Diabolik is a masked outlaw, the sworn enemy of injustice. You know what's the name of his girlfriend? Eva Kant."

"Like the German philosopher?"

Renzo bursts out laughing. "Not if you pronounce *kant* the Italian way, like my granddad used to do." He gives Anton a taste of how that sounds. A most un-pc word. "After all, it's an Italian comic strip. It was created by two sisters from Milan. I think Eva Kant's name was a deliberate pun on what sexual liberation amounted to back then."

"I see," Anton replies. "A short step from philosophy to profanity."

They keep laughing and Renzo does his granddaddy's impersonation once again.

"Poor grandma, she wasn't in on the joke. She complained to him, 'Eva Kant here, Eva Kant there, why's that name always upon your lips?' And of course she pronounced it just like my granddad did, the only way she ever heard it spoken."

Would my father pronounce that German word any better? And he isn't even Italian.

It turns out Renzo is a childhood friend of Margherita and married to Carlo's younger sister. His wife Veronika is in Berlin with their twins.

"Now An-dre-i-no goes down-stairs to grand-dad and grand-ma." Margherita pulls up her son and puts him in Carlo's arms to have him delivered to her parents on the first floor. While they wait for Carlo to come back, she tells Anton that this house has been her family's for several generations.

Bitcoin and the Ritual of Kyudo Archery

"Old money?" he asks, sort of out of turn.

"Let me put it this way," she answers. "My family is as wealthy as Carlo's dirt poor."

Dinner is served, course after course after course, by her parents' cook: Italian dishes on whose formidable flavors Anton's dining companions waste no words. They like it better to debate tiny marginal details – marginal to Anton – like what's the best device to slice a white truffle, what's the best knife to slice a steak diagonally, or what's the stem's best angle to swirl the wine around in the glass. They turn these issues inside out, tackling them from a large variety of supposedly irreconcilable views. Anton does not fail to notice that Carlo is much more tentative in his manners of expression than he used to be in Palo Alto. There's no kinder way to put it: he has become a stutterer.

Anton has never tried any of the red wines they taste through the meal (Renzo calls them *black wines*), but swayed by the conversation, he finds himself sipping from his glass with a sense of awe. He grabs his glass by the stem and grapple with swirling the wine in it, till a red crest overflows the rim and blends with the food in his plate.

Sooner or later in these sorts of conversational situation, he is stricken with panic the moment he becomes self-conscious of his poor contribution to the general merriment. Then he squeezes his brains for some topic of conversation, any topic.

"Carlo, I never had a chance to ask you," he says. "What led you to Robinson's scheme for prediction markets"

Carlo scratches his pink hair for quite some time, then he stutters, "Rob... Rob... Rob..."

"Robinson?" Renzo volunteers.

Beau de Rubempré

Margherita throws her white napkin on the table, staring furiously into her plate. "Carlo, you are not on your usual stage here. This one is Renzo, your brother-in-law. This one is Anton, your kyudo mate in Pal Alto, remember him? I am Margherita, your wife." She lifts her eyes on him. "Would you please, in the name of everything holy, stop faking it like you are our genius-in-residence? Okay, you made our initial token sale, nobody's taking that away from you. Just look at us now. Unless this Crypto Winter ends soon, we're fucked!"

A dismayed expression screws Carlo's face, and he starts talking in a pleading tone, without a trace of his previous stutter. "I just meant to say that Robinson's algorithms gave me the idea that, taking into consideration…"

Margherita cuts him short. "You just meant to say that somehow you cobbled together your Master's degree, we were penniless in Palo Alto, you were unemployed, I paid my babysitter fifty thousand a year, and you rushed headlong into the first idea that came your way!"

Why do I lack the gift for promoting trouble-free chat? Anton asks himself.

Somehow, Renzo's quietly unconcerned attitude reminds him that the logo of Futura is an owl. Renzo starts talking of the recent accomplishments of his two girls as though it were the natural prolongation of what's going on. He is addressing Carlo most of all, who is the twins' uncle. Anton adjusts with some effort to the abrupt change of climate: it looks as though Renzo is well acquainted with this sort of situations. Dwelling on the painless subject of his marvelous twins, Renzo brings a degree of mutual benevolence back to the table. In the initial-token-sale days of Palo Alto, Anton used to think that if Carlo was ever to grow a pair of wings, Margherita would be sure to nip them in the bud. Now that fame and success have pushed Carlo to posture like he is a pink-haired stuttering genius, she can't help demolishing his self-esteem.

Anton's fellow diners are back to the original synergy when Margherita throws herself into a tirade over the *nouveaux riches* of the crypto space.

"*Nouveaux riches?*" Anton say, mimicking her pronunciation. It certainly sounds like French.

"Those with the Lam… those with the Lam… those with the Lam…" Carlo tries to explain.

Renzo spells out the whole phrase. "Those with the Lambo."

They must be speaking Greek now. "The Lambo?" Anton asks.

"The Lamborghini, a luxury sports car made in Italy, is the favorite of the *nouveaux riches*. More expensive than a Ferrari…" Renzo explains.

Anton sneers distractedly as he thinks of Daniel's two red Ferrari. He wonders if Carlo and Margherita were ever aware of how much him and Daniel liked sports cars. he says once more in an enquiring tone, "Yes, but: *nouveaux riches…*?"

"It – means – new – rich – in – French," Margherita tells him, enunciating syllable after syllable in the affected way he saw her speak to Andreino before dinner. "I forgot, I bet you never set foot in France, Anton. It's a stone's throw from here, you know."

He smiles graciously. The libations have magnified the apple-red spots on her cheeks, and Carlo's re-energized stutter doesn't seem to bother her anymore, thanks God. "Indeed," he replies, crossing his fingers in the hope nobody will ask him what airline he flew on from San Francisco.

CHAPTER TWENTY-SIX

On their way back to the hotel, Renzo suggests they take a walk along the river. It's almost midnight, but it's quite crowded on the left bank. they climb down a narrow flight of stairs and end up walking on a large cement pathway on water level. Here and there the crowd of boys and girls is so thick you can hardly move forward. There are dark openings in the wall on their left, which disgorge waiter after waitress carrying food and drinks to the tables spread all around. There are rock and jazz bands trying hard to outplay one another. And plenty of colored lights like an amusement park. Anton's bow and quiver don't go unnoticed.

"This area is called *Murazzi*," Renzo tells Anton as he returns the greetings from a couple of girls sitting at a table. They climb back up to street level, turn left into a huge rectangular square, and walk under the arcade that frames its length.

"Piazza Vittorio," Renzo says, calling Anton's attention to the parallel arcade on the opposite side.

They take the next arcade. Anton has the feeling that Renzo is looking for the right words to justify the recent scene between Carlo and Margherita. He reassures the Italian that he saw plenty of those scenes in California.

Renzo goes into some details. "For some time now, Carlo got into his head that he is a stutterer. He isn't at all, if you ask me."

"Why would he fake it, then?"

"I haven't the foggiest idea. Is he pretending he is an absent-minded genius, as Margherita thinks?" Renzo replies.

"Whatever his reasons, he couldn't have come out with a speedier way to madden Margherita. Margherita is a firm subscriber to clear enunciation. As a child, I'll tell you why in a minute, Margherita hated anybody who didn't enunciate clearly."

Renzo's and Margherita's families were very close, and the two kids grew up together, he goes on. Margherita suffered from a congenital defect in the ear canals. She was born deaf.

"Now I get it!" Anton says. "Her scene tonight reminded me of something. She speaks strange when she's annoyed, alternating high-pitched words and inaudible words. I noticed it in Palo Alto."

"Yes, that's the reason, Margherita learned to speak normally very late. Deafness is a terrible condition for a child. I've seen it up close. We played together all the time that I wasn't away at kindergarten. She couldn't come to kindergarten because of her condition. Later on, she got most of her schooling from that house on the river. Expensive private tutors, you know. She and I played games which to me were spy games, but to her were sort of survival training. I would speak looking at her and she learned how to read my lips. We did it for hours on end. When we were both in the company of adults, I had fun enunciating my words soundlessly, and no one but she knew what I was saying. Later on, I would speak while staring away from her. Even if she could only see me in profile, she learned to read my lips that way too. She wasn't mute at the time, but her speech was hard to grasp."

"You mean, she was cured eventually?

"Only nineteen years ago, in 2000, near the end of high school. Her parents brought her to the Mayo Clinic in Arizona, and there they implanted her with two titanium prostheses. It seems the prostheses vibrate with external sounds and stimulate her inner ear. From then on, Margherita snapped free from her seclusion and started living a normal life: school of engineering, career, wedding, childbearing... I admire her enormously for all that. Not just anyone can overcome such drawbacks. I'm not convinced though that Carlo's crypto project was worth giving up her scientific career."

"What you tell me explain many unexplained things."

"Most of all, it explains why Carlo is a true idiot if he stutters on a whim. In her youth, Margherita could only communicate with people who enunciated words with clarity. It must be sort of a phobia to her. At times I wonder if Carlo can rise to the challenge of his awesome wife. At times his sister Veronica, my wife, wonders too."

"You must give him that Margherita is a domineering girl."

"That, we agree on."

During this conversation, Renzo makes sure Anton notices that, still walking under the same never-ending arcade, they have reached and gone beyond a large square surrounding a castle with real fortified towers: *Piazza Castello*, it's called. They keep advancing under the arcade, deserted now, and pick random topics of conversation which get them better acquainted with each other. Anton tell Renzo of his past as a child prodigy and the passion for computers that brought him to Palo Alto. Renzo tells him of the passion for fintech that brought him to Berlin. Renzo shares with Anton professional secret, on condition that he'll keep it to himself. Since the start of Crypto Winter, he says, most of Futura's FTR tokens are traded daily on the crypto exchanges. There're close to no hodlers left, only dogged traders.

"I own a good stash of Futura's tokens," Anton says.

"Me some."

They leave the arcade and keep going for another while, till Renzo shows Anton with a smile the neon sign of the Boston Hotel.

They are too tired to keep talking in the room. On a single walk through Turin, Anton feels he has used up a month's supply of words. "I'm dead tired," he says, collapsing into bed.

"Such luck!" Renzo replies. "We sleep under the watchful eye of the masked avenger, enemy of evildoers!"

CHAPTER TWENTY-SEVEN

Anton wakes up much too early, troubled by an obscure sense of foreboding. He can't stand his bed anymore. The hotel's restaurant won't be open this early. He is not even hungry anyway. He looks out from the window: the street, the cars lined up along it, the shutters hiding all windows, everything looks dark and lethargic. He gets stealthily dressed, leaves the room, goes downstairs – the reception is unstaffed at this time of night – and walks out into the street. He can't think of a single reason for this foreboding squeezing his entrails. Too much wine tasting last night? Too much rosé the night before? Yet, he hasn't got the slightest headache. He'll go look for a café already open, or *still* open, even if he is sure it's a waste of time. Besides, just the thought of an espresso brings a wave of acidity to his mouth. He can't recall the last time he woke up in this dark mood; maybe once or twice in Pittsburgh, but on those occasions it would've been caused by a plain, super-hangover. He wishes he was in Paris. It was a stupid mistake to come here by himself. It's too early to WhatsApp Sophie.

Right now, he could be in place de l'Alma, asleep side by side with her. Upon awakening, he would leave her to her federal auditing business and patent filing business, and tackle his own mission on rue Blanche 38 with a will. So far, in the apartment of rue Blanche, he has kept himself from trying hard on the pretext that he couldn't see the point of it anymore. He has pushed his mission on the back burner, and even called into question his own certainty about the identity of Daniel's attacker. This thought, the thought of Daniel's attacker, makes him dizzy: it's as though a blood-red membrane poured down from his eyelids and blinded his eyesight to the street around him. He comes to himself, but now he has before his eyes the scene of Daniel betraying the secret of his Dublin map to Nessim, while Nessim recites from the Latin of Saint Augustine and shows Daniel a naked odalisque in his iPhone.

It's barely starting to get light.

He walks through a pedestrian area, its streets lined with stately mansions that must go back to when Turin was the Capital city of the Italian kingdom, and he finds myself facing the School of Engineering. *Should I go back to school?* he wonders against his better judgment, while trying to decipher some political posters near the gate. This is a question he asks himself in the dark moments, and each time he regrets doing so. As far as coding and hacking go, he is far beyond many doctoral candidates, including that Nick who, out of their Palo Alto comfort zone, he is as good as invisible to. Yet, he could never enroll in a PhD program till he gets his bachelor's degree. And undergrad programs are childish for someone like him. So, he is stuck in the golden limbo bestowed on him by a decade of generous gifts from Daniel. His lucrative minority stake in the mining plants in Iceland, his broad stashes of cryptocurrencies: he controls sizable assets and revenues that nobody but he knows about fully, and that he would be hard put to justify in the eyes of the tax authorities. He handles a huge payroll in Iceland, paid out in the large amounts of US dollars that he trades monthly on crypto exchanges. From time to time he loses track of his checking, credit, and debit accounts, but anything he need he buys cash online, inclusive of the expensive spying toys he has been hoarding up in the

Bitcoin and the Ritual of Kyudo Archery

apartment of rue Blanche. As to saving accounts, treasuries, or securities, why waste his time on such small-time instruments? There's no escaping it: he belongs in the ranks of Margherita's *nouveaux riches*.

In spite of her upper-class family, Margherita has no qualms about asking him to share a hotel room with another conference attendee. Maybe she offered single rooms in better hotels to her more important guests? What face would she make if someone told her that a few taps on Anton's Mac's trackpad could paint this Crypto Winter totally pink for her – or the darkest black, if he felt like it?

Every time he asks himself the question of dark moments: *Should I go back to school*, he ends up picturing a world run by bean counters.

When he gets back to the hotel, Renzo is already gone. After a quick shower, he skips breakfast, gets a cab, and asks the driver to bring him to Lingotto, the location of the conference venue. Not even the sight of this colossal, post-industrial venue helps him shake off the sense of foreboding which weighs him down. At the main gate he finds Renzo, wearing a t-shirt emblazoned with Futura's stylized owl, who helps the Futura's personnel direct attendees, speakers, and exhibitors. Renzo gives him a warmer welcome than he can reciprocate, and ties around his wrist an attendee's blue plastic band. If Anton feels like it, Renzo says, he is welcome to put on the owl-emblazoned t-shirt too. In his place he wouldn't, though: he missed orientation, so, too many attendees would seek him out to ask information I'd be unable to provide. There is a limited number of brochures of the conference's complete program, but Renzo slips one out of the reception's package and gives it to him.

What he ought to do now is clear enough: get into an elevator to the top floor of Lingotto.

Renzo just told him that the testing circuit on the top floor is quite a sight. There's time enough to go up there and back before Carlo gives his keynote address. About half a century ago, Lingotto was a car-making factory with a pioneering assembly line: the workers took hold of basic raw materials on the first floor and delivered a finished car on top of the building, ready to be tested by professional pilots on the elliptical circuit.

But Anton lacks the resolve to follow Renzo's lead. Instead he drags himself to the main conference room, still deserted, and collapses onto the first chair at hand. He is unrecognizable to himself. He feels purposeless, rancorous toward the whole world (Renzo's pleasantries gave him such a hard time!), and is still struggling with the same unexplainable sense of foreboding. Is he being told something about something? By what, by whom? Is it about some impending danger?

He has to get up on his feet a thousand times to allow the incoming people to reach their seats in the long row of chairs to his right. Time after time, the friendly exchange feels ludicrous to him. Time after time, it feels as though an underhand, accusing glare was thrown at him: why doesn't he shift himself to a center-row seat already and stops making a nuisance of himself? Nothing doing. He stays where he is, his eyes on his feet – stand up, sit down, stand up, sit down – till a roaring applause tells him that Carlo has come up on stage. He lifts his eyes: after a few false starts, a tad of stuttering, and some serious scratching of his pink hair, Carlo welcomes the members of Futura's ecosystem and kicks off the annual conference.

Anton takes a look at his brochure. The names of several crypto celebrities are listed among the speakers. He recognizes the logos of the crypto companies that have their stands at this venue. Almost all of them are information technology companies born after April 24, 2017, the day when Futura's initial token sale turned the tables on conventional capital harvesting.

For a while after Futura's initial token sale, Anton had trailed all subsequent initial token sales, which came one after another at mind-boggling pace. Carlo's success had started a never-to-be-repeated novelty, or so it felt like to the contributors to those other initial token sales. He used to browse their chats on specialized chatrooms: they saw themselves as an army of dwarfs imposing their will on the giants of venture capital. It was pure FOMO, and it gave rise to a myriad of over-funded crypto companies, most of them listed here on his brochure – some of them boasting, at the time of the initial token sale, no more than a white paper and a few dozen lines of code.

Daniel's favorite image for what the future had in store for those enthusiastic dwarfs of investment capital was a deflated soufflé.

The speakers who succeed one another on stage are the front men of those same crypto companies. Anton starts feeling restless as he tries unsuccessfully to grasp what they're talking about. He switches from seat to seat till he has bothered so many people sitting in his row that he has to move to the next row, where he keeps doing more of the same. He rushes out of the room to the concession stand for some food, but once he is facing the barista, all that comes to mind is the word *espresso*. So, that's what he feeds himself. He comes back to the main conference room, takes a discreet corner seat, but must get immediately up to climb the stairs down to the toilets. As he does so, he has this vague recollection that no longer than a quarter of an hour ago he was climbing these stairs back up to the main room. Did he? He goes back to his corner seat. He tries to focus on the equations on the screen behind the speaker. That's better: they start making sense… But now the next speaker is talking of a different subject altogether, yet, aren't those the same equations? There must be some very bad speakers among Futura's guests, he tells myself. The brochure mentions a smaller stage in the venue: why doesn't he just switch to there? They must've kept all the good speakers to themselves in that more intimate room. He rushes out and reaches the concession stand. There is something weird to the face of the barista: the moment he gives Anton that inquisitive look of his, he can't help uttering the word *espresso*. This makes two on an empty stomach. As he sips his dark poison, Anton does a reconnaissance of the path between the concession stand and the entrance to the smaller stage: it's spread with groups of people chatting with one another, eating sandwiches and licking ice creams. He would have to zig-zag between them, no way he would make it to his destination without being tackled down by some eager conversationalist.

There's one thing to this conference he is absolutely sure about: all the attendees have better haircuts than him.

Bitcoin and the Ritual of Kyudo Archery

Lost in thought, Anton takes a glance at the barista. The barista glances back at him and Anton hears his voice say *espresso*. The cup he holds in his hand is empty anyway.

This brings the count to three.

All those guys chatting in small groups, it's clear, they're all well acquainted with one another. They may have come from New York, London, Milan, nonetheless they have been at some point in life employees of the same company, alumni of the same college, writers of the same white papers, foodies on the same restaurant scene. And then some of them are just celebrities, like Carlo.

Anton senses his brain is luring him into some sort of trap.

Some of those others are stellar PhDs turned crypto advocates, like Margherita. Some are highly regarded financial mathematicians, like Renzo.

And then there's him: the *nouveau riche*. Irrelevant, invisible, sentenced to his golden limbo of anonymity. Whom not a soul in this ecosystem of Carlos' invention would give the light of day to.

Thanks, brain. I fell into it, didn't I?

He wonders where did everybody get those sandwiches? The poisonous black pitch in his stomach would even welcome a vanilla ice cream, he muses; he dumps compulsively a bag of sugar into his fourth espresso.

He walks back to main stage. Takes a corner seat.

Now he dozes off, his chin on his chest, and when he opens his eyes again, the speaker on stage has changed, but he would swear he is speaking the same exact words that his predecessor put Anton to sleep with. He checks his brochure.

"Infrastructure is the same for all of us," the speaker just said.

It's even written here on the brochure, black on white. *Infrastructure is what it is.* Futura found itself over-funded by contributors who expected it would create a prediction market. But prediction markets are illegal in the States, unless you're licensed to sell gambling services. And Futura is incorporated in Delaware. Hence, waiting for better times, Futura keeps busy creating infrastructure, namely, a wallet where you can hold your Futura tokens and an exchange where you can trade your Futura tokens with the tokens of the other companies in the ecosystem. The same applies to those other companies: most of them over-funded by their initial token sale, most of them stuck with an impossible-to-realize project, most of them killing time by creating their own wallet and their own exchange. The beauty of it all is the comparative advantage bestowed on them by over-funding. Why compete with one another when profit is not a priority? They can trade business secrets instead, technologies even – that's why they meet at conferences like this one in Turin – and work together inside an echo-chamber where everyone is a clone of everyone else.

I've had enough. I go back to Paris.

Anton looks around to take leave of Margherita and let her know there'll be an extra bed tonight at the Boston Hotel. He catches a glimpse of her apple-red cheeks on first row, on the opposite side of the room. She must have sensed his eyes on her because she turns her head his way. She smiles. He makes an effort to smile back. His lips are dry. Instinctively, he enunciates soundlessly, "I need to talk to you. Right now, if you can." She looks down to type into her iPhone and WhatsApps him: "Right now? Is it urgent?" He raises his eyes from the screen trying to feign one more smile. But as he does it, a blood-red membrane pours down from his eyelids and blinds his eyesight to what's around him. Just like this morning on his way to the School of Engineering. A red liquid screen is all he sees. It shields him from something, something that's on the other side of it. The noise it makes is familiar though, just so much louder than normal: *lub-DUB, lub-DUB, lub-DUB*. It's as though his own heart was pumping and pumping right up there, against his pupils. He sees moving pictures on that red screen: Daniel betrays his secret to Nessim, Nessim recites words from Saint Augustine, Daniel writes on his red Moleskine that Margherita watches from the couch. *Watch out your lips!* Anton hears himself scream. Too late. The screen gives way and red-hot blood rushes down to fill up his lungs. He is drowning in liquid hate.

The red screen has faded away. Anton is back in the conference room. Did he really scream? It looks as though he did not: nobody is staring at him. His eyes are still in Margherita's eyes. Hers in his. How long did his breakdown last? How long have they stared at each other like this? Margherita isn't smiling anymore and the apple-red spots on her cheeks are gone. Her face is the color of ash. She stares at Anton with an enraged expression that, he realizes, is the mirror image of his own. He sees her get up and walk toward a beefy guy standing by the wall. It's the first time he is noticing that strange character, so out of place in this world of geeks: how many times do they break your nose before it takes on that truffle-like shape? Even if Margherita is a tall woman, the truffle-nosed guy bends down to put his ear near her lips. She whispers and he nods. Margherita looks down into her iPhone and WhatsApps to Anton: "At the party after the conference. My office."

He is still staring at her. It's the insolence of his anguish that moves his lips. "See you there," they mouth.

By now the barista treats Anton like an old buddy, even if the only word they trade in their lingua franca is *espresso*. A few more of his espressos get Anton through the next several speakers and the few mumbled words by which Carlo adjourns the meeting until tomorrow, extending a collective invitation to tonight's party at Futura's headquarters. Shortly later, Anton is traveling on a minuscule German car driven by Nadia, Futura's content writer. Renzo is on the back seat by his side. Anton does his best to show some interest in Renzo's comments to today's presentations. Luckily, Nadia has something of her own to argue with Renzo. Anton keeps his mouth shut.

They are approaching their destination when Renzo jokes with Anton, "You remind me of Steve Jobs, Anton. Black sneakers, black jeans, black t-shirt, black socks even… Ever considered dyeing your hair black too?"

"Jobs' jeans were blue, like in *blue jeans*" Anton reply, surlier than he meant to sound.

All he needs now is that they take his outfit for a costume, like one of those pathetic black hats!

The party is in full swing when they get there. Plenty of food, drinks, waiters and waitresses in black uniform. Anton can't help worrying that everybody will be comparing his black uniform with the waiters'. Plenty of live music too. Renzo grabs two plates loaded with exotic bites and two glasses filled with a gray liquid with a plastic straw in it. He puts one plate and one glass in Anton's hands, and guides him in front of a sunny window, away from the crowd, where he's all but ready to start an in-depth discussion on the future of the blockchain. Again, Anton does his best to show himself interested in what Renzo has to say.

What's my move?

Anton brings a tasty-looking pyramid to his mouth and his lips take to salivating wildly. He regurgitates some undefined acid while sweat runs down the sides of his head. He spits the unchewed bite into his hand and asks Renzo to help him find a restroom. "You are as white as a sheet," Renzo says, looking worried. He takes Anton by the arm and elbows their way through the festive crowd. There is a line of young women at the door. Renzo jumps the line altogether without a word, pretends not to hear their rising voices behind them, and when the door opens, he pushes Anton fast inside. Anton sees him turn around to face the music.

Renzo, my new-found friend. Am so sorry.

Anton tries to vomit but it only makes things worse. He washes his hands and face with cold water, which helps a little. He pees. He washes his hands again, staring at himself in the mirror. He can feel his heart pump, *lub-dub, lub-dub, lub-dub*. He can't hear his brain think, though. *Anybody's home?* Not a sign of life in there. He is aware of what he is supposed to think: *Go home, Anton, just go home.* But his brain is out of order, just can't think it. Or won't.

He speaks to himself in the mirror: "Now or never," and walks out of the restroom, thankful that Renzo is not behind the door waiting for him.

Beau de Rubempré

The offices of the Futura's personnel have glass walls and glass doors, all except Margherita's, evidently. Someone points him toward it. On the wooden door there is her nameplate. He walks in without knocking. She's sitting behind a large, old-fashioned desk. The room is in semidarkness: heavy curtains keep the sunlight away. On the wall to her right Anton makes out the black and yellow circles of a toy target, same as the one which Carlo and Andreino shot at last night. Tottering on shaky legs, he crosses the room to a chair facing the desk, then takes a seat before she asks him to. *Time to go for the jugular*: the effort this thought takes him burns out what's left of his mental energy.

He points a sarcastic finger at the black-and-yellow target. "A mini-makiwara for Andreino?" He can't do better than that, it seems.

No sooner does he utters these words than a hand as large as a baseball glove springs up before his eyes. The beefy guy he saw talk with Margherita at Lingotto is standing by his right side. Anton had all but forgotten about him. He cranes up his neck to look at the guy's face. That truffle of a nose…

"Anton, this is Chiacchiera. Chiacchiera, this is Anton."

Ludicrous as it is, here they are, nodding at each other like two gentlemen.

"Chiacchiera is a man of few words, Anton. Hence his nickname. It occurred to him they might have put it into your head to record our conversation on the iPhone."

"Why should they?" Anton replies in anger. "Who are *they*?" *Why didn't I think of it?*

"In fact, we have so little left to tell each other," she says.

Bitcoin and the Ritual of Kyudo Archery

Chiacchiera's knobby fingers make an impatient come-on gesture in front of Anton's face. He takes the iPhone from his pocket and hands it to him. Margherita says something in Italian. Chiacchiera grabs Anton's hair as though he were going to scalp him and pulls backward till Anton is staring at the ceiling. Margherita speaks in English: "Allow Chiacchiera to borrow your face a minute." Chiacchiera places Anton's iPhone's screen in front of him, face-recognition unlocks it, and he hands it to Margherita after pushing Anton's head back forward.

She swipes a finger up and down and sideways on his iPhone while Chiacchiera comes back to his right side. Then she puts the iPhone face down on her desk. At that moment they hear his WhatsApp's ringtone.

"Don't be afraid, I won't read it!" Margherita says. "It's not everybody that can be a snoop."

What Anton wouldn't give for some punch in his reply! "A mini-makiwara, huh?" he says again with a snigger, pointing his chin at the target to her right.

Is that all I've got?

Margherita too must find Anton's irresolution hard to bear. She gives him a long sullen look with the dismissive face she had often on in Palo Alto when she rebuked Carlo for something. An inner debate seems to be raging in her head. Then she comes to a sudden conclusion, bends down in her chair, opens a lower drawer in her desk, and when she straightens up again, she's holding in her hand what looks like an electric drill. She points it at the black-and-yellow target, clicks the trigger, and *plop, plop, plop*, three nails in a row make a cluster on the target. Anton's lethargic brain coughs up the picture of Daniel in a pool of blood on the floor of his Palo Alto apartment. His nostrils smell Jesus's stinky sweat. In some other life, ages ago, he was filled with red-hot hate for the woman in front of him. When he looks away from the target, he finds the round black eye of the nail gun staring at him. From this close, a couple of nails could make some real damage. A wave of sweat rolls down his back.

He feels so sick and nauseous that even his hair hurts. Right, Chiacchiera's pull on his scalp must be in it too.

He may just as well throw a Hail Mary, come what may. "You didn't wring a single passphrase out of Daniel. This morning one bitcoin was worth eight thousand four hundred dollars, and there you are, still frightened by the Crypto Winter. Much good it did you, stealing his Mac."

"What do you know about it, you bum!" she screams. "You've never really belonged to the crypto community anyway. A sleazy stowaway, that's what you are. I'm up to my neck in this muck! Think I didn't know it? You were Daniel's kept man. You don't know *a fuck* of crypto, if you want my honest opinion."

Anton opens his mouth twice but thinks better of it and shuts it back both times. His brain is not up to this shouting game.

Truth is the safest bet when your brain can't think. "I'm knee-deep in it too," he says. "And that's thanks to you. But it isn't mud, Margherita. It's blood. Daniel's."

She crosses her eyes and speaks sideways, as though she was addressing Chiacchiera instead of Anton. "Daniel didn't get it, did he? You don't either, Anton. Why are we in crypto? Crypto is anonymity, crypto is above the law, crypto is above the state.

Bitcoin and the Ritual of Kyudo Archery

I thought it would be obvious to everybody by now: code is law. I did my best, Chiacchiera is my witness, to talk Daniel into our true calling. And you know what he tried to sell me into?" The pitch of her voice jumps up and down between octaves. "Of all things, he was giving me ethical coding. Can you believe it? Like I worried about the ethics of particles when I split them open at SLAC! Nature too has laws and my job was to break them. Give me a band of real crypto operators like Chiacchiera and me, a fulcrum like I'll turn Futura into, and I'll lift you the world!"

"What does Carlo..."

She cuts Anton short. "Carlo is our figurehead. He does it well, poor thing."

She gestures to Chiacchiera to come closer and hands him Anton's iPhone. Anton is under the impression that Chiacchiera's knobby fingers rest a second too long on hers. Chiacchiera comes back to his side and hands him the iPhone back. *Just like that? What now?* Anton waits for their next move. Margherita gives him again the long silent look of her dismissive face, an amused smile on her lips. Then she loses interest and makes a get-off-my-face gesture with the nail gun in her hand. Anton screws his eyes questioningly. She repeats her gesture, more flippant this time.

We are done?

To lift himself up from the chair, Anton needs to push with both arms. He walks around the chair from the opposite side to where Chiacchiera stands, then drags his legs, heavy like lead, to the door. He feels a harsh imaginary pain in the back of his head, where in a minute Margherita's nail will bore into the bone of the skull. Did Daniel turned his back on her this way, after standing up to their coercions? Doesn't she know that within Anton's skull hides an *Open Sesame* too? Anton has now touched the doorknob with his hand and his head is still whole. As he turns the knob, the picture of a different Anton flashes before his eyes. Black from head to foot like Diabolik, he turns around and gets the final say: "BITCOIN WAS INVENTED TO MAKE ESTABLISHED ORDER FAIR AND JUST. CODE IS LAW, MY ASS!" But no, that's not him talking. He, Anton, is opening the narrowest crack to slip through the door and his hand shakes horribly as he does it. He crawls out, clumsy like some drunken rat. When he pulls the door shut – *boom* – the tip of a nail pierces through the wood.

The party in the Futura headquarters keeps going but to him it feels as though they turned off the soundtrack. He sees a hand pluck the strings of a bass, a waitress offers him a whole trail of polyhedral bites, everybody's mouth is busy talking, chewing, drinking, and singing, and when a stranger walks on his foot, he doesn't hear himself groan: it's a silent movie. He walks unscathed through the silence – *am I truly invisible?* – and a moment later he is boarding a cab outside. As they drive toward the hotel, he checks the message he got on WhatsApp while he was in Margherita's office. It's from Sophie, it says: *st positif.* He blows his cheeks out and then releases the air in a fit on impatience. He does it once again just to listen to the noise he makes, his short-lived deafness all but gone. *You didn't pick the right time for riddles, Sophie.* His tongue sticks to the palate; his mouth feels as dry as a bone.

And now he is in his hotel room, mocked by the sardonic grimace of Diabolik.

Bitcoin and the Ritual of Kyudo Archery

He ordered some plain food and this time it goes down right. He gulps glass after glass of mineral water. Then he puts on his black hoodie on a clean t-shirt, grabs his backpack, bow and arrows, leaves his key card at the reception, and walks to the Bentley.

Renzo, my new-found friend. Yesli tol'ko… if only…

There are several parking fines under the wipers. He rolls them into a ball and throws them on the sidewalk.

CHAPTER TWENTY-EIGHT

I'm a creep, I'm a weirdo. What the hell am I doing here? I don't belong here.

He has been sitting in the Bentley for quite some time, waiting for it to get real dark. The Bentley is parked on the right side of a small alley leading into the avenue which runs along the river. The top is up, the radio tuned in to a vintage rock station. He has a partial view of the entrance to the rowing club which faces the terrace of Margherita's mansion.

He guessed right: the rowing club shuts down at sunset.

Time to get moving.

He turns off the radio, silences his iPhone, lowers the hood on his face. Holding the unstrung bow in one hand and the arrows against his chest under the black hoodie, he waits for a lull in traffic and jaywalks across the avenue. Some of the houses along the avenue have windows looking on the river, but there is nothing to be seen, except for a moving black target carrying a lopsided stick. He plunges into the dense vegetation of trees and bushes surrounding the right bank.

The front gate of the rowing club is a length of chicken wire fence hinged on a metal stake. It's secured by a large padlock at the height of his head. All he needs to do is push against its lower edge, it bends at will. He throws bow and arrows in the dirt beyond the gap, then squeezes himself in. He has to grope for his bearings in all this darkness. He can't turn on the Apple watch's torch, it could be seen from the opposite bank. Little by little, his eyes adjust to the darkness. He moves forward till he is a few steps away from the two rowing shells docked to the pier. He strings the bow and then sits down on the cement

Bitcoin and the Ritual of Kyudo Archery

floor. He keeps the bow upright, its bottom nock resting on the cement floor, to prevent the bowstring from sponging up the river dew.

Carlo and Margherita aren't back from the party yet. On their dark terrace there shines only the light of a small sconce. Two windows downstairs are lighted by a bluish glare: Andreino watching TV with his grandparents. Far to the right, Anton can see the bright lights of the Murazzi, but the silence around here is absolute, broken only by cricket chirping. Tall apartment buildings scattered with lighted windows tower beyond and above Margherita's mansion. The surface of the river is crossed by quivering strips of light, white and yellow. They seem to converge on him.

He stands up and takes the shooting position, his left shoulder pointed at the wall sconce shining in the dark. He notches the arrow and pulls back the bowstring. He must stop right away to lower the bow and wipe sweat off his eyes. Never mind the heat, he won't pull the black hood off his face. He takes the shooting position all over again. This is new territory for him. Faced with a similar ordeal, five centuries ago, the unbeatable Wasa Daihachiro would've had, say, two chances out of three of hitting the target? How many does Anton have? In the kyudojo, the arrow flies horizontal to the ground, but at this distance he must shoot a parabolic trajectory, which he has never done before. Besides, he is on the water's level, and the target is higher up. And lastly, between him and his target there will be the brick railing. Margherita is tall, but even if she'll stand by the railing, more than half of her body will be shielded by it. Not the head though… He wishes he could test his aim, shoot an arrow at that bright sconce. And screw the element of surprise in the process... No, he can't afford that.

I have one chance out of ten to hit my mark in one try, he mulls as he kneels back down on the cement floor, wiping the sweat off his eyes again. Nine chances out of ten, that is, of screwing it all up. He feels stomach cramps like he hasn't felt since the days of his binges in Pittsburgh. There is also an unfamiliar pain in his lower back. Daniel was right, kyudo archers are not Samurai: pure-bred specimens, nice to watch in competition, sure, but they suck at the arts of war.

He counts to three. One: *calm*. Two: *elegance*. Three: *flow*.

He feels the metal of the arrowhead. *It looks like it could break through a wall*: words of his friend the policeman back in Palo Alto. Tonight, it's through a human skull this arrow must break through. Soon he'll find out if he has it in him.

One chance out of twenty?

Just as the top-floor windows of Margherita's house light up, Anton's Apple watch vibrates against his wrist. It's Sophie calling from Paris. It must be some emergency; he can't recall the last time she used the iPhone to call him. He presses the green button and brings the watch close to his lips.

"Hi," he whispers softly.

"I don't hear you! I don't hear you! Hallo? Do you hear me? Hallo?" she says.

He tries to whisper less softly. "Hi. Can you hear me?"

"Yes. Now I hear you."

"Here I am."

"Did you get my WhatsApp?"

"Yes, I did," he whispers, choking back the guilty feeling for the snort that was his response to it. "I got it, but didn't get it."

"Don't act stupid, please," she says. "There was nothing to get."

He has taken the iPhone from his pocket. He is looking at the WhatsApp screen as he shields its light from the opposite bank. "Your *s-t-positif* sounds like Turkish to me," he whispers. "What does it mean?"

"How about '*test positif*'?"

"*Test positif*," he mimics her voice. "Something tells me it means *positive test* in our lingua franca? You threw away a t and an e. A case of fat thumb syndrome?"

"As you like it."

Silence.

"So?" he whispers.

More silence. At last she bursts out, "You kept asking and asking! Now that it's for real, you play it cool?"

His peripheral vision tells him the roof terrace on the opposite bank is brightly lit now. Meanwhile, an even brighter window opens wide in his skull. "You mean to tell me…"

"It's what I wrote you hours ago. It's what I keep telling you since you started mumbling into that phone of yours."

"It's my watch." Now he is cruel just to be kinder in a minute.

"Look, Anton. We both know what *positive test* mean, right? POSITIVE TEST, okay?"

He surrenders to the joy. "I can't believe it, Sophie. It really happened!"

"You'd better believe it. Happy?"

"Am I *fucking* happy? You need to ask?" He is just too exhausted, his happiness calls for profanity. "You are my Eva Kant!" He mimics the Italian accent of Renzo's grandad.

"Are you reading Charles Bukowski these days?"

Renzo grandma didn't study literature at Wycombe Abbey, that's a fact.

"I never heard of this Bukowski, but I know Diabolik and his girlfriend Eva Kant."

"One of these days I'll tell you of Bukowski, he was a mailman. But I never heard of your Diabolik or that deplorably surnamed Eva girl. If you are done with acting stupid, I have a question for you: when do you come back home?"

"Now."

"What do you mean, *now*?"

"I mean that I'm on my way to Paris."

"What about the conference?"

"What conference are you talking about?"

"You are the boss, Diabolik."

He is already back at the gate of the rowing club. He turns around. Margherita is leaning on the brick railing of her terrace, her back to him, speaking into her iPhone. The phone's screen shines by the side of her face: the perfect target. The pain in his stomach and lower back is gone. Four catlike jumps stand between him and the docking pier. The width of the river stands between the metal tip of his arrow and that shining screen. The iPhone flies away from her hand and Margherita turns around to face the river. This fantasy brings to his face the same sardonic grimace that seemed to mock at him from the wallpaper of his hotel room, a few hours ago. He laughs a roaring laughter as he gets rid of his hood. He pushes his hands against the chicken wire, bends down, and squeezes himself out of the gate. When he straightens himself out, he feels as though his eyes crossed Margherita's, for hardly an instant. She must have heard him laughing because her iPhone's torch is on now and she is scouring the bank underneath her terrace.

CHAPTER TWENTY-NINE

Rue du Massacre. Anton is in Chartres, rue du Massacre, about seventy miles from Paris according to his GPS. He is in the dark as what massacre in French history they dedicated this street to. Did it happen here under his feet? Was there a day, back when, that the watercourse in front of him was a river of blood? Last night Anton went a small step away from shedding Margherita's blood. He was acting under cover of the night, or so he wanted to believe. In all likelihood, the conjurors in Chartres acted under cover of the night as well. Not that here, whatever the goals and means, night or day would have made much of a difference: Anton is surmising that most bloodsheds follow an elementary algorithm. They turn *historic*, a plaque on a street corner, if the conjurors have history on their side. Otherwise they lead to the gallows.

If he had fractured Margherita' skull with his arrow, last night, his fate would soon be sealed. Forget the night cover. Forget historic deliverance. Private revenge is expensive.

He leans on the brick railing that runs alongside the watercourse. On the opposite bank are the ruins – maybe it's not ruins, just a crumbling side wall – of a church that must have grown out of layers from different epochs. The weather turned ugly as he wasted the afternoon napping in a small hotel downtown. They say that sleep brings counsel. Indeed, he opened his eyes with a smile on his lips. But shortly later he was prey again to the oppressive feelings that got ahold of him yesterday morning in Turin. He lived all over again his brush with Margherita: sick like a dog, at Futura's party, he had thrown himself into the deep end with no plan but a blind thirst for vengeance. He hears again his sarcastic laughter last night, the nightly avenger renouncing his ambush on the bank of the Po river, but it sounds like the feeble titter of a procrastinator.

A swan skims across the water before him, followed by a procession of cygnets, closed by a duckling. The swan's feathers reflect the undifferentiated gray of the sky, and the cygnets look even grayer, as though they were undernourished, while the duckling is bright yellow from beak to tail and has a bulging breast. Are they all from the same brood? Did the duckling join the procession for lack of better options? Are the cygnets aware that there is a stranger in their midst? As to the duckling: what does it feel like to him – or, fifty-fifty, to her – to be a misfit in their company?

Anton hears in his mind the faraway echo of Bashir's voice. *I'm a creep, I'm a weirdo. What the hell am I doing here? I don't belong here.*

He counts the procession on his fingers: *one, two, three, four...* There are six birdies, seven counting the duckling.

He keeps counting on his fingers. That's why he stopped over here in Chartres, after all: to count. But first, he must unlock the iPhone and check the exchange rates of Futura's FTR tokens against the other cryptocurrencies in his portfolio: bitcoin, ethereum, zcash, and ripple.

Okay. Done.

He lists on his thumb how many Futura tokens he can buy with his bitcoin balance, on his index finger how many Futura tokens he can buy with his ethereum balance, on the middle finger how many Futura tokens he can buy with his zcash balance, and on the ring finger how many Futura tokens he can buy with his ripple balance. That's the entirety of his crypto portfolio. It all adds up. Private revenge is expensive in more ways than one.

He WhatsApps Sophie: "I'm in Chartres."

"What are you doing in Chartres?"

"I was tired. It was a mistake to set off at night."

"When do you plan to get home?"

"Tomorrow morning. Tonight."

"Which is which?"

"I'm not sure yet."

"I'll see you when I'll see you. We are waiting for you!"

… *we. The three of us?*

The hotel's receptionist has suggested a restaurant downtown, the *Pilgrim's Lodge*, owned, she said, by a cosmopolitan woman who serves exotic dishes. Not the best of recommendations, but he is not in the mood for finding himself a better alternative. He walks into a sort of witch's hovel, dark, deserted, and encumbered with gewgaws galore. The old lady owner is bent in two with age, chatty beyond redemption, and totally bonkers. She seats Anton at a table for two, sits down herself, uninvited, on the other chair, and, talking in a labored sort of English, takes to describing her travels in the Far East. Each one of her gewgaws has an adventurous story behind it. Then she wants to know if Anton spoke Arabic or Mandarin in his previous lives, and tests him with weird-sounding words. Then she declares herself fluent in Anton's obvious mother tongue, and to prove it, starts spewing even weirder, Russian-like sounds.

He praises her facility with foreign languages.

Through the dim light surrounding them, Anton catches sight of a miniature shrine on a small table against the wall. It holds a black Madonna on top of a pillar, framed by a half circle of tiny red lights. The old lady notices the direction of his gaze and explains that it is the crypt of the black Madonna of Chartres.

"Just a few days ago, I saw a black Madonna in Lyon," Anton says.

"A pilgrim!" she blurts out in a piercing voice. She grasps his hand and stares meaningfully into his eyes before he can add that he was just passing through Lyon, took a hike up the hill, and paid a visit to the local cathedral. "Welcome to your lodge," she adds.

Anton is standing now. Holding his hand with surprising energy, the old lady leads him to a much smaller room, even more dimly lit, with a single table in it. And one single chair in front of the table. She pulls back the chair and invites him to take a seat. He is now facing a larger version of the miniature shrine he saw in the other room. Only, the pillar and the black Madonna's multi-folded mantle are gone: what's left is the life-size statue of a naked girl, blacker than black opal, with breasts like a wet nurse, holding a black baby Jesus on her left arm. The shrine is framed by the flickering lights of seven red oil lamps.

"You deserve pride of place in my restaurant," she says. "I knew it the moment I saw you."

"Table for one?" Anton says.

"Your dining companion is facing you. The black virgin."

"That's what you call the black Madonna?"

"The keepers of the cathedral call her Our Lady of the Pillar. But you and I know better, don't we?"

"We do," he says.

"Surrounded with seven red moons and a sphere of stars... Doesn't it remind you of something?"

"I'm afraid it doesn't," he says.

"It tells you where to look for the origin and the center, Chosen One. You see the golden radial pattern above the black virgin?"

"I do."

"Stop pretending, Chosen One. That's the reason that brought you to Chartres!"

"Is it?" Funny as it all is, he tells himself not to push it too far.

"It's the black star! The fulcrum of all black arts."

Now the old lady appears totally depleted, as though that climactic revelation was beyond her meager forces. She walks backwards to the door, her head down, and the moment she leaves the room, all lights go off, except for the seven red oil lamps around the shrine. When a beanpole of a waiter appears, not much younger than the old lady but silent like a slab of rock, carrying the first course, only then does Anton realize that he was not even shown a menu.

After laying down Anton's dish on the table, the waiter puts a smaller serving in front of the statue. He does the same with all subsequent courses. The meal is plainly awful, and the bites in Anton's plate are indistinguishable in all that darkness, making him a natural candidate for food poisoning. In the second course, Anton recognizes two thick slices of raw bacon, which he pushes expeditiously on the side of the plate. But that's not why he keeps his eyes riveted to the plate throughout the meal. It is because there is a sinister flickering of life in the eyes of the statue, and when he looks at her, he sees Gala: same flashy lips, curved around her same scornful smile, and those same round breasts and narrow hips he pictured under Gala's gauzy veils every time he saw her. And he hears Gala telling him in uninflected English that Nessim knows he is here.

Here.

Under Gala's demanding eyes, the best he can manage is to keep his own eyes down.

Bread is most fragrant at home. This is the weirdest thought to have, he tells himself, given the predicament he finds himself in. But a moment later, he realizes that this thought was just a forerunner to the heartburn that is making it acid way up his throat. He must have heard it said somewhere by somebody, that your bread is best when eaten at home, but who said it and where, he can't recall. It must have been someone who knew how to find his way back home, and it must have had something to do with how salty the bread on your table is. Or how sweet.

This train of thought gives him a brave new idea. He pushes his plate aside and WhatsApps Sophie again.

"I'll be home tonight, but I need to work undisturbed till around noon."

"Fine with me," she says.

"Tell that Dambreuil too, please."

"I will."

Then he throws his Hail Mary. "Pack a small bag with a change of clothes, will you?"

"What for?"

"Around noon we take off."

"Where to?"

"It depends," he replies. "Bring some dry food for Elvis too."

"How long you said we'll be away?"

"I didn't say."

"How long, then?"

"It depends."

"You are the boss, Diabolik."

He has before his eyes a different Anton, black from head to foot like Diabolik, who crawls out of Margherita's office like a drunken rat. If you want to get yourself the final say, he ponders, you must become the real thing. A lame impersonator won't do.

He checks the Google Translate app, fishes out some childhood memories, and when the old lady comes back to his table with a complicitous light in her eyes, and asks if he is ready for a shot of her *vin santo*, he says, "*Ya schitayu sebya osvobozhdennym.*" What he means is that he deserves an exemption from farther digestive atonement at the shrine of the black virgin. But he takes pity on the old lady's stunned expression: she doesn't understand his Russian, or does she find it inexplicable that he is passing on her *vin santo*? So, he just shakes his head with a smile and asks for his check. She walks robotically out of the room, and an instant later, *pop*, the room is rawly lit by neon lights.

As he waits for his check, he takes a good look at the black virgin. In this raw light, her magic is gone. There's not a hint of animation in her pupils' blobs of black paint, the breasts seem each molded over a large ball cut in half, and the hips are freakishly tiny. A wooden statue sold out by some itinerant carnival, that must be it. Painted black.

Bitcoin and the Ritual of Kyudo Archery

How 'bout another staredown contest, Lady Madonna? I'm ready when you are.

At the hotel he pays his bill and warns them I'll be leaving his room a bit after midnight. The hotel restaurant is closed this late, but he manages to have a basket of fruits sent to his room, to chip away at the bad taste in his mouth.

After a brief Google search, he finds out there are a total of ten crypto exchanges where Futura's tokens are traded. He already has an open account in four of those exchanges: once a month, if the fees of more established exchanges like Coinbase are too steep, he switches to one of those accounts to trade bitcoins against the US dollars he needs to pay his staff's salaries in Iceland. He registers himself on the remaining exchanges. Four of them are decentralized, so his new accounts are opened in the blink of an eye. When they offer him the opportunity to take on a username, he writes down *Diabolik Cash*. But then he doesn't bother to use a masked email address; his regular one will do just fine. The remaining two exchanges are centralized; they use the Know-Your-Customer process to verify the legal identity and potential risks involved with each new customer. He has got nothing to hide, but it is a tedious process. In the end, his legal identity is fully verified by one of the two. The second one will take another forty-eight hours before his new account may be opened.

Nine out of ten is good enough.

Before calling it a day, he Google searches: *Nessim Hosnani*. Loads of entries. Loads of pictures too. There he is at the Cannes film festival a few weeks ago, escorted by a fat-assed girl in jeans and niqab whom Anton barely recognizes as Gala. Olive-skinned, a far cry from the jet-black panther he met twice. Dambreuil's words come to his mind: *That girl is a beast, a wild beast.* Not a panther for sure, though.

All things considered, he wouldn't mind a short nap before taking off for Paris.

CHAPTER THIRTY

Anton pulls out the first orange flag from his street map of Paris and as it falls down to the floor, the echo of Jacqueline's coughing fits on rue de la Tournelle fades forever away. He pulls out another orange flag, and Jean inhales his last dose of ether in bed with Jacqueline on rue des Bernardins. He lets a third orange flag fall down, and the door to 160, boulevard Haussmann is shut forever before Jean's eyes. Never again will he spy on Jacqueline's secret trysts with Pierre Cartaud.

He pulls out four more orange flags – quai de Passy, Porte d'Auteuil, boulevard Suchet, Porte Maillot. These are the flags that hide the *Open Sesame* of his bitcoin portfolio. He initializes a blank Trezor with the twelve words of this passphrase, his bitcoin balance appears on the screen, and he send all of it toward some of his accounts on the crypto exchanges where Futura's FTR tokens are traded. He wipes the Trezor clean. The bitcoin portfolio is his largest one. As it falls down on the floor, the flag of Porte Maillot erases the adulterous encounter between Jean and Jacqueline, now called Thèrése, at the Bois de Boulogne.

It's now the turn of the pale-blue flags, linked to one another by the black ribbon that circumscribes the adventures of the protagonists of *Youngsters,* one of Belmondo's novels whose characters take refuge in Nice. The pale-blue flag of Gare Saint-Lazare is on his floor now, followed by the pale-blue flag of Gare du Nord. He initializes the Trezor with the new passphrase, and a minute later all of his ethereum tokens appear on the screen, only to leave the gadget right away and fly into some others of those crypto accounts.

Beau de Rubempré

He moves on to the dark-purple flags, linked to one another by the green ribbon which circumscribes the adventures of the protagonists of Belmondo's *Poisonous Plant*. The same Jean who eloped to London with Jacqueline is back in this novel, side by side with Dannie this time. Dannie is a pseudonym, she is known to the police as Mireille Sampiery, Rue Blanche 21, Paris 9ᵉ, but her real name is Dominique Roger, a willing prostitute when in need of cash (just like Jacqueline-Thérèse in her youth). Anton recites by heart under his breath: *Do we have the right to judge those we love? If we love them, it must be for a reason, and this reason forbids us from judging them.* He reminds himself that Patrick Belmondo was christened Jean. Is Patrick a pseudonym? Just like Guy, the pretend-British writer who sold Anton the Villa Baroness Orczy?

He transfers his zcash balance to the one of those crypto accounts that's still empty.

Now it's the turn of the red flags and his ripple balance. He had run out of colored ribbons when he pinned these flags to the street map. He used a network of arrows drawn with a black marker instead, to circumscribe the adventures of the protagonists of Belmondo's *In the Environs*, the novel which inspired him to buy the Villa Baroness Orczy in Nice. In this novel Jean's surname is Dekker. In Paris, Jean Dekker rents a room in a hotel on rue Troyon. At his side, the nameless girl from the suburbs of Saint-Maur who lures him away from the aged charms of Carmen Blin. The nameless girl resurfaces twenty years later, when she is Carmen Blin's age, and now she lives on boulevard Sérurier, XIXᵉ arrondissement. By now, though, Jean has become the writer Guy de Guise. In Belmondo's novels, sooner or later Jean discovers his vocation as a writer. The Jean from *Deeper than Forgetfulness* becomes a writer on the long sleepless nights spent waiting for Jacqueline to come back, or maybe not, to their room in London. And the Jean from *Poisonous Plant* becomes a writer by mourning over the loss of his manuscript, while his girlfriend Dannie wants him to make up for it by rewriting a novel picked up at random from the used-book stands by the Seine.

Dannie-Dominique-Mireille juggles three identities at once under the nose of the police. It is in character that she thinks it'd be easier for Jean to rewrite someone else's story rather than write his own.

All of Anton's ripple tokens go feed the same crypto account where his zcash tokens have just gone.

On the floor at his feet is a tiny, multi-colored heap of ribbons and flag pushpins. *Farewell, my Kripta*. No need to kill the white flag at the intersection of boulevard de Montparnasse with rue de Chevreuse, though, where the Tschann Bookstore is: it commemorates Anton's reunion with Sophie under Belmondo's eyes.

Now for the hard part: buy as many of Futura tokens as he can.

The windows of his nine crypto accounts are open side by side on the giant curved monitor on the desk. He enables the applications' interfaces. Since he means to buy at market price, it is a matter of placing his buy orders at the same time on all nine exchanges. The element of surprise is crucial. If he were to give the traders too much time to gauge his real intentions, they would raise their ask price much too fast.

Here we go. The nine buy orders are launched on the order books, all that remains for Anton to do is follow the red-and-green blinking of the order book in each single exchange. The Futura token price climbs at an impressive pace, but it would be worse if he had come out in the open one exchange at a time. After hardly ten minutes, there is a slowdown in all order books: they are running out of asks. It is about time for the traders on the tenth exchange, the one which Anton failed to register his new account on last night, to put their feelers out. In fact, yes, the pace picks up again in some of the order books Anton is monitoring, as new supplies of Futura tokens are transferred into the exchanges. The token price jumps up at a faster and faster pace. There is nothing much he can do about it. He just keeps buying. Two minutes. Three. It's finished.

The Futura token price has risen so much and so fast that the first half of what he bought today is already valued at a lucrative premium. At his own expense, of course.

An hour ago Anton owned 3% of Futura's total token supply. He just squandered all of his crypto portfolios and now he owns 77% of the total supply, spread over nine exchanges. Margherita and Carlo own roughly 10%, but their share is frozen for another eight years or so. Another 3% is frozen forever in Jesus's plugged-up memory. According to the latest dispositions of the Security and Exchange Commission, Anton is now Futura's majority shareholder.

No longer than a quarter of an hour from now, the ten crypto exchanges where Futura tokens are traded will find out that the volume of these tokens' transactions on their individual book orders has fallen down to zero. They'll sound the alarm. A myriad of alternative explications of the unexplainable will follow one another. Then it will be time for harsh accusations right and left, unfounded rumors and fake news on Crypto News, Cointelegraph, and all other crypto social networks. In the end, someone will ask the fatal question: "Who is this Whale and why did he do it?"

The Whale is Anton, pure and simple. In a few more days, some mole will come out with the real name behind the *Diabolik Cash* username, and he will be outed as the owner of the accounts which hijacked most of Futura long-standing token supply. That day, he hopes that Margherita will remember the roaring laughter she heard come at her from the rowing club, two nights ago.

Now for the third and last phase: transfer the whole of his Futura token balance to the Trezor, away from the greedy reach of hackers.

The Trezor walks him into its browser. Anton confirms the Futura address on the Mac against the address shown on the screen of the Trezor, then he copies that address, and one by one, from each of the nine windows of the exchanges open on the giant monitor on the desk, he sends all of his Futura tokens to it.

All that is left for him to do now is verify that the nine transactions are brought to completion. It won't take long.

He steps into the walk-in closet and puts on the kyudo outfit. In the linens section he finds a pile of elegant handkerchiefs. He selects the largest one, a sort of silk bandana, brightly colored, folds it into a rectangle, and ties it to his forehead while the elevator brings him down to the kyudojo. Daniel's bow is still in the Bentley, together with the backpack he brought to Paris. He walks into the garage to get it. Now he kneels down in the kiza position on the shooting platform, the bow in the left hand, the arrows in the right, takes a good look at his surroundings, and then lowers the bandana before his eyes.

He plunges deep into himself. All he hears is silence. All he sees sis darkness. He keeps his eyes shut behind the bandana. It's weird, in this pitch dark it feels as though he could *think* the silence of the kyudojo. The thought of silence, the void of darkness: he makes them last some while longer.

He gets up to his feet, takes on the kai position, and shoots his first arrow into the darkness. The silence is broken by the thud of the arrow piercing the target – it is the thud that spells *bull's eye* – and right after that the bowstring's sound pierces the air. He waits for his left wrist to absorb the bulk of the vibrations in the bow, then he shoots the second arrow into the darkness again. The thud of the arrow hitting bull's eye is preceded by a chafing-like noise this time, barely perceptible: the two arrows scratching each other.

We both know what's a blind archer worth on the battlefield: Daniel's words flash soundlessly through his mind. *No, Daniel, you didn't know it, and I didn't either, not yet*: the blind archer in a state of grace is a most formidable opponent. His arrow is in the bull's eye long before he shoots it. No oracle, however unchallengeable, has power over him.

As the bowstring's vibrations die down, Anton keeps both arms stretched out in a straight line: the left hand holding the bow and pointed at the target, the right hand, gloved, pointed in the opposite direction. He stands like that till the sound of the bow folds upon itself and he can hear again, and *think* again, the silence of the kyudojo.

Bitcoin and the Ritual of Kyudo Archery

It's finished. He takes the bandana off his eyes, walks to the garage to put the bow and two new arrows into the Bentley, and climbs back to the third floor.

The nine transactions add up on the Trezor. He smashes the Trezor to smithereens.

A shiver runs through the length of his spine. Numbers, shares, budget, projections, governance: he can't wait to preside over the next meeting of Futura's board of directors. Served this roundabout way, ice-cold, his high-tech revenge has something graceful to it. He is ready to bet it is not too late to set Futura, *his company*, back on the proof-of-work path. He finds it hard to believe that no longer than thirty-six hours ago he was after a bloodshed in Turin.

All flags and ribbons are gone from his Michelin street map, except for the white flag. So many *Open Sesame* wiped off, so many of his anonymous crypto identities drained into the microscopic holes left behind by the pushpins. There is still, at the heart of the map, the geometry of streets he highlighted with a black marker: that network of arrows can't be erased. At its center is the hotel on rue Troyon where Anton first met the character of Jean Dekker. Jean Dekker's story goes beyond the boundary of this two-dimensional geometry of streets traced in black, though. Jean will find fame and wealth as a British mystery writer under the pseudonym of Guy de Guise, while the nameless girl who lures him away from Carmen Blin will age in the middle-class anonymity of a suburban neighborhood. They too shake off their old identity to take on a new one: there still is, after all, an unsolved murder in their past, minutely described in the dossier of a police case. But Anton wonders, how much of your castoff identity can you remove from your own memory? Belmondo would know, his life went through so many parallel plots – about one per novel. Would he be willing to share the secret with Anton, though?

How many of the crypto identities bunched up at Anton's feet in a heap of ribbons and colored flags can he get rid of for good? Wipe them even from his memory? All he cares for is the one identity, still marked with the white flag, he took on in the arms of Sophie here in Paris.

EPILOGUE

Anton grabs his second backpack and puts it on after filling it with some extra briefs and t-shirts, basic gizmos, and the Dell too, just in case. He slips the iPhone into his jeans' back pocket and the keys to the Villa Baroness Orczy into a front pocket. He goes down to Sophie's apartment on the elevator.

She's sitting in front of her Mac, guarded by the black-onyx statue which Elvis pretends to be from time to time.

"Ciao, Diabolik."

Sophie lowers the lid of her Mac with a smile. She gets up, tall and slender in spite of the bulging fantasy that Anton's eyes project onto her belly, puts on her backpack and walks toward him.

He shakes his head. "Don't forget the Mac. The iPhone"

She turns around, slips her iPhone into a side pocket of her backpack, and holds her Mac under one arm.

As Anton picks up the leather leash and the bag of dog food, Elvis' entire body takes on a brief, frantic quiver, as though he swallowed a jackhammer, and then he is back to his normal state of three-legged dog. They go down to the garage. Sophie selects a bow and two arrows from her collection.

Anton crams their luggage into the trunk of the Bentley. With the top up, two bows in the cabin feel a bit awkward, but it will do.

"It's about time you learned to drive," he jokes.

"I will the day you give up on your fancy cars," she replies.

Anton never owned a fancy car in his life, least of all this one. Go argue that with her.

Beau de Rubempré

The Bentley rolls out of the ramp with a high-pitched squeal, and he skids it the wrong way, straight into the bridge. Is he hallucinating, or the woman waving a white handkerchief in his rear-view mirror, from that second-floor window, is really Dambreuil? The GPS is still off. He heads south as though he was driving back to Italy; the highway A6 signage can't be missed. He goes faster than the speed limit; at every other intersection some hidden camera records their passage with a flash of light. More delinquent traffic fines for Nessim.

It'll help you keep track I was here, mon ami.

When she realizes they are southbound, Sophie asks Anton where they are going.

"City of Nice, French Riviera," he replies.

"Why Nice?"

"Nice is the perfect spot to make a fresh start," he says.

She keeps silent.

"Forget the past and make a fresh start," he adds as he earns Nessim another couple of fines. For the life of him, he can't take his foot off the pedal.

"Who told you that?" Sophie says.

"That, what?"

"That you must go to Nice to make a fresh start?"

"I read it in a novel by Belmondo," he replies.

Sophie is silent again and keeps to herself, pensive, till they leave Paris behind and Anton can speed up on the highway. He had no idea the Bentley could run this fast.

He laughs out loud as he says, "Let bygones be bygone!"

It's past noon. He is of half mind to dine and sleep somewhere midway. Tomorrow they will get there in no time.

"Which one?" Sophie says.

Vroom-vroom. He is passing a string of cars and trucks as though they were snails. What's she talking about?

"Well, yeah," she replies, "which novel by Belmondo says you must go to Nice to make a fresh start?"

"Can't remember."

She's silent again, staring into the highway ahead of them. But then she bursts out laughing as though Anton said something very funny. She waves an admonishing finger under his nose and says, "Never forget a thing, not a thing!"

"Share the joke with me, would you?" Does she take him for a machine, he wants to know. *Vroom-vroom,* more snails out of his way. "It's not that I can remember everything I know, right?"

"Is that why we are going to the seaside?" She laughs even harder now. "They say eating fish is good for memory."

He swerves into a slower lane, steals a quick look at the confession in her eyes, and ends up saying, "Come clean with it, you've been peeking into my black notebook when I wasn't there."

She replies with a question. "So, I didn't give you a bellyache back in Palo Alto, huh?" and laughs again, silently this time, just with her eyes and dimples. "Should I call you Monsieur Holmes de Baskerville?" she asks.

He won't take it the wrong way. The secrets of his black Moleskine can follow down the drain the crypto identities he shed this morning. Sophie still has no idea that in Turin he found the culprit of the aggression against Daniel. Maybe she will never know. Unless, that is, he was talking to her all along in the black Moleskine?

Beau de Rubempré

"No way," he replies. "My name is Anton Gunzburg, soon-to-be father of Daniel Gunzburg. Or, fifty-fifty, Danielle."

One of them three, regardless.

Four, counting Elvis.